running as fast as we can

Molly Hurford

about "running as fast as we can"

High school is an uphill battle... especially if you run cross-country.

Juniors Krista and Elle might be have been best friends once. Not anymore. But they do have one thing in common: A distaste for school sports, and need for an athletic extracurricular on their college resumes. When they both show up to the first cross-country practice of the season, it's a surprise to both of them.

Writer and wannabe punk Krista wants nothing to do with preppy go-getter Elle, at least not anymore. But what caused the rift between the former childhood friends... and what will happen when the reason for their mutual dislike shows up with swagger?

Competitive sparks will fly, but it's going to take the two girls finding common ground if they're going to make it through junior year and fight back against the real enemy.

Content Guidance: This book explores themes around disordered eating as well as sexual harassment.

For Lindsay

chapter
one

Krista

FROM: Lisa Smith, Guidance Department <smith.
lisa@nhhschool.org>
   Sent: September 15, 2021
   To: Krista Hitchcock <hitchcock.k@
nhhschool.org>
   Subject: RE: College Applications

Krista—

Thank you for meeting with me yesterday. After reviewing your list of colleges that you're hoping to apply to and looking through your overall grades as well as your current list of extracurriculars, I think you're going to need to add to the extracurriculars in order to show that you're a well-rounded young woman (which I'm sure you are!).

At the moment, you have every single English class and elective possible, and your current extracurriculars are all literature/journalism-related. Many of the top schools are looking for students with a broader range of experience. But don't worry, there's still time!

As I told you in our meeting, in your position, I would seriously consider joining a sports team for the fall semester, before your applications go in.

Please let me know if you have any more questions.

Sincerely yours,

Lisa Smith, Guidance Counselor

From: Krista   Hitchcock   <hitchcock.k@
nhhschool.org>
    Sent: September 15, 2021
    To: Jane Tsai <Jane@janesayswhat.com>
    Subject: HELP! FW: RE: College Applications

Jane, I need your advice.

    See below. Ms. Smith, the guidance counselor from hell, has informed me that I need some kind of sporty extracurricular to "round out" my college resume. You got into Columbia and are crushing it, do you think I need to rethink my plans for this year and actually *shudder* join a school sport?

    (Tell me no, please.)

    Anyway, hope you're doing well in the big city. Miss you around here. There's no one to talk to and the newspaper staff is seriously weak this year without you at the helm. I'm doing what I can, but the freshman are just so… freshman-y. And I have no time to do the music reviews, so that's all turned into an I <3 T Swift column and I can't believe I even typed those words.

    Anyway, help!

    -Krista

Chapter One

From: Jane Tsai <Jane@janesayswhat.com>
    Sent: September 17, 2021
    To: Krista   Hitchcock   <hitchcock.k@
nhhschool.org>
    Subject: RE: HELP! FW: RE: College Applications

Bad news, girl. Smith is right. Everyone on my dorm floor played some kind of sport, or instrument, or did theater in addition to doing school paper. I was lucky I squeaked in thanks to my mom pushing me through Girl Scouts all these years (bet you didn't know that! I kept it pretty under wraps).

Seriously though, get into a sport that doesn't require a ton of teamwork. You don't have time to learn an instrument, you hate public speaking so acting is out, which leaves athletics. What about cross-country? Running alone in the woods is kind of punk rock, right? At least it's easy to phone that in, unlike something like soccer where a coach can see you the entire time. Just put in your headphones and get it done.

I'll see you in the city soon enough. For now, I gotta get to class.

-J

From: Krista   Hitchcock   <hitchcock.k@ nhhschool.org>
Sent: September 17, 2021
To: Jane Tsai <Jane @ janesayswhat.com>
Subject: RE: RE: HELP! FW: RE: College Applications

Ugh, thanks for nothing. (I kid. I'll give it a try. Though it could kill me.)

What am I doing here? I ask myself — silently, of course. Right this second, I really, really don't want to draw any attention from the students milling around me. I feel like an idiot, wearing my old gym shorts from elementary school. They're black, of course, but with hot pink piping that makes me feel like I Googled 'how to be punk' and found a site from 2013 or something. I wanted to wear my Bad Religion t-shirt, but at the last minute, my mom found an old tank top from her rowing days at college, so Rowan 1997 is emblazoned on my chest in what I'm calling ironically collegiate lettering. It's so not punk that it's punk. My tube socks are the same level of ironic, and I'm hoping my Converse low tops are going to be okay to run in.

Guidance counselors are supposed to be on our side, I think furiously as I stomp between the linebacker and the running back, both still attaching pads for practice. As I make my way to the center of the field, I barely contain a huge sigh, and shove my just-bleached bangs up and out of my face. It still feels like summer out, and I just know that as soon as we start running, my bangs are going to be sticky and plastered to my forehead. I suddenly regret cutting them, and also the texturizing wax I pulled through them this morning because I can already feel the wax slicking my forehead with grease. The rest of my hair is yanked into two tiny pigtails, the only way I could get it all to stay somewhat contained.

"Are you here to join the cross-country team?" asks one of the volunteer parents, smiling cautiously at me and holding a clipboard.

"Yep," I say, trying to convey a deep sense of ennui in my monotone. She hands me the clipboard and I take it, scrawling out my name and emergency contact information while she looks on, and I can tell she wants to make conversation but doesn't know where to start. So instead, she turns and starts talking to one of the other girls — one who was on the team last year and showed up in Nike shorts and last year's team singlet, clearly ready to run in the heat with her hair braided into a perfect ponytail and her clean sneakers. Now that they're both ignoring me, I set the clipboard down by her feet and awkwardly slide away towards the group of scruffier-looking guys.

Okay, don't panic, I tell myself firmly. *It can't be that bad, right?* The teacher in charge is one of my favorites and also happens to be the teacher who manages the school paper, so I'm hoping she lets me sneak out of some practices and races when deadlines are looming.

Seriously, why are colleges so crazy about 'well-rounded' people anyway? Ms. Smith has a lot to answer for, if you ask me. I was just minding my own business, helping run our school's poetry slam, editing the student newspaper (#1 in the state for hard-hitting news reports three years running!) and writing for the literary magazine (no awards, sadly, but I'm working on it). How is that not going to get me into NYU or Columbia?

Normally, I'm not exactly self-assured. But when it comes to writing and journalism, I've always known that this is what I'm meant to do. It's never even occurred to me that there's another career path out there, and NYU and Columbia represent two of the best schools to go to for that, and since they're in the city, I'll be surrounded by great internship opportunities. I can't imagine a worse fate than going to some school in the middle of nowhere and having to intern at a local paper, gathering stories about knitting circles and minor house fires. Ugh.

I've wanted New York City since I was maybe eight years old and got my hands on a copy of *Teen Vogue*. But I never wanted to be one of the models on the glossy pages. For one thing, I'm too short. Fashion design? Not even a little bit. However, writing those stories? That's what I've always wanted to do.

So there I was, sitting in the guidance office, waiting to hear that my dreams were almost positively going to come true, when Ms. Smith shook her head sadly. "No sports?" she asked, like she was almost begging me to prove her wrong.

"No," I answered shortly. "Why would that matter for journalism?"

She looked at me almost sympathetically, but then shifted to a grumpier know-it-all look as she took in my black button-down tucked into high-waisted black jeans and topped with an undone white bowtie. My bleached white hair, cut in a short and straight bob, almost glows against the black-on-black combo, which is why I picked that outfit. And my trademark red lipstick was still perfectly done.

"Colleges look for students who are well-rounded, Krista," she said matter-of-factly.

"I know that," I replied. "That's why I'm working on the newspaper *and* the literary magazine."

"That's nice," she said in a way that implied it absolutely wasn't. "But what colleges mean by well-rounded is that you do well academically, while also participating in a wide variety of extracurriculars. A school like NYU may notice you based on where you are currently" — she gestured to the papers scattered on her desk dismissively, as if to say 'yeah right'— "But you'll increase your chances of getting into both of these schools if you also have a sport."

"A ... sport?" I said, disbelievingly. "You've got to be kidding."

She shook her head. "Otherwise, you're looking good, but if you don't round out your activities a little more, your application will look pretty sparse," she warned me.

"Do..." I struggled to figure out how to ask this next question. "Do I need to be good?"

She laughed a little. "No, they won't care about that."

And before I can either argue that that makes no sense, or just leave, she also adds a little dig about my public speaking class grade not exactly being amazing. "Maybe consider re-taking that class?" she says.

Honestly, what is the point? I said a curt thank you, then I slammed the door a little too hard on my way out.

I mean, come on. Retake public speaking? After what happened last time? (Long story. Vomit involved. Don't ask.)

And signing up for a sport? What could cheerleading or spiking a volleyball have to do with filing a story on time? I fumed my whole way down the hall, and even my favorite English teacher couldn't get me to crack a smile despite the fact that we were reading my favorite TS Elliot poem in class. ("Do I dare eat a peach?" Well, I would if I liked peaches. Just like I would have joined a sports team if I liked sports. Which I don't.)

And all of that led signing my name on the sheet for cross-country, which in addition to Jane's advice about being a solo sport was the only one that didn't require tryouts. While the idea of joining the team might make me feel slightly ill, the idea of not getting into my dream school for a reason as dumb as not playing a sport is just inconceivable.

Jane was my co-editor on the literary magazine, where I spent a lot of my time trying to gently convince her that some of her more 'subversive' work was just a little too dark for high school audiences. Now she's in college, and it turns out, the subversive work that kept getting her in trouble in high school has boosted her career and she's already getting internships at magazine in her freshman year. When she was here, she spent a lot of time at the guidance counselor as a result of her writing, even the tamer stuff, though secretly, she's as well-adjusted as they come. Her parents are happily married, and each summer, they go on a six-week vacation somewhere amazing—and apparently, she was big into Girl Scouts, which she thinks was shocking, but I wasn't all that surprised, honestly. She shares goth-y pictures of her grumping on a beach in a long black dress on her Instagram (GothGirl2003 — so cheesy), but I've been to her house and seen the actual vacation photos: her grinning in a bright pink bathing suit rocking a scuba mask, her arms thrown around her mom and dad and sunlight in the background. It was always kind of funny, seeing her try so hard to be maladjusted. Her parents just laughed when they got called in because a teacher doesn't approve of her black lipstick, and seem to take her offbeat fashion choices in stride. (Part of that is probably because like me, Jane was a secret nerd who gets straight As. We spent a lot of time studying together before she graduated and abandoned me.)

All that to say—I trust her. I'll go to a couple practices each week, but I won't have to give up my newspaper editing duties. And there are only a few meets throughout the season, none of them totally mandatory, so I figure I can go to one, completely suck, and be dismissed from needing to be at any more.

Problem, solved.

Except for, you know, the fact that I'm here now, while the newspaper is supposed to go out in just a couple days and needs a lot of work done on the first issue for the year, but I'm stuck out in the middle of the field trying to avoid being jostled by the overeager freshmen trying too hard to stretch.

Me, I'd rather skip the attention and just get that participation credit, so I don't bother with stretching. I just slouch and examine my nails: black, chipping *just* enough. (Don't tell anyone I said this, but I usually paint them, and then pre-chip them so they look cooler. Perfect black nails are so faux punk.)

The sun is beating down, and I'm getting even more nervous about the integrity of my bangs, and worrying that my mascara and eyeliner are definitely not waterproof. I want to look punk, not like a cut-rate Marilyn Manson (gross). Not even Jane goes for that look.

When I look back up, I see that the head coach is gesturing for everyone to gather around him. I saunter over, careful to stay on the outskirts.

"You—you running?" I hear the coach yell, not too nicely, and at first, I panic that he means me. But then, I see he's not looking in my direction at all.

"I'm coming, I'm coming," I hear someone squeak from somewhere on the field, which is now also teaming with football players milling around before tryouts, trying to out-bro each other, and the school marching band, who've somehow become a lot more aggressive and are currently marching directly through said football practice like they're in that American Pie song. Despite all the commotion, the voice is familiar and it hits me in the solar plexus.

As she steps out from behind the curtain of shoulder pads, torn pinnies, and second-hand helmets that reek of teen boy, ducking her way around a trombone player, I gasp. *She's* trotting towards us, short shorts just a little bit too tight, smile just a little too bright.

"What is she doing here?" I ask, this time unintentionally out loud. But luckily, no one hears me.

chapter
two

Elle

WHAT AM I DOING HERE?

I waited until the last girl was out of the locker room before I slipped in to get changed after the last bell rang today. Then, I gave myself a long pep talk in the mirror. And then, of course, I realized I was late, and had to dodge the marching band (that simply refused to yield) to make it to the field before practice started.

Of course, they wouldn't be in my way if, in the process of clawing my way to the top of the high school social structure, I hadn't also eaten pretty much every bag of Doritos from the vending machine, and sipped iced coffee with cream and sugar like it was water every day. Maybe if I'd kept dancing, I wouldn't be struggling to pull my jeans on every morning, and maybe I wouldn't be hiding in the locker room waiting for everyone to leave so I could change. I definitely wouldn't be huffing and puffing just from walking fast over to the football field.

Cross-country is my only option. At my last yearly appointment with my gynecologist — yay, first week of school fun! — she told me gently that it might be time to start thinking about getting a little healthier. She didn't tell me I was fat, but I didn't need her to. I figured that one out on my own. She just listed things like my blood pressure being a little high, and mentioned that the rate of type 2 diabetes in my family history was a little worrisome for her. When I asked her what I should do about it, she asked if there was any sport that I could play.

Chapter Two

I told her that wasn't really an option, but when I went home, I was freaked out enough that I found myself scanning the electives and sports page on our school's website, bypassing the stupid student newspaper in the process.

"No tryouts, no pressure" was the slogan under the cross-country team's banner, and the blurb from the coach read, "Want to PR your 5K? [No.] Want to win some races? [Also, no.] Want to feel healthier and have fun? [Yes.] The reason you join doesn't matter, we're happy to help you meet your goals." It sounded a little cult-ish, but it was also the only option on the list that didn't have tryouts and team cuts, so really, the pickings were slim.

And so here I am, trying to sneak way towards my first practice and failing miserably. In my borrowed workout clothes, this is the most uncomfortable in my own skin I've felt in a long time. Ironic, right? The voice of the student body trying really hard to pretend like she doesn't exist, and not even doing that very well.

As everyone stares as I make my way over, I want to hunch my shoulders, but I remember what my mom has told me pretty much every day of my life. "Shoulders back, chin up, walk proud, and fake confidence," she says — sometimes gesturing with her spoon if she's eating cereal at the time, or with her wineglass if it's a Saturday night.

Mom and I are close, but her career trajectory and take-charge vibes makes my rise to the student body presidency look like a bloodless coup, even though I fought really hard for it. She's a lawyer and well-known on her firm's softball team for not just being fiercely competitive, but *brutally* so. And watching her in court is just freaking scary. She's a lady who expects a lot from herself, and unfortunately, that spills over into those of us who share her DNA. Maybe it would be easier if I had a high-performing sister, but it's just me and Mom in the house, which raises the bar pretty high.

I know she hasn't been thrilled with my weight gain either, since she went through a similar up-and-down (I just haven't gotten to the 'down' part yet) when she and my dad divorced a few years ago. There was the eating phase — and I helped her out a lot there — before she hit her triathlete phase — which I had no part in. She started running, biking and swimming, getting up before dawn to get her workouts in, her jawline and cheekbones slowly coming back into sharper definition, like I'd been seeing her with bad reception and finally, she was back in HD.

In fact, it's her old running shorts from when she first made the declaration that it was time to get fit that I'm wearing right now. They're a little short and a little tight, but I wasn't about to admit that my mom, even at her biggest, was smaller than I am now so I squeezed into them, and now, I'm walking with my shoulders back and head proud.

I dodge around the first football player, and then the second — he's also on the prom committee, so I give him a little smile and wink and try to act confident. He grins back, and lets out a loud whistle, which makes the rest of the players stop and stare. I might not be the skinniest girl in school, but I'm pretty good at talking to guys, and most of the guys I know don't seem to mind a few extra pounds. Not for nothing, I got a lot curvier as I gained weight, so compared to the stick-thin girls on the track team or cheerleading squad, I have much more impressive... assets. Every girl needs a little edge, right?

I wind through the last few players assembling for tryouts and I can see the cross-country coach standing surrounded by a herd of kids — some look athletic, some look scared, some look bored. One very familiar face catches my eye and I'm absolutely perplexed... so much so that I do a proper double-take.

But I hear mom's voice, so I square my shoulders again, set my jaw, and smile hugely, greeting everyone but not making eye contact, all the while thinking:

What is she doing here?

chapter
three

Krista

MY FORMER BEST friend apparently had the same plan as me: junior year, time to join a team. But why did it have to be this one?

Elle and I have a complicated history.

Actually, it's not so complicated. We don't like each other. That about sums it up. To say we're mortal enemies might be pushing it slightly, but not by too much. We're not quite mortal enemies since we rarely are in direct competition for anything anymore, though there was a time when...

Well, anyway. That's ancient history. Finished. Finito. The end.

Except here she is, strutting onto the field like she's queen of the freaking world. Unlike my choice to hang out on the sidelines, she walks straight up to the coach and starts animatedly talking to him, despite showing up late. From what I can see, he's looking mildly amused by this short, curvy animated blonde girl explaining what she's doing there and what she hopes to get from the season.

He doesn't need your life story, Elle. I want to say, but I know that's not exactly going to score me points with the coach or the rest of the team, including the few freshman who look thrilled that their student body president, their leader, has deigned to grace us with her company. At least I'll be able to outrun her, I think, and bend over to touch my toes. Now that I have a reason to run fast — to get away from someone — I feel a little more motivated to stretch.

But it's been a while since I've stretched, and I'm realizing that my toes seem incredibly far away, and even though I'm barely at a 90-degree angle at my hips, I can't really go much farther. I strain my upper back, trying to get a little closer to the ground, but as I'm panting, I feel a gentle hand on my back and glance up.

It's the assistant coach, Miss Carmichael, better known as Miss C to those of us who work on the newspaper. "Don't stress your back trying to buy flexibility in a day," she says in a low voice.

Ugh. I can't help but be a little annoyed watching her walk to the next student. She's smaller than most of us, maybe only 5'2" and tiny, and in addition to being assistant coach here, she's also an advisor for the newspaper, the student council and the tennis team. She's everywhere, and somehow always manages to be calm, collected and dressed just right.

When I grow up I want to be just like her. But maybe wearing a little more black, since she tends towards a more pastel-but-still-funky wardrobe. (I even — though I'd never admit this in public — bought a pair of clear-framed glasses to look more like her. I don't need glasses, but wearing them makes me feel significantly more writer-ly.) I guess if she can tolerate cross-country, I can too.

Of course, that would be easier to do if I wasn't so acutely aware of my new teammates side-eyeing me like they know I don't belong there. And it only gets worse when I spot my uber-cool punk friends literally pointing and laughing at me from their slouched hangout under a tree in the shade. I was hoping I could fly under the radar, but apparently, my scene cred is going to take a beating, just like my poor legs. I know I shouldn't care that they're laughing at me, but it stings. As a closeted nerd, I already always feel on edge around them, and now I'm going to also have the 'jock' label attached to me. Perfect.

I take Miss C's advice and stand up from my awkward stretch attempt. And of course, as I do, I see that Elle is already surrounded by people on the team, all chatting with her as she beams like she's in the running for Miss America, soaking up all the attention.

chapter
four

Elle

WALKING over to the coach ("Just call me Coach") and saying that I wanted to be on the team wasn't exactly my first choice... but I remembered reading in *How to Win Friends and Influence People* that being bold and taking those first steps in communication is really important.

After I finished talking to him — *such* a fun guy, if you can skip over the blatant misogyny and sexism, which I opt to do in this case — I turned to my constituents. I mean my fellow students. Classmates. Teammates. I stretch my trademark smile across my face, blink hard once, and start saying hello while I try to ignore the panic in my stomach and the glare from Krista that I feel all the way over here.

What's her problem, anyway? It's not like I did anything to her. She's the one who stopped coming over every Friday for sleepovers, she's the one who doesn't even call on my birthday, she's the one who untagged herself from all of our pictures together on Instagram.

Oh, and she's the one who ruined my life.

There is a tiny voice in the back of my head that's buzzing even as I'm smiling and laughing at some dumb joke a sophomore boy just cracked about our physics teacher. That voice is reminding me that maybe that's not *entirely* what happened, really.

But I don't have time to listen to it. The coach is starting to gather us into a circle for warmups. If this is what the season is going to be like, I have nothing to worry about. A few arm circles, forwards and backwards. Some toe touching, no problem. Even the couple of planks and lunges don't hurt too much, though I am starting to sweat a little. Maybe I'm in better shape than I thought. But I surreptitiously glance around and see that no one else seems to be turning red, though I can feel my face starting to pink up a bit and my breathing is getting harder.

Then, it's time for "strides." Coach lines us up into four lines and I pick one of the last spots. Of course, so does Krista, and there we are, next to each other. She doesn't so much as glance over, just keeps her eyes glued to the back of the guy in front of her. (Trust me, it's not because he's cute. He isn't.)

"We'll start with skipping," Coach says, and goofily demonstrates a skipping motion that I haven't done since I was probably 10. I sneak a look over again, and Krista's lip has curled up in a bit of a snarl. That just inspires me to want to skip like I'm 10 years old again, so when it's our turn, I put on a smile and skip for all I'm worth down to where Coach is standing. He nods in approval and I beam back, even though I'm already starting to feel the effects of the skipping fast. We'll probably get a break after this, I tell myself sternly. Stick with it.

I experience a little thrill when he barks at Krista to hustle.

The next drill is butt-kicks, which I have a bit more trouble with and stumble once. Krista glances over disparagingly as I move a little close to her on a butt-kick gone wonky. I move away. Coach either doesn't notice or pretends not to.

Then, he announces we're doing 'accells,' which confuses me until I watch the first few kids go and realize that it's a gradual speed up to sprinting. Ahhh, accelerating. Can't be that hard, right?

Wrong. Suddenly, it's my turn and my smile has vanished and the butterflies threaten to fly up to the surface, and it won't be pretty. GO, Coach yells, and even though it's "just a casual warm-up," my heart leaps and I take off, speeding up faster and faster and faster. I'm practically flying. I'm doing it, I'm sprinting.

Abruptly, my breath catches and I wheeze, instantly slowing. As I do, I look around and realize that I'm barely halfway to Coach and everyone else is already jogging back to the start, except Krista, who's just reached him and, putting her hands onto her knees, gasps for air.

We do this again, twice. But I don't go hard these times. Now, I'm way at the back, just trying to make it to Coach jogging. He doesn't nod in approval now.

He calls for us to come back to the circle, and we group up. "Some of you have been doing this for a long time," he says. "And some of you are having your first practice today. Whatever reason you're here, whether you want to win states, beat your personal best, or maybe even just get in better shape..." (Here, I swear he looks right at me.)

"Whatever your reason, there's a place for you on this team. There are friends for you on this team. Do me just one favor," Miss C says, sliding in front of him and smoothly cutting him off. "Don't make today your last practice... No matter what happens."

That sounds a little ominous, but I nod along with the other kids.

"We're going to keep it pretty simple today," she adds. "We're going to run the two kilometers to the trail, do a few accelerations and mini-intervals, then we'll jog back to the school the same way we came. Sound good?"

I'm feeling a little dizzy as she says that two kilometers is going to be the warmup. I've never run one, let alone casually jogged two. I'm actually not sure how long a kilometer is, honestly. I look longingly at the school, thinking that I could be comfortably ensconced in one of the cozy library chairs, working on my speech for the next pep rally. Instead, I'm standing in the slightly chilled September air, wondering why my mom's shorts had to be so darn short and wondering what happens if I just stop and sit on the sidewalk part of the way there.

We start to jog, en masse, and pretty quickly, I'm out the back, jogging solo down the road. Miss C breaks from the pack and falls back to where I am, looking unfairly glamorous and not at all sweaty, while I can feel my hair sticking to my neck and sweat beading down my back. I'm huffing and trying really hard not to cry.

"Doing okay?" she asks sympathetically. Everyone loves Miss C — even Krista is friends with her — but I haven't ever really talked to her, except to discuss student government business for publication in the school paper, in order to avoid connecting with Krista.

"I'm fine," I say, pasting that smile back on my face. "I'm just a little out of shape is all." I'm hoping she'll let me suffer in silence, and despite my best efforts to make it to the stop sign before I stop for a walking break, a cramp in my stomach comes on so quickly that I'm forced to stop my slow crawl and grab at my side.

"Side stitch?" she asks sympathetically. I nod.

"That's the worst. Keep walking, though, I promise it will help," she says, gently putting a hand on my back, guiding me forward a bit, and pushing just hard enough that I straighten up from my hunched position. A few steps later, it's already feeling a little better and I can breathe again. "Keep breathing nice and deep," she adds, "And try to belly breathe."

I look at her with an expression of horror.

"Yeah, I know, sticking out your stomach is no one's idea of a good time," she laughs. "But it will help the cramp go away."

I try inhaling and letting my belly expand, and even though I want to clap my hands back on my stomach and suck in, she's right. It eases the cramp that was threatening to boil over and leave me with a migraine.

"You're not alone," she says, and points just up the road. There's Krista, leaning heavily on a mailbox and holding her stomach in the same spot I'm holding mine. Of course, on her, it looks like she's a model for some artsy magazine doing a piece on trending mailboxes, because her tall and thin frame looks artistic even as she's clutching her flat tummy. Tyra Banks would be proud, I think, and I feel an inexplicable pang of sadness and for a second, I'm tempted to yell at her to start smizing. It's a joke she would have loved a couple years ago, I think.

But we're not friends.

When we reach her, Miss C urges her to start walking and belly breathing along with us, so for a few minutes, we're not friends or enemies, we are comrades in arms as we make our way to the end of the road, where the rest of the team is waiting patiently (and impatiently in the case of Jenny, our school's track star, who's pacing and doing random jumping jacks and huffing as she looks at her watch).

Coach gives us the thumbs up and Miss C returns it and he turns to the group again and explains the plan. "We're going to run for one minute hard," he says. "Then, when I yell time, those of you at the front of the pack, turn around and jog back to the last person. At the back of the pack, just slow to a nice easy jog. When we're all bunched up again, we'll go again. Sound good?"

I'm a little confused but considering I'm certainly at the back of the pack, it sounds like my job is to just go hard, and then not go hard anymore, which I can handle. The not going hard part, anyway. We file onto the trail and Coach yells GO.

Everyone else takes off like a herd of gazelles, Krista included — her stomach cramp is obviously forgotten. I feel more like a buffalo, and I stay back, trying to go fast enough that I'm not too far away from the last person other than me, but not so fast that I'll run out of air.

Well, I don't think I'll run out of air. I'm confident that the minute is almost over as I run past a thorn bush that catches me on the ankle, I'm positive there are only seconds to go when I dodge a gopher hole and I'm sure we're finished as I pound my way down and over a dried up creekbed.

"Halfway there!" I hear from down the trail in front of me.

You have got to be kidding me. My lungs and legs are on fire, my feet hurt, I feel like my vision is graying at the edges. Time or not, I'm done.

It's tempting to flip around entirely and just head back to the school, but I'm not sure we're allowed to do that, and I don't think that breaking a rule like that will reflect well on me as the student body president.

I see movement to my right, and realize I'm right next to a side trail and someone is rustling their way down it. Krista appears in front of me, and grimaces. "Tell Coach I'm going back to school?" she asks, though she's looking at me like I'm the last person in the world she wants to talk to. She's also clutching her side tightly, like her internal organs are going to spill out if she's not careful.

"Are we allowed to do that?" I ask her. "I don't think you should go alone."

I spot Miss C in the distance and wave my arms frantically at her. She sees us, and speeds over to where we're standing, looking like it's taking her no effort at all to race across the field. She's so efficient it makes me want to push her into the woods, but I paste back on my smile instead. "Krista's stomach is cramping, and I'm exhausted," I admit. "Would it be okay if we went back to the school and called it a day?"

Krista glares at me for a second, and starts to say something, but realizes quickly that while I might not be the person she wants to jog back with, I'm the lesser of two evils — me versus more running.

"Sure," says Miss C. "Just follow the road back. And promise that you'll both come to practice tomorrow too?" We both look at her incredulously.

"Seriously, come back to this?" Krista says exactly what I'm thinking, to my horror and relief. A few extra pounds won't kill me, but this running thing might.

chapter
five

Krista

CLEARLY, me doing a sport is a huge mistake. My side feels like it's on fire, my feet hurt — Converse may not be the shoes for the job — and my (former) favorite teacher is telling me she expects me to come back for more of this tomorrow? Oh, and my current archnemesis and former best friend (and she knows why) is supposed to WALK ME HOME?

What. Is. Happening?

"I know the first day feels like crap," Miss C says sympathetically. "Okay, to be honest, the first few weeks aren't going to feel fantastic. But you will get better quickly, and you'll start to see it happening soon, I swear. Just trust me — come back tomorrow."

We both nod, grudgingly on my part, perkily on Elle's, and thank her for our early dismissal.

"Want one tip before you come back?" Miss C asks as I turn to start our walk back.

"Sure," I say, not actually sure that I really can handle any advice right now.

"Get a pair of actual running shoes and it'll make a big difference," she says. I want to refuse, because that style definitely doesn't match the look I'm going for, but as I shift my weight from one foot to the other and my arches shriek in pain, I realize I might need to give in and wear ugly sneakers for a few practices. I can probably swipe a pair from my mom for now, but I'll be shopping for some black-on-black sneakers as soon as possible — the last thing I want is to end up with a pair of light pink puffy-looking glitter bombs like the monstrosities that Elle is wearing right now. Miss C waves at us before merrily jogging back to the lead group, and we turn and start the long trek back to school.

"You don't actually have to walk with me," I say grumpily to Elle, who's practically skipping along at my side.

"Are you kidding? I told Miss Carmichael that I would, and besides, you just got me out of that thunderdome of a practice. Did you see how Jenny was looking around eyeing the competition?"

I can't help it, I snort just a little. "I don't think either of us counts as competition for her," I say. "And it's Miss C, she hates being called Miss Carmichael."

Elle looks so crestfallen that I momentarily feel bad for her, but then I remember who I'm talking to and look grimly straight ahead.

We walk back to the school in painful (physically and emotionally) silence, and thankfully, my mom is already there waiting by the bike racks for me. Normally, I ride home by myself, but since practice lets out late enough that she can ride to school from work, she wanted to meet me. I grab my backpack from under the bleachers and head over to unlock my bike. I pop my helmet on and swing a leg over, and see that mom is waving furiously. Not at me.

"Is that Elle? ELLE!" she yells, oblivious to my look of horror. I shove her arm.

"Mom, stop it!' I whisper furiously. But Elle is already waving back, her politician-style vote-for-me smile plastered on her face.

"Oh, come on, you aren't still holding a grudge, are you?" my mom says, adjusting her cycling cap under her helmet. (My mom is entirely too casually sporty sometimes, and it is annoying.)

"Yes," I say with a dignified sniff, before I start pedaling away from the school and towards our condo three miles away, leaving her no choice but to sigh and follow along, rather than chat with Elle. Luckily, we can take the bike path most of the way there, otherwise she would never let me go to school by myself on the bike. She definitely won't let me drive — I have my license but until I go to college, she says we don't need to use the car for anything other than emergencies. My mom is what you might call a new-age hippie.

By the time we get home, my stomach is feeling better, and I'm actually starving. "What's for dinner?" I ask, and mom looks at me like I've grown another head.

"Since when are you ready for dinner at 5 PM?" she asks, but dutifully starts rummaging around in the kitchen, seeing what we have that's cookable (answer: usually a lot of vegetables). It's obvious dinner isn't happening anytime soon, so I join her in the kitchen and try to spot any junk food that's languishing on the shelves. There isn't much, but I do come up with an almost empty bag of tortilla chips that have lost all of their crunch due to the aging process. Still, a chip is a chip, and I grab hummus out of the fridge to use as dip as mom pulls out arugula, tomatoes, fresh mozzarella and olives.

"I had cross-country today," I say in a bit of a whine. "I'm starving!"

"How was practice, anyway?" she asks as she starts chopping the tomato for our salads.

"It was okay," I answer, looking down at the book I grabbed off the coffee table and trying to send a message that I don't want to talk about it. Which, of course, in mom-code means that I need to talk about it. The problem here is two-fold. First, as previously mentioned, mom is what I call casually sporty. She runs marathons on the regular — not even marathon races, just a relaxed 'I'm going to go out and do a 26 mile run because it's Saturday and I feel like it' which is somehow more intimidating than someone who trains for a marathon race once a year. I hate to have to tell her that I'm not good at running, nor do I want to be. I think she was hoping I'd be world-class on day one, a secret phenom.

And second, she's never really understood what happened between Elle and I, and now that she knows Elle is on the team as well, she's going to pry for more details about that. Me, I want to forget that Elle ever existed.

"What was today's workout?" she asks, trying for a second, more-specific question. Classic parenting move.

"Two miles to warm up, then some one-minute efforts on the trails out by Kilarney Street," I mutter.

"I hated one minute efforts," Mom says sympathetically. "It's such a long time and a short time all at once," she adds. "I mean, how do you know how hard to go?"

"Exactly!" I say, waving a chip for emphasis. "And my stomach cramped really bad even on the warmup jog."

I look closely at her face, searching for traces of disappointment. I can't see any, but it might be lurking there. Still, if it is, she hides it well: "It's your first run in... well, in forever," she says. "It would be shocking if you didn't cramp."

That's pretty much what Miss C said, but I don't know that I believe either of them. There were a couple of other equally non-sporty kids on the team and none of them seemed to have any trouble, except for Elle and I. I think there's a chance that we're just not athletic.

Wait, did I just say *we*? Scratch that.

"I'm going to shower," I announce, trying to ignore the fact that I just lumped me and my mortal enemy into the dreaded 'we' category. Stomping a little on my way to the shower, I catch a look at myself in the mirror while I wait for the water to heat up. Eeep. It's about as bad as I had imagined, if not a little worse: My hair is stuck to my forehead in weird, sweaty clumps, my mascara has migrated to down my cheeks so I look like a cut-rate scary clown, and my face is still bright red — which against platinum blonde dyed hair looks even worse than it would have if I'd stayed a brunette.

I vow to stop at CVS on the way to school tomorrow to buy extra-waterproof mascara to avoid that problem again, and maybe pick up a headband as well. Then, I spot one of mom's cycling caps with its small brim and jaunty black and red colors lying on top of the pile of magazines sitting in the bathroom. I grab it and experimentally try it on, pushing my bangs up and under. It doesn't look too bad, I think. It's not a cheesy running cap like some of the girls have, and it's not a lame headband. It's just different enough to feel like me, but practical. And Mom has a dozen, so she won't even know it's missing. I just need to swipe some shoes and I'm all set.

I'm not quite singing in the shower when I finally get in, but I am feeling a little better about heading to practice again tomorrow. Remember, I tell myself sternly, you don't have to be good, you just have to make it through enough practices and meets to technically be 'on the team' so NYU wants you. How hard can it be? Miss C let me leave early today, and still counted the practice, so if I do that most days, it won't even take up much of my time.

Famous last words.

SECTION: Op/ed
  DRAFT: V1
  TITLE: Why sports shouldn't count in college

~~Look.~~ I get that going to college means big changes, and that being flexible and adaptable are healthy traits. ~~But since when does adaptable also have to mean "can run a 10 minute mile" or "serves a volleyball and makes it over the net most of the time"? I mean, can't schools look at a student's academic record, consider all of their other extracurriculars, and see that for some, sports just don't matter? And what if someone wanted to do a non-school sport? Like, what if I was a yoga lover or super into krav maga? Would that count against me like working on the literary magazine rather than running laps up and down a soccer field does?~~ *~~Would it?!~~*

College shouldn't be a time where we're forced to belong in certain groups or cohorts, it should be a time of self-exploration. ~~And what's less self-exploratory than team sports that force you to befriend total bitches who definitely don't deserve to be in your life anymore and you haven't talked to them in years and they don't matter at all to you, and that's to say nothing of the guy you once thought you were madly in love with and~~
  Oh no…

chapter
six

Elle

WHEN I GET HOME from practice, taking the late bus after stopping into the library to fill out some forms for the student council meeting later this week, I immediately head to the shower, feeling grimy and greasy. As I head up the stairs, as is our usual tradition on long days like this, Mom and I grunt at each other—an actual grunt noise, rather than conversation. It started out as a fun ironic thing a couple years ago, but I think we really mean it at this point. She's still tucked in her home office typing away on some legal brief, just like she usually is. When I get under the hot water in the shower, I nearly whimper, it feels so nice. My muscles — very unused until today — feel like they're tied in knots.

"Chinese or Mexican?" Mom yells through the door after I've stood (okay, fine, *sat* on the floor of the shower curled up in a ball while water pelts me) for what feels like an hour.

"Definitely Chinese, the usual stuff," I respond as I turn off the water. That shorthand conversation means, like most nights, we're getting take-out for dinner, which means it's going to be a working meal for her and therefore, a working meal for me. I briefly think about maybe ordering mixed vegetables or tofu instead of my usual orange chicken — fried chicken covered in sweet and savory and delicious gloop — or even changing my white rice to brown rice for the sake of 'health,' but I can hear my stomach growling and can practically smell the orange chicken already, even though I know that until Mom shuts her laptop, she won't even think about calling and *actually* placing our order.

I'm right, of course, and when I get out of the bathroom, I can still hear her clicking away, so I grab my cell phone and navigate to my Favorites, where Choy Wong has a spot right near the top of the list, between my debate team partner and student council VP. When Jan picks up the phone, I can hear the bustle of the restaurant behind him, and either he sees my caller ID number pop up or I just have called enough that he knows my voice, because he greets me by name and asks if I want the usual. "Yes, and can you deliver it super quick? I'm starving," I beg, and he laughs and promises to ride over with it the second it's ready.

I already know that I'm going to grab an extra few bucks out of Mom's wallet to tip him extra big if he makes it here (with the extra crispy noodles he knows I like) in under 40 minutes.

While I wait, I check my manicure — the one I get every other week because Mom noticed I was biting my nails — and my pedicure (that's just for fun, I don't bite my toenails!), and make sure that there aren't any chipping issues that need to be dealt with. When I'm sure that my nails haven't been wrecked from a day of running, I flip open my notes for tomorrow's debate team meeting during lunch, and start underlining, highlighting and mouthing along with my own arguments to prepare. But my mind keeps drifting back to practice. Nothing about it felt good, and my legs are still screaming at me, but I do feel an odd sense of satisfaction. It's quickly shot down by the look on Krista's face as she took off once we got back to school grounds, like she couldn't bear to be seen with me.

She wishes.

Next time, I'll be able to get away from her faster, I vow silently. She just happened to be the one to do the fast exit first this time.

I get changed into comfy sweats and a t-shirt from one of mom's soccer tournaments from a few years ago — I'm not trying to impress anyone, but I also don't want to greet the delivery guy wearing a robe — and exactly 39 minutes after I called in dinner, the doorbell rings. I almost fall down the steps trying to rush to answer it, because my calves are so cramped and also because I am a bit of a klutz. But mostly the calves.

Jan is standing in the doorway, and it occurs to me that he's probably the guy who visits the house the most often, which is pretty sad for both me and for my mom. She and my dad divorced a long time ago when I was little, and he moved to London for work soon after, so we're not very close. That's the understatement of the century. And boyfriendless wonder that I am, I've only had a few guys over for study sessions (not quote "study sessions," we really do study) and a couple of utterly un-noteworthy dates. I get asked out often enough, but usually to the kind of parties where keg-stands will be the highlight of the evening. And that's not really my vibe.

But Jan, I can always count on — and actually, he's kind of cute, come to think of it. And I don't think he's older than me, or at least, he doesn't seem to be. Maybe it's his family's restaurant?

Today, I'm in no condition for flirting so I backburner that idea, instead giving him a big smile and big tip before grabbing my bag, which is already starting to glisten with oil overspill. I take a big, deep inhale of my dinner. "Thank you," I say with as much sincerity as if he was giving me diamonds.

"I hope you have a good fortune in there," he says, and gives me a wink before he turns to leave. Huh. Maybe I should order Chinese more often than we already do. Or, you know, figure out if he goes to school anywhere near here.

"Mom, dinner's here!" I yell.

"Be out in five," she yells from behind closed doors. I know what that means: it's going to be a while. So, instead of waiting, I bring our meals into the kitchen and lay them out on the counter, building us each a plate. For Mom, I put her spring roll and shrimp lo mein on a plate with a fork (so she can eat and type, she says), and for me, I drop my rice and orange chicken onto another plate and toss a dumpling on the side, along with the chopsticks that Jan stuck in the bag with — *Thank you, Jan!* — extra crispy noodles, which I'll have later for dessert.

I grab myself a can of Coke and a can of Diet for mom, and bring her plate and soda into her office. She nods in acknowledgement as I set them down, then gives herself a little head shake ("I should probably say something to my daughter," she's probably thinking) and she looks up from her work. "Thanks, sweetheart," she says absently.

"No problem," I say. "I had my first cross-country practice today," I add. She looks surprised, even though I wrote it on our shared Google Calendar.

"That's right!" she says, trying to recover. "Was it fun?"

"Not really," I say honestly.

"You'll learn to love it," she says. "It's always hard in the first few practices."

"That's what Miss C says," I tell her, excited to start talking about how my teacher gave me advice today.

"Well, she's right," Mom says, but I can see her side-eyeing her computer, longing to get back to what she was doing.

Clearly, she's done with our conversation. "I have a lot of homework to get done, too, so I guess I'll just..." I gesture towards the door, but she's already turned back to her computer.

"We'll catch up later, okay?" she says, clicking away. "I know I haven't been much for conversations lately, it's just..."

"This case, I know," I finish for her, and turn around with my plate and Coke in hand, and make my way back upstairs. I hear the click of the study door shutting before I even make it to the top step. It's always the case. Such a cliche, but I know she genuinely thinks she means it and has some vision of us spending more time together 'later.' It's just that it's been 'later' for the last five years.

I bring my dinner up to my room most nights, to be honest. And usually, that's fine with me: my desk is plenty big enough for my dinner, my notes, and my laptop. I would normally eat while I watch some kind of debate or TED Talk, but tonight feels more like a *Buffy the Vampire Slayer* night, and thankfully, you can still watch the whole series on Netflix. I click on Season 5, and watch Buffy start to reject Spike's advances. I can't say I'd do the same—he's super cute, even if he is a killer vampire, though I am staunchly Team Angel.

I can multi-task and work on my speech notes while I watch. That's a solid compromise.

Debate Team To Do List

Do:
Remember to stand up straight, but stop doing that weird thing where your chin tilts up too high. You are not the queen.
Project ... but not in that booming voice that you get where it sounds like it's about to crack.
Smile—but not so much that it's an even teeth-to-gum ratio. Keep it sedate, but friendly.
Blink. Remember last time when the video afterwards made you look like a weird bullfrog? (Note to self: skip turtleneck sweater when on camera. And maybe ask teacher to shift camera angle slightly for more flattering effect?)
Put on an extra layer of mineral foundation before practice, you get far too red and shiny when you're excited otherwise.

Don't:
Cry. Again. Even when Nathan disagrees with your arguments. Remember that it is debate club—he literally has to disagree with you, that's the entire point.
Wait until two minutes before it's your turn to go up before realizing you need to pee. And if you do have to run and pee, definitely check that toilet paper isn't stuck to your shoe.
Mess up James' new pronouns—they/them. Get used to it. And if Victoria keeps rolling her eyes when they correct her, call her out. Be an advocate!
Overdo it at lunch beforehand. A gassy argument is never a good argument.

chapter
seven

Krista

IF ANYONE ASKS, I generally claim I like to watch artsy documentaries, which is partially true, but definitely not what I do when I'm alone. And since I have no one to impress at the moment, *Buffy the Vampire Slayer* is queued on our big TV in the living room, and Mom is already cozy on the couch by the time I finish my (very poor) attempt at an editorial. There's a big bowl of stew sitting on the counter with a chunk of sourdough bread and arugula salad next to it, and a glass of kombucha is, naturally, both of our drink of choice, served in short whiskey glasses with ice cubes. And of course, all of it is home-made. Mom is *such* a hippie! And in times like these, I'm thankful for it. Back when I had tofu in my lunch box in third grade? Not as ideal.

I grab my bowl of stew and dump myself onto the couch next to her, putting my feet in her lap as I do. "What, you do one day of running and you already want a foot rub?" she asks, laughing at me as she presses play. We're both *Buffy*-obsessed right now, and Mom especially loves it because she remembers when it was first on TV. She keeps telling me what a big deal it was when the one character on the show realized she was gay (on the show, not in real life) and how it changed a lot about network television. My mom was in her mid-20s at the time and had always known that she was gay, but she says having that happen on a mainstream show meant that a lot more people were suddenly accepting of her 'alternative lifestyle.' Total eye-roll these days. Being gay barely counts as alternative anymore. It used to be exciting and a little scary to tell people I have a gay mom. Now, *yawn*.

"How are your legs feeling?" Mom asks as I struggle to eat stew while perched on the couch. It's a messier process than I realized it would be.

"They're a little sore, but my stomach was what was killing me during practice," I tell her. Mom has always been a long run type of person, and lucky for me, she's never been pushy about me joining her. But I'm starting to slightly regret that, because if I was even a little better at running, I wouldn't be that girl in the back of the pack dropping out because of a cramp. Feels kind of lame, now that I'm home and relaxed.

"You really do get used to it," she says. "But the best advice is to just breathe into it and don't actually stop running. Slow down, but don't stop."

How the hell does she expect me to keep running when my stomach is burning, or to 'run slowly' when I can't run, full stop? I keep that thought to myself, because that's just going to open a can of worms about nutrition and nutrient timing and all that fun stuff. Mom, in addition to being a hippie and sometimes runner, is a holistic nutrition-ist, which basically means that it's a huge fight to eat anything unhealthy in the house (so I smuggle Snickers bars and potato chips up to my room to snack on), and any chance she gets to start talking about macronutrients, you can bet she will. I love her, but if I have to hear the lecture about eating a balanced lunch "yes, even at school in that terrible excuse of a cafeteria" lecture one more time, I might throw her sour-dough starter out the window. And while that may not mean anything to most people, that would be a really mean thing to do to my weird mother.

So I just nod and keep eating my (nutrient-dense) stew and enjoying the dulcet tones of Spike singing in the graveyard while Buffy just glares at him. Total dreamboat. Team Spike all the way. All in all, it's a solid way to spend the evening after a stressful day.

After I help clean up the kitchen, Mom shoos me upstairs to get ready for tomorrow, which is much more complicated now that I'm running after school, but also need to get to the newspaper studio in the computer lab after practice to prep the paper for its Friday release, and have that whole 'regular classes thing' to deal with. I have a piece to write about the quality of breakfasts served at school — citing my mother heavily, of course, because it's both easy and efficient — and I have a bunch of articles from the freshman class that are coming in that I already know will eat away my day as I try to make them readable. So I dive into a few of them now, to get ahead.

If NYU doesn't accept me, I don't even know what I'm going to do. I have the vision board set up in my room and look at it every night when I'm reminding myself that all the extra hours spent making those edits to freshman monstrosities are worth it. It's covered with pictures of New York, cool loft apartments in Soho, black skinny jeans paired with oversized tweed blazers and funky black-rimmed glasses, big desks with views of Central Park, taxis and fashion shows, Instagram pictures printed out from my favorite magazine editors with their bleach blond pixie cuts and black eyeliner, and of course, covers of the best issues of my favorite magazines boldly placed front and center. One day, I'll be covering offbeat fashion choices, underground plays and shows, and avant garde art exhibits.

And I certainly won't be running, I think to myself as I click from one article to the next, scoring the headline out with a red slash halfway through reading it. Sigh, freshman.

I can hear my mom downstairs, settling down on her big armchair with her laptop open, working through her stack of emails. Like mother, like daughter, I suppose — especially now that I'm running too.

By the time 11 PM rolls around, my edits for the day are done and I'm caught up on homework. My blog is lagging a bit, and I'm a little nervous since this is the first year it's going to be directly linked to the school newspaper website and it'll probably get more readers than, well, just my mom and my friends on the literary magazine committee. But I figured a bold step like that, making my private life a little more public, might be looked on favorably by NYU, for journalistic integrity.

By the time I finally switch off my desk light and pull my black comforter up to my chest, I figure I'm about as ready as anyone can be for the next day of school—with the exception of slightly sore legs and late bedtime, that is. I don't care what my guidance counselor says, I am not sure about this running stuff.

chapter
eight

Elle

```
TO: [SPEECH 101 FULL CLASS]
   From: Elle
   Date: September 19, 2021
   Subject: A few tips to remember!
```

Hey everyone!

Mr. P asked me to send out a quick email with a few of my top bits of advice for you all as we get closer to your first public speaking assignment. So, here you go!

DEBATE TEAM TIPS AND TRICKS
By Elle Winchester

1. Don't look at your notes, look at the audience
2. Don't make creepy eye contact, make casual eye contact
3. Pause to breathe
4. Be passionate, but not dramatic

5. Keep it tight, don't lose focus
6. Emotion has a time and a place, and debate team is not it
7. End decisively
8. Do Not Cry.

When I wake up at 6AM, birds are chirping outside my window — shut up, birds! — and my legs are feeling so cramped that getting out of bed seems almost impossible. I slowly make my way to the bathroom, wincing the whole way, and grab for the bottle of ibuprofen in the medicine cabinet, hoping that it kicks in before I have to walk downstairs for breakfast.

Mom either didn't sleep last night or got up crazy early for her morning workout, because even as I'm heading back into my bedroom to get dressed, I hear the door slam and the kitchen sink start spouting water so she can fill up the coffee pot as she stretches out from her morning spin session on the exercise bike. I grin just a little as I hear the music turn on and it's upbeat and funky. Mornings like this are the best. It means her work has gone well — otherwise, Mom would never make time for her workout — and the coffee starting to brew plus the happy music generally means she'll actually sit with me while I eat breakfast and we can talk.

I'm dying to try out one of my debate arguments on her, and I've been thinking more and more about the cross-country team and how I can get better. I'm hoping she'll have some good running advice for me, but I'm also hoping for some mom-style encouragement, like you'd get on a sitcom.

Before I head down though, I want to get ready for school so when I do sit at the breakfast bar, I'm not rushed. Today is definitely a leggings and Uggs day — there's a chill in the air, and more important, my legs are so battered-feeling that the idea of trying to jam them in jeans seems just plain cruel. And ditto my poor feet. Uggs sound like heaven. Cozy, cozy heaven.

All that topped with a big deep purple cashmere sweater (Mom might farm out her Christmas shopping to her personal shopper, but that woman knows how to pick out great clothes!), and with my recently highlighted hair tossed into a messy bun, I'm in good shape... the sweater covers my bum and highlights my boobs, while staying loose enough on my stomach so you don't notice the bulges at the top of my leggings. It's my go-to outfit for feeling normal.

Of course, if today was an actual debate team day, I'd be wearing one of the suits Mom actually did go shopping for, but thankfully, no button-downs for this girl today. I'm already a little nervous about re-tying my shoelaces to go to practice this afternoon (if I can't walk, do I have to run?) but I'm hoping as the day wears on, I'll start feeling those #gainz that Miss C was promising.

Sure, she said it might take a few practices, but that's for really unfit people, right? I should pick it up pretty quick. Maybe. I look in the mirror and do my usual smile-grimace-smile combo. The first smile is for face and hair. My skin is pretty clear, and thanks to Mom not stressing over money anymore, my hair is cut and highlighted by the best salon in town and it always looks pretty good. The grimace is for the neck down. I don't know exactly when the weight creeped on, but sometime between sophomore year and a couple of months ago when I went to try on my shorts and bikinis from junior year for the summer before senior year, I realized that they no longer fit — or if they did, just barely. My stomach and thighs took the brunt of the weight gain. I never used to worry about how my body looked because it was just.... I don't know, my body? Sort of neither here nor there. I wasn't skinny, but I wasn't fat. But now, I don't like wearing anything tight on top, and I make sure that the sweaters I wear over leggings (to avoid any discomfort of buttons poking into my stomach) cover my butt and upper thighs.

Even my leggings are wearing out faster, and I realized after the third pair last winter it was because my thighs were starting to chafe any time I walked. And when Mom gave me this purple sweater for Christmas, I was worried that it was half genius on the part of Martha, her shopper, and part gentle hint, since it was a size large and longer than what I had been wearing.

So, the grimace. And the reason I joined cross-country. I don't want to start college as the fat girl, or be the pudgy one pledging at the sorority.

But the last thing — the smile — is courtesy of the lipstick writing on my mirror that actually just says SMILE. I read in a magazine that if you smile, it can shift your brain chemistry and actually make you feel happier, so I stretch my lips into a grin as often as I can. I can't swear that it's working, but leaving my room with a smile on my face feels less depressing than moping out with the grimace.

By the time I get downstairs — slowly but surely making my way down, pausing between steps so my legs could recover — Mom already has her egg white and spinach omelet on a plate, her coffee cup in one hand and phone in the other. But she puts down the phone when I walk in.

"Omelet?" she offers, which means her work went really, really well last night. Mom never cooks unless she just composed a case-winning argument and is feeling wildly smug.

"Sure," I say, and slide onto the stool at the counter. She pushes a steaming mug of tea towards me since I can't stand the taste of coffee, though I do love the smell.

"So tell me *everything* about yesterday," she says, back to me as she pulls more spinach out of the fridge and tosses it in the pan. Her capri tights showcase obnoxiously good legs and thighs that only touch because they're so muscular, and her sleeveless top is streaked with sweat down the back, which is the only indicator that she already did a workout today. Her hair, slicked back in a blond ponytail (her natural color, of course), is photo-shoot perfect. Thankfully, I got the hair genes, but why did the jeans genes have to skip me by?

"Cross-country was okay," I say slowly, "But my legs are on fire today."

"DOMS," she says knowledgeably.

"Don who?" I ask, confused.

She laughs. "It stands for Delayed Onset Muscle Soreness," she says. "Your legs hurt more a day later than they did right after practice."

"Exactly," I say. "I didn't even run much."

"You ran, though, right?" she asks.

"Well, of course," I respond.

"Then that's a lot, considering I haven't seen you run since maybe the seventh grade when you were on the rec soccer team," she says, and slides the fresh omelet off the pan neatly onto a plate. She turns and hands it to me. "Any running is a lot when you're starting from zero, and cross-country teams are brutal for beginners," she adds. "Your team has some of the best runners in the state on it and they're doing the same workout as you are, so of course it's going to feel terrible at first! You're not going to quit, are you?" she asks, and now her tone is a little menacing, her gaze a little sharper.

Remembering how my legs looked in the mirror a minute ago, I shake my head no. "I want to be in shape for college," I tell her.

"That's my girl!" Mom says approvingly. "Did you put that on your vision board?"

Mom got really into vision boards a few months ago, and I have to admit, it made for a super fun Saturday together — the only one we've really spent together in ages. We sat with stacks and stacks of magazines and two big bulletin boards, and we each cut out words, pictures, and articles that symbolized what we wanted in our lives. When we had hung them in our rooms — well, mine in my bedroom by my desk, mom's in her study — I secretly attached one last picture: the cute surfer boy I'd cut out of one of mom's sport magazines. That's my secret vision for this year too, and I know if I can just lose a few pounds, I'll find a boyfriend that cute. Mom wouldn't exactly approve of my vision board being used for finding a boyfriend, it's about academic and career goals to her, but I want one, dammit.

To that end, and in order to avoid the college embarrassment of being relegated to fat best friend, I also stuck a few pictures of girls running happily, smiling, sweating artistically, and looking in charge of their lives. That's the feeling I'm craving. It didn't quite happen in that first practice, but I bet by the end of the week, those endorphins will be flowing and I'll be a lean, mean running machine.

I realize I didn't answer Mom, and nod my head as I bite into the omelet. It's not her tastiest effort (it's a little soggy if I'm honest) but Mom isn't much of a cook at the best of times. Still, it's here and it's healthier than the PopTart that I had been planning to have, so I manage to finish eating it while she tells me all about the case she's working on and the loophole in the manual that she found at 2AM. That's why she's so chipper.

"Will you pick me up from school later?" I beg as I start to gather my books to get to the bus stop.

"What time is practice over?" she asks. "I have court today until at least four."

"I won't be done until six," I promise. "I have debate practice with Angela and Tony after I get done at cross-country, we're going to be in the library."

"In that case, sure," she says, and I sigh in relief. I hate trying to catch the town bus home, and the last school bus leaves at five, so I'd be stuck at the mercy of public transit. "You'll eat dinner there, or wait until you're home?" she asks, though I know she isn't asking so she knows how much to cook — she'll probably order takeout on her way to get me and we'll pick it up together once I'm in the car. It's sort of our thing.

"Definitely eating at home," I say. I like Angela and Tony fine, but they're not really my friends. More... colleagues. And I don't want this to be a working dinner. Unlike Mom, I prefer eating my meals either reading a good book or watching a good show, and right now, *Buffy* is calling my name. I'm definitely not a work-and-eat person when I can avoid it.

I grab my backpack, kiss Mom on the cheek and wish her luck, and she says the same for me. As I'm about to walk out the door, she calls me back, holding up the gym bag with all my running gear. "I think you're forgetting something?" she says.

I laugh and grab the bag, but wonder if my subconscious was trying to tell me something — you know, 'take the day off,' 'don't go back,' something like that. But now, I'm stuck with it.

chapter
nine

Krista

I AM NOT A MORNING PERSON, so all that happens when I leave for school in the morning is that I roll out of bed as late as humanly possible, pull on whatever I laid out for the day the night before — in this case, black tights, tight black knit dress with long sleeves, black and white checkered cap, leather (fine, faux leather) jacket, and white high-tops — and put on my foundation and a lot of mascara. If I was feeling kicky, I would add red lipstick, but today isn't one of those days. The vibe is very much almost veering into mime territory, but I don't have the energy to figure anything else out.

My backpack and bag with my cross-country stuff — including a fresh pair of sneakers that Mom insisted I borrow after I told her I ran in Converse — is ready by the door because night owl Krista is smart, prepared and studious. On the other hand, morning Krista has no idea what the hell is going on as she drags herself through the apartment to the door. My mom is gone on her run, but she left a thermos filled with coffee and coconut milk and a protein powder — my special morning latte that she finally caved on. I am not a breakfast person, despite a nutritionist mom who claims the day can't start without it, but I do need caffeine to get through the first few periods of the day. So our reluctant compromise is the latte. Mom makes it almost every morning, sometimes switching it up and doing almond milk with a vanilla protein, or a shot of mocha for a chocolate taste. As it gets more into the fall season, she'll add some nutmeg and cinnamon for a pumpkin spice vibe. It's tasty enough, caffeinated enough, and nutritious enough that we're both okay with it. Plus, I don't need to stop and eat it.

I toss it in my backpack and drop my gym bag into my bike basket before fastening my helmet over my cap. 'Safety first' was Mom's other rule when I begged to be allowed to ride to school without her. It's bad enough that I don't have a car and can't drive myself; I really didn't need my mommy pedaling alongside of me too.

It's earlier than usual when I leave since I want to get into the newspaper computer lab before classes start so I can upload last night's edits before first period. As I pedal in, it's even brisker than I expected and I'm getting annoyed at myself for thinking this thin jacket was going to be enough. Time to bust out the heavy peacoat again, a fact that I'm not entirely unhappy about. It's much harder to pull off a chic punky look when your mascara is sweating off of your face and your black clothes absorb heat.

But the bright side is that my brain fog is lifted by the chilly ride so I can get straight down to business when I get into the newspaper lab and have some solo time to work. My energy crashes after that and the rest of the school day crawls on at a snail's pace, but at least my stomach isn't aching like it was right after practice. I even manage a smile and conversation with Miss C when she asks how I liked practice yesterday.

"Are your legs sore?" she asks sympathetically.

"No, why would they be?" I respond, and she looks at me strangely.

"Well, you're not exactly used to running," she says.

"I feel fine," I tell her, shifting from one foot to the other, testing my muscles. All good. "My stomach just hurt yesterday, that's all."

She nods and we move the conversation away from running and back to where it should be: the newspaper. These next couple of issues are super important for college applications, she tells me. Like I don't know that already. Still, this fact annoys the hell out of me, since it's also apparently essential that I run cross-country for a sport this semester, right when I need to be as focused as possible. "It's not fair," I whine, just feeling a little sorry for myself, the weight of a thousand editorials draping over my shoulders.

"I know," Miss C says, patting my shoulder. "But you're going to do fine. You just need to adjust."

She didn't see my late night edit session and I don't feel like she'd approve of me skimping on sleep, so I don't mention that, only nod and smile. "I know. I've got it," I say, before waving and moving briskly down the hall to the cafeteria for lunch.

I could sit with the other punk kids — and sometimes I do — but days like today when I'm tired and there's still a lot of hours left before I get to pedal home, I just want to have some *me* time, so I grab a peanut butter and jelly sandwich from the lunch lady, fill my thermos with water from the fountain, and slip out of the cafeteria and across the hall to the library. I'm technically not supposed to eat in there, but the librarians have gotten to know me since it's where we hold our poetry slams and lit mag meetings, so they let me sneak in when I need the quiet. I sink into a beanbag chair that's out of sight from the doorway and the tables, and open my book and unwrap my sandwich.

I'm embarrassed to admit that I'm actually just re-reading *Little Women* — and loving it — instead of some Henry Miller or Henry Rollins über-hip or über-punk volume. I'm just about to dive into the part where Jo turns down Laurie (noooooo) when I hear the door creak open and someone else slips in. I don't look up, until the rustling gets close enough that I can't help but peer over to see who it is.

Of course it's her. I can't seem to escape Elle. She picks a table almost directly across from me, spreads out a huge pile of index cards and unscrews the cap on her water bottle, sipping quietly. She's reading the notecards silently, but her lips are moving so she's clearly practicing for something.

I know Elle has spotted me as well, because she refuses to look up and make eye contact, and we spend an uncomfortable lunch hour ignoring each other. I eventually get wrapped up enough in the trials and tribulations of women in the 1860s (Corsets. The Worst.) to stop noticing Elle's annoying breathing habits, but it does spoil the mood somewhat and I'm almost relieved when the bell rings and I can head to physics.

By the end of the school day, I'm ready to sink into some newspaper editing and almost start to walk towards the lab before I remember that there's practice again today, and I actually groan out loud before I do an about-face and head for the locker rooms, causing a few confused freshman to scatter as I tear past them. Today, I have a t-shirt from a Bikini Kill concert mom went to back in the nineties. The sleeves are cut off and it's been worn out to a dull gray perfection. It's my comfiest t-shirt, and if Mom ever asks where it is, don't tell her you saw it. I leave on my leggings instead of putting on shorts because it's cooler out today, but change my Converse high tops to the bright purple sneakers mom had in the closet that were my size. They aren't particularly cool looking, but at least they aren't pink. I'm in and out of the locker room before any of the other girls are done changing, so I manage to avoid conversation with any of these other — ugh — "athletes" before I head out to the field.

I don't, however, manage to avoid the stares from my normal after-school crew that hangs out on the other side of the football field. They aren't the burnouts, exactly, but they are the punk kids that definitely spend most of their time hanging out after school trying to look intense while mocking the football players and other assorted jocks.

And I guess I count as a jock now too, or at least, they have no problem catcalling and mocking me as I walk onto the field towards where the team is gathering.

"Nice legs," yells Vinnie, while the rest of them just hoot and wolf-whistle and Frankie does some mock butt kicks and high knee drills.

Great. I'm trying to keep the whole athletic thing under wraps and was just kind of assuming that they wouldn't notice, since I'm rarely hanging out after school because of newspaper anyway. But apparently, I stick out like a sore thumb on the field.

For a second, I consider heading back into the building and changing, then coming back out to hang out with my friends instead of running laps. Or — more likely — heading back in the building, changing, and putting in some time in the newspaper lab instead.

But then I remind myself that Henry Rollins, the lead singer of Black Flag, is all about fitness. "Keep your blood clean, your body lean, and your mind sharp," he wrote.

And yes, I totally looked up 'punk musicians exercise' on Google. Joe Strummer of The Clash ran marathons in the 1980s, Henry Rollins lifts weights, Stuart Murdoch was running before he formed Belle and Sebastian, Kim of Matt & Kim was a runner, and Ben Gibbard, the Death Cab for Cutie singer, runs a ton. So I'm in good company, I tell myself as I walk onto the field, trying to project more confidence than I currently feel. I also give Frankie the finger behind my back.

Running is punk as hell.

chapter
ten

Elle

MY LEGS ARE STILL sore from yesterday when I head out to practice, but I try to put a smile on and pull my shoulders back as I walk towards the huddle of runners. "You've got this," I grit out to myself, saying it out loud before nearing the group. "Be a leader."

I'm still totally the biggest girl there — darn it, I was hoping for some latecomers to the team, and counting on someone being more out of shape than me! — but I try to not think too hard about it and focus on the positive. I'm here. The fall weather has kicked in and it's brisk out, the leaves are starting to change color, but the sun is still beaming down. It's a great day to be outside. My boobs look great in the top I borrowed from Mom.

I'm keenly aware that my stomach is growling, so I cough a couple of times to cover it up. I didn't have lunch, so that egg white omelet isn't doing much to keep me feeling full at this point. But I'm determined that I'm going to lose some weight starting this week, and that means making sacrifices.

We start with the same stretches and strides — "Skip like this, use your arms!" Coach demonstrates, awkwardly skipping down the track, unaware of how uncool he looks. We follow, though I try to stay towards the back. Coordination isn't exactly my middle name. The static stretching on the ground is worse. We're doing leg lifts from lying flat, and every time I raise my legs, I feel like I'm going to die, and worse,

I feel like everyone can see my flabby, ghost-white butt. I never thought of applying self-tanner there, but I'm rethinking my whole grooming regimen at this point. My ponytail, at least, doesn't get messed up while pressing my head into the grass. Dirt is getting under my nails when we get into plank position, but I'm finding myself struggling so much to hold the form that I don't even care anymore. I can see Krista is struggling too, and at least for a few seconds, I'm able to use that as motivation to stay in position. She crumbles first, and I feel a tiny ping of victory.

By the time Coach declares that we're warmed up and ready to run, I feel like I've already done a full workout, and half of me is feeling like I should just quit and head back to the school, but the other half is thinking, 'well, how much worse can the run itself be?'

Today is hill repeats, Coach tells us, so the answer is 'very.' To make matters worse, he reminds us that we're less than two weeks out from the first meet of the season, and before I can make up my mind to be ill that day, he reminds us that in addition to it being the first meet, it's going to be the smallest and the easiest. "And if you're hoping to put cross-country on your transcripts," he adds ominously, "you need at least 25 practices and three races this season."

I gulp, audibly. I look around and almost everyone else is nodding seriously, like that makes perfect sense. Only Krista, who's standing on the edge of the crowd, looks as appalled as I feel. Three races? I had no idea I was going to race. I just wanted to drop a few pounds and improve my odds of Ivy League. This seem unfair, I think to myself. But I don't say it out loud, and again, I bust out the big smile in case anyone is looking. Krista looks scornfully at me for a half second before turning away. Whatever. It's not like I need her to be my ally on this team.

But it would be nice if it wasn't quite so lonely.

"Let's get going, just an easy mile jog to get to the hill," Miss C tells us, and she starts to run. Her jog is faster than my top speed, and almost immediately, I get swarmed by the pack of faster runners and left in last place again. I try to catch up, but I'm quickly panting and my legs are threatening mutiny. The front yards along the road are looking mighty tempting, and a couple of leaf piles look almost feather-bed-like. But not this time. I know today I need to make it to the hill. Once I'm there, I'll get a break, I promise myself, and keep moving, slow and steady. I have to walk every so often, but I try to turn it into a game.

Walk between one set of mailboxes, run between two. The driveways go by faster, and by the time we get to the hill, I'm still far behind but it's not as bad as yesterday. Improvement!

And then, it happens. Like a slow motion moment in every romantic movie I've ever seen, *he* appears, his black hair breezing behind him just enough that it looks like it's floating. Jess, the dreamiest guy in our class (my personal opinion)... and a major part of my middle school history, and my first real crush, and my first real heartbreak.

What is he doing here?

I knew he was the school's track star, but I didn't think he ran cross-country. If I'd known that, I would have tried out for field hockey, rugby, wrestling, literally anything else. Maybe. Or maybe I would have been the first on the cross-country sign up list. Oh no. Did my subconscious do this? Did *Krista's* subconscious do this?

Seeing him jogging in my direction like some kind of Greek god, I can almost hear strains from Phil Collins' "In the Air Tonight" in the background. It's the worst thing, but somehow it's also the best thing, and I can feel my heartbeat creep even faster.

Oh lord, oh lord...

I have had a huge crush on Jess since we were about 10 years old. Past-tense. Had. Definitely don't feel that way now. At all. But as he gets closer, he gives me his trademark cheeky grin and I almost forget just that we don't speak anymore, and why that's the case. I'm caught off guard by the fact that he's running towards me when the rest of the team must be waiting at the top of the hill.

"Come on, Miller," he says, using my last name like he always used to do, back when he and Krista and I were a single unit, best friends forever, peas in a pod, inseparable. "You're almost there."

I blush furiously, which luckily, he likely doesn't notice since I'm already beet red from exertion, and huff my way towards the finish as he gives my hip a quick brush with his fingers and lightly treads away, looking like he's barely breathing. Meanwhile, my hip where he touched it is on fire. And then I notice the platinum blonde head bobbing a block in front of me, and see Jess run casually by her, saying something as he jogs by. She responds by giving him the finger, and I bet she's not blushing.

Shit. Krista, Jess and I all on the same team. It's so ridiculous that I almost laugh out loud. The triangle that got blown apart at freshman year homecoming, suddenly reunited by my need to get ready for freshman year of college. It's so ironic that for a second, the magnitude of how uncomfortable I am is swept away by sheer hilarity.

I remember in vivid color screaming at Krista that I hated her and never wanted to talk to her again, I remember Jess saying we were both acting like children and he never wanted to talk to *either* of us again, and I remember Krista glaring at both of us, silent and cold.

Looking back, it seems so trivial, but at the same time, still so earth-shattering. For a minute, I actually stop dead in my tracks and relive it, like I really am in a cliche teen movie.

It was the worst night of my life. My only solace was that it happened within the first semester of high school. Realistically, there was no way that the three of us—the newfound punk, the old-school jock and the perpetually preppy—were going to stay friends for the next four years. In some ways, the huge fight we had that night was like ripping a Band-Aid off: it hurts for a second, but it beats the slow, painful process of peeling it back bit by bit.

The logical part of my brain, Mom's lawyer-speak, tells me that no matter what actually happened, we were always going to end up growing apart. The *why* didn't matter, the *how* was inconsequential. No one stays friends from preschool to adulthood, it's just not practical. If we didn't burn out, we would fade away (that metaphor is admittedly cribbed from one of Krista's Kurt Cobain posters she hung up just a month before our friendship went to hell).

What we fought about barely mattered. The three of us had gone as a group to the homecoming dance, the same way we did everything: together. Of course, Jess didn't know about my huge crush on him then, but I harbored fantasies that the first slow dance of the night, he'd take me in his arms and he'd realize that our friendship had grown into something much, much stronger than that.

Krista knew.

But it wasn't me that he asked to dance when the beat slowed. No, he turned to Krista, who looked so chic in her short black dress compared to my long, soft pink one. Even then, before she'd gone full-on punk rock, her edgy vibe had started to work for her. She said yes and they never even glanced back at me before heading into the sea of couples swaying.

And she knew.

She knew how much I *loved* him and she went and danced with him, smiling into his stunning green eyes while I just stood there and watched. I kept hoping someone else would come back and dance with me, but no one asked or offered, so I just stood by the doorway, awkward and alone.

Afterwards, Krista told me out in the hall that she really wanted to spend more time with Jess, and could I hang out with someone else for the rest of the night, pretty please? She said it so kindly that at first, I had no idea what she was asking. And when it did sink in, I was almost speechless. In retrospect, being fully speechless would be have been better than what happened, in which I spewed out some of the most mean, vicious things that I've ever said in my life. And I didn't just say them to her, I said them about her. Loudly. To everyone who would listen.

I wish I had kept my mouth shut, looking back on it. My rational brain knows it wasn't worth it, that she probably didn't mean to break my heart any more than he did. But *She Knew*. She knew how I felt, and didn't care. She knew how I felt, but she chose him anyway. I let my emotions get the best of me. Sure, my heart was shattered, but I could have been dignified, and really, if Jess chose her, that meant he didn't choose me. But it was her, and I freaked out, and then she freaked out, and Jess, who had wandered out to find us, overheard as we were just tearing into each other's personal style, personal hygiene, deepest secrets, tiny flaws. It was one of those moments where a betrayal becomes an avalanche of unleashed disappointments, and the friendship we'd started at the bus stop on the first day of kindergarten vanished entirely.

As far as I know, Krista and Jess haven't spoken since that night either. He ditched her almost immediately, as soon as he saw us having that fight. It definitely didn't help that after all of that, instead of the three of us sulkily hanging out or at least riding home together, Krista had her mom come and pick her up and I spotted Jess making out with another girl on the dance floor later, which I immediately texted to Krista to let her know that she ruined our friendship for nothing. I had to hitch a ride home with another girl in our neighborhood, because there was no way I was getting in a car with Jess.

"Teen hormones," Mom sighed at me when I came home that night and started sobbing. She rolled her eyes, looking up at the ceiling like some higher power was going to help her deal with the mess that was my life. Then, she patted my shoulder as I cried on the couch and told me that no guy is ever worth this level of drama, and that maybe now, I could start to focus on school and my future. So I did, and I have ever since. No dates, and barely any friendships since Krista, because why bother when it'll just end when we leave for college? I'll save the social life for the Ivy Leagues.

But now, Jess is here, still dreamy, and okay, fine, I'm still secretly half in love with him, or at least, deep lust. Of all of us, he was technically the most innocent: it wasn't his fault that I was head over heels into him, and that apparently, so was Krista (though she never mentioned it until that night). And yeah, he could have been less obvious about immediately finding another girl to dance with — and make out with — but after the way we all screamed at each other, I can barely blame him. And it has been years and years.

I shake my head just the slightest bit, like I'm trying to knock the memories out of my brain, and I dig deep to speed up so I can pull alongside him at the top of the hill. I give him my most dazzling smile that I can possibly muster.

"I'll race you on the next hill," I say in my flirtiest voice, stifling the need to take a huge inhale or collapse on the ground. As Coach blows into the whistle signaling us to get moving again, I make every attempt to catch up to the group as fast as possible, while making sure I don't trip or accidentally vomit or something.

Right before he passes me—which, I'll be honest, is pretty quick—he moves just a few inches closer to me and quietly says, "I missed hanging out with you."

And right then, I know I'm absolutely done for.

chapter
eleven

Krista

JESS

It's been a minute.

You there?

KRISTA

Who is this?

JESS

You deleted my number?

It's Jess

I miss hanging out with you.

You there?

KRISTA

"I MISS HANGING OUT WITH YOU?" What the hell is that supposed to mean? I'm raging my way to the car, oblivious to the fact that Miss C is trying to have a conversation as she jogs alongside of me. Well, not oblivious — I just don't care. Where in the hell does Jess get off not speaking to me for THREE FREAKING YEARS and then just giving me that knowing smile as he sped past me on the hill and then texting me that after practice while I'm trying to cool down? How does someone cool down with that popping up on their phone?

Scumbag.

But still, a pretty hot scumbag. I blocked him from my radar since freshman year, and I had no idea that he was on this team. Really. Hopefully my subconscious didn't know that either. I thought he was strictly the golden boy of the track team, but apparently, he's here. He's a running phenom, naturally. He wasn't even breathing hard when he passed me on that first hill, said hi, and then somehow managed to text between intervals.

I'm fuming. I'm pissed. I'm... okay, fine, slightly into it.

"KRISTA!" Miss C is shouting now, and she breaks me out of my complete frenzy.

"Sorry, Miss C," I say — I'm not normally this out of it, so she seems to just shrug it off. Hopefully she assumes I'm just exhausted from practice, which is partially true.

"How did you feel today?" she asks.

"Pretty good," I tell her. I'm not lying: the jog out to the hills wasn't pleasant, but once Jess got my blood boiling when he said hi, I channeled all of that irritation and confusion into my legs and just raged up the hill, panting, pumping my arms in time with my legs.

"You were one of the fastest girls on the hill today," she tells me, and I admit, it's not very punk, but I get a little glow of pride as she compliments my athletic achievement. "You definitely didn't run on your own this summer?"

I shake my head.

"If you keep practicing, you might be really competitive at our first meet," she tells me. "It has a few big climbs that might really suit you."

"Thanks," I say, even though doing well in a meet isn't particularly interesting to me. "Have you had a chance to read the new editorial column from that junior in band?" I ask, trying to shift the topic to one that I deeply care about.

We chat about that and the new website layout — designed with some help from one of the graphic design students, but using my concepts — and how we might actually be up for some bigger awards this year, and I realize that she's sneakily walked me around the track twice as we run through what needs to happen before the new edition is published online. "You made me do a longer cool down!" I say accusingly.

She doesn't look sorry at all, she just looks smug. "It's important," she tells me, before pointing over at the parking lot. "Isn't that your mom?"

It is. She's standing under the lamp by the side door to the library chatting with someone, so I grab my backpack and start walking towards her. I can always shower at home, and I'd rather not brave the locker room. Even if it is a girls' room, it still reeks of sweaty socks in there, plus Elle might be lurking and I know she saw Jess too. That's an interaction I'd rather avoid.

As Mom waves at me and I get a better view of the woman she's talking to.

"Great," I mutter under my breath. Today is just a day for reunions, I suppose, because while I spent the last two practices realizing I've reluctantly reunited with my two former besties in Elle and Jess, I completely forgot the potential for my mom to reconnect with hers: Elle's mom, Stephanie. They're both smiling wide when I get over to them.

"I remember that Bikini Kill shirt!" is the first thing out of Stephanie's mouth as she looks at me, and she's grinning at my mom as she says it.

"I was wondering where that was," Mom says, giving me a mock glare before turning back to Stephanie. "Remember that one long run we were doing when we got caught in that rainstorm..."

"And you had to use that shirt to wrap your cell phone so it wouldn't get wet, and did the rest of the run home in that awful old sports bra!" Stephanie finishes the story and both of them burst out laughing. It never really occurred to me that when Jess and Elle and I stopped being friends, it meant that Mom and Stephanie didn't have much time to hang out with each other anymore, and I feel momentarily guilty.

That is, until I see my mom pull her classic move — she gently leans over and nudges Stephanie's shoulder with hers. "Those were good times," she says.

Is my mother *flirting with Elle's mom*?

Oh, hell no. Absolutely not. No. Nope. Nyet. We are going to have a serious discussion about this later.

"Mom, I have a ton of work to do and I'm starving," I say, knowing that the work might not matter, but the nutritionist in her can't help but need to feed me as soon as possible.

"I'll send you that meal delivery service link I mentioned," she says to Stephanie before giving me a look and getting in the car. "You've got to start taking care of yourself better. Chinese takeout is not a food group."

Stephanie giggles back, destroying my notions that she's not at all interested in my mother.

As soon as we load my bike on the rack, shut the doors and pull away, I twist in my seat and look at her, as serious as I possibly can. "Mom, you cannot hit on my teammate's mothers," I tell her patiently.

"I wasn't hitting on anyone," she says innocently, but doesn't totally meet my eyes. "I was just catching up with an old friend. Honey, you didn't tell me Elle was on the team with you! Have you two been catching up?"

"You know we don't talk anymore," I say, and cross my arms to signal the end of that conversation. But after a few seconds of silence, I feel even more guilty, partially because I know I cost Mom a best friend, and partially because I'm acting like a spoiled brat. "Guess what?" I say, to change the subject. "Miss C said I was a natural on hills — the fastest one on the team!"

Instantly, my mom's slightly pouty expression shifts to a happy one, and she starts babbling about how much she loves hill running too and maybe we can get out on the trail for some extra practice this weekend. I have a sinking suspicion that this 'easy' sport that I've signed up for is going to take up a lot more of my time than I expected.

I do have a secret, though: when I was pounding away up that hill today, I felt like I was unstoppable, like I was on top of the world, ecstatic. It's the best feeling I've had since I became editor-in-chief, and this time, I wasn't even trying to accomplish anything really.

I haven't been competitive about anything other than writing, ever. In fact, right now, Mom is laughing at a story she's telling (she laughs at a lot of her own stories) about when I was six years old and she tried to get me to go play tee ball. "I left you sitting on the bench looking so grumpy that the coach came over to you and said that you could be his special helper for the day. Naturally, you just started bawling immediately. I was almost at the car and I could hear you wailing," she says, laughing. "I had to go back and get you because you just wouldn't stop. I thought I was going to die of embarrassment."

"I don't know why you wanted me to play tee-ball anyway," I say, kind of grumpy hearing this retelling. As I recall, the coach scared the crap out of me by telling all the other kids to be extra nice to me that day, and when they started talking to me, I just got overwhelmed and kind of freaked out. Like *any* normal kid would.

"My parents always wanted me to play sports but I hated it," Mom says. "I didn't really care if you played— hence why we never went back — but I wanted to give you the opportunity in case you loved it."

Fair enough. "So when did you get into running, then?" I ask. Funny how I never wondered about it — I've always just wanted to hear about her escapades traveling around the country following punk bands. Which is, of course, where my current Bikini Kill t-shirt came from. The stories about her selling merch and waiting tables in random cities for a week or two at a time have always been way more interesting.

"It was just after you were born, actually," Mom says. "I was going stir crazy being in the house, especially the first few months when my mom was living with me. She was so good with you that she didn't mind if I would go out for walks on my own to get a bit of time to myself, so I'd leave you two together. And then the walks got faster and somewhere along the line, I turned into a runner. It just sort of... happened."

By the time we get home, Mom has given me advice on how to tackle downhills — keep your weight back and focus on taking longer strides— and criticized my shoe choice, despite the fact that they're her shoes. "They're road shoes," she says, "Not trail shoes."

Who knew sneakers were so complicated?

Dinner is quick because we both have work to do — Mom has a client consult call (say that five times fast) at 8PM and I still haven't finished my personal blog entry that I want in the school paper. But when I sit down in front of the keyboard, I can't really find words to write. I'm still spun up from the events of the day — the good and the bad. Mainly, I can't stop thinking about Jess, why he said he missed me, what Elle would do if she heard that he texted me and not to her, and what's going to happen with the three of us on the same team.

I don't miss either of them at all, I think mutinously, staring at the band posters behind my desk, their black-and-white and blocky fonts looking stark on my gray walls. For a second, my vision blurs just a little and I get a flashback to how this same desk looked just four years ago, with a bulletin board covered in pictures of the three of us: Elle and I wearing each others' clothes and looking terrible, Elle and I on the beach watching the sunrise, thinking we had actually managed to sneak out without my mom noticing (who do you think took the picture?) and the three of us rowing a canoe — very poorly — down the river one summer, Jess at the front of the boat and Elle and I paddling along in rhythm behind him, all of us grinning in the sunlight.

Just as quickly, I snap out of it. 'We weren't going to stay friends before we had that one big fight anyway,' I tell myself, rolling my shoulders back, then forwards and rolling my head in a circle to release some of the tension that's built up. And it wasn't my fault anyway. Not entirely.

chapter
twelve

Elle

BY THE TIME I get home, I'm absolutely livid. First, Mom showed up an hour earlier than planned to pick me up. Not only did she show up early, she was talking to the enemy — Krista's mom. And they looked like they were having the time of their lives, even when Krista walked up. My mom should know better. Just because we're on the same team doesn't change anything. She still screwed me over, she still abandoned our friendship, she's still dead to me. Krista, I mean. Not Mom. But she's also on my list at the moment.

So, I wait behind the door to the school until Krista pulled her mom towards the car and my mom is left looking suddenly lost and a little lonely. For a moment, I consider not coming out until six — when she was *supposed* to be coming to get me — but I feel sorry enough for her standing there by herself that I text my debate colleagues (let's face it, they aren't my friends) that I need to leave early and we'd catch up online later.

For a second, I can see what people mean when they say mom and I look alike: We're both sort of natural blondes, we have the same small nose and brown eyes, and our cheekbones slant upwards a bit more than most peoples' do. Before she spots me, I see her fidgeting with her sweater, trying to subtly pull it so it sits looser. She always has been in such athletic shape that I know the last couple years of late nights at work have made her much less happy with herself, since she has much less time to exercise and is self-conscious about it. At least she has an excuse though, I just straight up hate working out and haven't... until now.

Once I'm in the car and buckled up, she asks how practice was today. My stomach growls in response — I'm still starving. "Better," I say carefully. "I'm still the slowest one there, but it didn't hurt quite as much."

I'm lying. It actually hurt a lot more, honestly, but that was because when we rejoined the group, I was so conscious of Jess watching me that I tried my hardest on every hill repeat, finishing wheezing and sore, and the jog back to school felt more like a death march than a casual cooldown, but I didn't want to seem like I couldn't handle it. Every part of my body is screaming for a break, though I'm also pretty proud that I made it back without stopping.

That said, I was still the slowest one.

"I wish I wasn't so out of shape too," Mom responds, and adds, "I can't believe how fit Elle's mom still is! She doesn't look like she's changed at all in the last few years."

I stay silent, willing the conversation to shift. I refuse to engage with any discussion of Krista or any of her relatives.

"What do you want for dinner?" Mom asks, taking mercy on me and changing the subject. And I know she really means, "What should we pick up for dinner," so suddenly, my appetite goes into overdrive and I almost shout "Everything!"

Instead, we hit the drive-through of the local burrito joint, where we both have regular orders. Mom just says her name and asks for the regular, and in minutes, we have a huge brown bag filled with chips, guacamole, two huge burritos — mine with extra cheese and sauce — and two Cokes. "I don't know about you, but I needed this pick me up," Mom says, sighing happily as she takes a sip.

"Ditto," I say. The calorie count flashes briefly before my eyes, before I blink it away and dig in for a handful of chips.

When we make it to the house, Mom actually grabs her TV tray and sits next to me on the couch, switching the smart TV on. "Want to watch something while we eat?" she asks, and even though I have a mountain of homework, I nod and grab my tray too. I take what I can get when it comes to time with Mom.

But before she sits down, she pulls out a sheaf of papers from her briefcase, parking them on her tray as well. It's definitely still going to be a working dinner for her, so I grab my history notes from my backpack so I can semi-study for tomorrow's test while we both pretend to be watching whatever sitcom is on tonight. It's not the perfect mother-daughter bonding time, but it's actually pretty pleasant as we sit in companionable silence, occasionally laughing when we catch a joke on *Friends*, but mostly I'm highlighting my notes as we devour our burritos.

For the first time in a while, I actually outlast mom — I'm finishing up calc homework, chasing the last of the guac with a couple of rogue chips, when I hear her softly snoring next to me, her head tilted to the side and resting on the arm of the couch. I put a minus sign on the front of my last answer (so sneaky!), cover her with the cashmere throw that's draped on the back of the couch for situations like this and collect our trash before heading up to my room. I can probably get through a bit more on my debate speech, but my main plan is to get onto social media and start scrolling through all of Jess's posts from the last few years.

He missed me, he said. But did he really? If he did, why didn't he ever get in touch? He must have known that the fight was never really about him — it was always about Krista and me. But I guess to him, the two of us were a unit. Maybe.

I'm just debating myself now, I realize, and while that might count as practice, it probably won't sound too great when I accidentally start expounding the he said/she said dynamics of freshman year fights in the next team meeting.

I can make him like me again, I tell myself before I turn off the lights to go to sleep. I just need to lose these few pounds and he'll see exactly what he's been missing.

chapter
thirteen

Krista

IT'S BEEN a long week of practices, but I don't feel like I'm at all ready to race. My readiness doesn't matter, though, because in a few hours, I'll be racing no matter how I feel. Sure, I don't have to be competitive, like my mom says. But still, it's a start line and a lot of people and despite my attempts to not care, it's pretty hard to completely not care. Putting out the aura of not caring is way harder than caring.

When I climb on the bus, the freshman are all excitedly talking about how great it is that we get to miss most of the school day, but I roll my eyes. Silly freshman don't realize what a giant pain in the ass it is to make up schoolwork when you miss a day, especially a day where you're trapped on a bus and then in a tent for most of it. I couldn't even bring my laptop!

The week itself has been frustrating too. A school-wide computer glitch knocked out some of my work on the paper so it's not ready to go out yet, and my mom keeps casually mentioning Elle's mom in conversation like I wouldn't notice. I finally snapped at her yesterday that she could just come to the damn meet and talk to her if she cared so much, and now I'm a little worried that she'll take me up on it. I know Elle's mom is going to be here: Elle made a huge deal out of telling everyone that her mom was going to come to help out at the first meet, and she's even — thank goodness — driving separately.

And speaking of Elle, we've miraculously managed to avoid each other every single practice. It hasn't been too hard, since it turns out that I'm able to keep up with the fast girls going uphill. It almost seems easy, to be honest. Elle still hasn't really improved, still huffing and puffing her way up the hill, almost always the last person to get to the starting point of our workouts. But I have to give her credit, she also hasn't given up. She's still out there every day. She's not looking too healthy, though. She looks great in her short shorts, and I do envy her curves — she certainly gets more stares on the hills than I do, despite how quick I'm going. But she's gotten really pale these last few practices and seems to be getting tired almost as soon as she starts, though she keeps pushing. I've noticed her talking to Jess a couple of times as well, and it hurts my heart just a little bit every time I notice them together. Not that I would want to be friends with either of them ever again. But still.

And not that I'm keeping track, but Jess hasn't messaged me since that second practice. I have caught him staring at me a few times, but then, he starts talking to the super-fast girl on the team, Jenny, and goes right back to ignoring me. Which is good.

I climb slowly onto the bus, swathed in a big black hoodie and black sweatpants that are a little bit too big on me, but are super comfortable. I know that this long bus ride is going to feel even longer because we're going to be crammed together, so I plan to sleep for as much of it as possible. I snag one of the last open seats in the middle and prepare to defend my territory.

Talk about the best laid plans going wrong though. I manage to keep a few people from opting for that empty seat next to me, and I think I'm almost home free... until Jess climbs on the bus, runs a hand through his hair as he surveys the scene (teen rom com protagonist cliché much?) and lets his gaze stop on the last empty seat. Next to me.

Of course.

I curse under my breath but I don't want to give him the satisfaction of seeing that I care, so when he plunks down next to me and smiles that lopsided grin, I don't smile back, just coolly nod. That'll show him.

He pulls out *This Band Could Be Your Life: An Oral History of Punk Rock* and starts reading it, and immediately, I'm intrigued... and suspicious. From what I've seen on Instagram — not that I follow him

— he isn't into punk music at all. He might remember that it was the book I was reading freshman year before things went to hell. I'm not sure if it's an olive branch, a power play, a dick move, or him just reading a book for the sake of reading. But I don't ask. I know better than to engage.

Jess didn't technically do anything wrong, other than be in the wrong place at the wrong time — right between Elle and I — but that doesn't really change how I feel about him. And besides, I've seen him on social media: every week he's with a new girlfriend or 'just hanging out' with some girl he just met. Even if we once had a mutual crush, we're not the same people anymore.

Except that he still smells the way I remember, and I can't help but think about the drives we used to make, him in the middle seat and Elle and I on either side as one of our moms drove us to the movies, the mall, or the little downtown lined with coffee shops and stores we'd never go into. I instinctively almost lean my head onto his shoulder, but catch myself.

Instead, I put on my headphones and lean my head against the window, trying to block him out.

It works, until the bus starts creaking away and it's so shaky that I'm forced to sit upright again, and he looks over. "Hey," he says.

"Hey," I respond.

Witty repartee, I know. But what can you expect from two people who spent most of high school ignoring each other? Which is somehow now something I can't ignore.

"What are you listening to?" he asks.

"You haven't heard of them," I say, a tiny bit snarkily.

"Try me," he says, holding up his punk rock scene cred book.

"River City Rebels," I say.

"Never heard of them," he admits. "But I've been digging the Jurassic Five lately—you like them, right?"

Ugh, he's right. I'm not really into current punk, but give me the classics and I'm here for it. But still.

"Why are you suddenly talking to me again?" I say, just throwing it out there like it doesn't matter to me at all.

He smiles again. "I just miss talking to you," he says. "It's not like we'll be in high school forever, so doesn't it make sense to make the most of the time?"

The seize the day approach. YOLO. While I generally agree with it, it feels a little like a line. (A *lot* like a line.) Still, I think, I don't owe Elle any loyalty anymore, so what would be the big deal be if I did decide to hang out with Jess again? She must be over him by now, but even if she wasn't, do I have an obligation to care? I don't soul search too hard about this.

"Fair enough," I say, and extend an olive branch of my own. "What's your favorite part of the book so far?" I ask, gesturing to *This Band Could Be Your Life*.

He starts talking more about Jurassic Five — huh, he actually has read at least a part of it! — and from there, we move to that time our parents took us to see *Jurassic Park* and I cried, and before I know it, I'm laughing so hard that I'm a little afraid I'm going to pee in my running shorts.

Luckily, I don't, and when we go to shuffle off the bus, Jess squeezes my hand. I don't pull it away, but I do feel itchy about it. "I'm glad we got to talk," he says seriously, and I nearly believe him this time. "Save me a seat on the ride back?" he asks.

"Sure," I say, and we go our separate ways, since I really need to find the bathroom, and I assume that as the team's super-star runner, he has a whole routine before his race he has to follow.

After I pee, I try to emulate what the other senior girls on our team are doing, which seems to start with snacking, sipping water, walking the start, stretching and scouting what the first big hill of the course looks like. One of the younger girls offers to lend me her running spikes when the coach notices that I don't have any, but they seem a little intense for me to be trying during my first race, so I say I'm fine in my sneakers.

Coach calls us into a huddle and Elle finally arrives, in pristine cross-country spikes that she's definitely never used before and a pair of shorts so crisp that look like they may have been ironed. She looks sort of like cross-country Barbie.

"Remember, make your starts count," Coach tells us. "Get out there and do some strides and accels 15 minutes ahead of start. Make sure you're at the line when they call you to the staging area, so you don't end up at the back of the pack. Start strong, and settle in to a comfortable but hard pace once you're over that first hill. And don't forget, look for...."

He pauses to let us fill this in, and all the older athletes who clearly have done this before dutifully say, "Spaces, not people."

"This is the number one rule for racing," he says, addressing all of us like the troops before a battle. "Don't look at the back of the person in front of you, focus on the empty space ahead of it or to the side of it and try to get there."

I don't get it. But I've never raced anything, let alone cross-country, so I'm sure I'll figure it out. Or not. I don't care. Really.

He tries to make us put our hands in and chant, which obviously I'm not going to do. Not exactly my style. So I'm surprised that I feel a little left out when it's not just the dorky freshman with their hands in, it's everyone, including Jess and the team's star female, Jenny, who puts her hand right on his and gives him a little smile and wink. Whatever. But they all look pretty excited afterwards, so maybe there's something to the whole rah-rah-rah thing.

I watch closely as the freshman racers get started — I'm not the cheering type, so I'm hoping that my smiling is encouraging enough. I want to see how the starts work... not like I care how it goes, I just don't want to make a fool out of myself either, running in the wrong direction or something. It's getting warm out, so I'm in my singlet with our school mascot — an alligator, which is weird but kind of cool — on the front, and my black shorts. Luckily, the singlet is black with green for the logo, so it's a pretty black-on-black outfit and I'm okay with it. My hair is braided in a few rows so it stays off my face — it took Mom a while to do it this morning, but she swears it was her lucky hairstyle the first time she raced a marathon, so I figured it couldn't hurt.

After watching their start, all I can do is awkwardly wait around for mine. I really wish I had a book.

chapter
fourteen

Elle

WE'RE ABOUT five minutes from the start of our race and the other girls are milling around the starting grid, waiting to be called up. I look over and accidentally make eye contact with Krista, who's playing with her braids and bopping along with her headphones, and instantly look away when our eyes meet. Angry ex-friend is not the kind of vibe I need right now, and I scan the crowd for Jess instead. I can't see him anywhere, so I'm nervously pacing and smoothing out my singlet, which feels lumpy over my perfectly fitted lululemon sports bra (it's the only bra I own that actually makes me feel like my cleavage is just right. It's kind of my lucky bra, I guess).

The other girls are doing strides up and down the starting grid, so I follow along — we skip down, do butt kicks back. We do high knees down, and skip back. We do a few accelerations (Coach's 'accels') and I end up at the back of the pack, breathing hard. I didn't get dropped from the group during warmup, so that's a plus.

I'm starting to get nervous, but an excited nervous. I can see my mom and Krista's mom are both over at the starting line, talking animatedly to each other. I momentarily feel guilty about the fact that they haven't hung out in years because of what happened between me and Krista, but I give myself a mini-lecture. They're grown women who could have stayed in touch if they wanted to. My mom is the one who suddenly started taking on more and more cases after her promotion, and she's the one who never has time to hang out with anyone (including me, usually). Even now, I'm willing to bet she's thinking about checking her phone and how soon she can start responding to emails.

The race director waves her arms and shouts into a bullhorn. Slowly, everyone makes their way to the lineup. There's some jockeying for position in the front row, and I can see my mom motioning me to start moving up, but I just hang out in the fourth row. I haven't gotten that much better in the last three weeks, and I'd really like to avoid being trampled in my first ever race. I feel like Krista especially would have no problem whatsoever stepping on me to get by.

The race director blows a long sharp blast on her whistle. I jump at the noise, but then surge forward, propelled along with the crowd. It's fast, and I'm already struggling to keep up the pace but I know that there are girls behind me who very well could mow me down if I make a misstep. So, I pump my arms as hard as I can, as my lungs constrict, my breathing gets harder, and my legs start to feel like they're being weighted down even though it's only been a few seconds.

We're only 30 seconds in and I can see the first hill. It's terrifying. My lungs are burning already. I hit the hill trying hard to stay right on the heels of the girl in front of me, her ponytail bobbing and weaving in front of my face. I'm there for a few steps, but I lose my breath entirely about halfway up and start to hike. By the time I make it to the top, there are only a couple of girls panting behind me, and there's a solid 100 meters between me and the girl in front of me. I'm dimly aware that I can hear screaming, that it's almost certainly my mother's voice, but the blood is rushing in my head and I can't make out what she's saying. I take a few more slow steps, trying to breathe as deep as I can to clear my lungs and my brain.

And then, as the fog lifts slightly, I try to pick up the pace. 'Jog just a few steps,' I urge my legs. They sort of listen, and I move forward just a bit faster than I was before. I'm not catching up to the girls in front of me, but I'm not getting passed by anyone else either and I'm able to ignore the burning in my quads.

The buzzing in my ears is getting louder though, and my stomach gives a huge growl — maybe this wasn't the morning to finally be good about skipping breakfast. I can almost feel the coffee sloshing around in my stomach, and I'm definitely feeling like I could use a nap. Or a donut.

But I keep going, because now I'm in the middle of the woods, and going back the way I came seems like it would take just as long as it would to keep moving forward to the finish. And Mom finally made it to one of my activities. I don't want to let her down.

As I pass through a sharp corner, I hear a tiny moan off the trail and look down. Sitting, leaning against a tree and holding her ankle tightly is Krista.

Of course.

I look around, and no one is in sight. There aren't any course marshals, coaches or photographers skulking in the bushes. It's just us.

For a second, I consider leaving, just pretending I don't see her. I even take a few more steps forward. But my conscience kicks in and I can't do it.

"Are you okay?" I ask.

chapter
fifteen

Krista

WHEN THE RACE STARTS, I immediately surge to the front. I get a few weird looks from the other girls around me, and I'm not sure if it's because of my extremely dark lipstick and bleached hair or because they've been racing each other for years, and suddenly, this b-word is out in front. It feels good.

Whatever the reason, they can just keep staring as I kick up dust and furiously pound up the first hill, trying to remember what Miss C told us about pumping our arms for more momentum. Things are going well according to my race strategy: Win. I don't know when this strategy developed. I don't know when I got so competitive. But my urge to crush the other girls and speed off the front is suddenly all-consuming.

My breathing is getting harder, but the adrenaline shooting through my body is making me feel electrified, like I'm hovering above the ground. It's the same feeling I get when I really nail a perfect line of poetry, or when I'm at a concert and dancing away to my favorite song. I'm floating, still leading the pack, and I know I can actually keep this up.

But then, suddenly, I'm falling, careening off the side of the trail and into the ditch on the side. My toe must have snagged a root and before I could put my arms out to brace, I'm rolling on the ground. The race leaders surge up ahead on the trail and are gone. Not a single, "Are you okay?" to be heard.

What happened to teamwork? I even spot a few of our school's singlets rushing by and actually catch the eye of one of the girls on our team. She doesn't even pause.

I try to stand, but as I make my way to my hands and knees, I feel my ankle on fire. I can't believe it. Pain shoots up my leg as the rest of the racers storm by me. I don't know if they don't see me or don't care, but I can't bring myself to shout to any of them. I'll just lie here for another minute and catch my breath, I think, and then I'll get up and hobble back to the finish line. It can't be that far.

While I'm contemplating my fate and scanning the area for sticks that I could use as a crutch, I hear the one voice that I absolutely didn't want to hear.

"Krista, are you okay?"

I groan, and this time it isn't in pain. It's more annoyance. Of course, Elle would be the only one to bother stopping, Miss Everyone-is-my-best-friend-and-I'm-perfect. While I'm cursing the gods in my head, she's made her way off the trail down to where I'm still awkwardly sprawled. I'm still planning to get up on my own any minute now, I swear.

"I'm fine," I say through gritted teeth, but even I have to admit the situation isn't great. The pain has become an eye-watering throb and I'm starting to get cold and shaky.

"Your ankle looks like a balloon," she observes, and I have to bite back a really rude retort about her face. Hate her or not, I would never.

"Thanks for noticing," I say instead. Still not the nicest, but not incredibly mean.

"Let me help you," she says. I try to wave away her hand, but she pulls me up. "Wait, should you even get up? Should I go get help?" Visions of a stretcher and the embarrassment that would cause flash before my eyes and I opt for the lesser of the evils. If Elle helps me most of the way to the finish, surely I'll be able to walk the last few steps before anyone notices us together.

Grudgingly, I grab her hand. "I'm fine, it's just my ankle," I say, hissing as I put the slightest pressure on it. Elle tucks herself under my right arm so I can hop on my left foot. She's stronger than I would have expected, honestly. She manages to get her arm firmly around my waist and we move pretty quickly down the trail, like we're in a three-legged race against no one.

And that alone brings back a lot of memories, and maybe it's the pain, but I'm suddenly almost nostalgic and before I can stop myself, I blurt out—"Remember the sack race in the third grade..."

"When you took out the substitute teacher as you crashed completely off course..." Elle adds.

"And there was Jello everywhere..." I groan.

"At least this time there isn't a video camera!" Elle says.

The situation is so ludicrous that I actually giggle, and she does too. And then, neither of us can stop. We're both laughing out loud now, even as tears are streaming down my cheeks. As we come into view of the finish line a few painful minutes later, both of us heaving to catch our breath, I try to shake off her arm, but the second I put pressure on my right foot to take a step, I stumble and yelp.

Bad move. As soon as I let out the short scream, all eyes are on us, and Elle has grabbed me again and is propelling me towards the finish line, panting with exertion. I barely register the fact that a few people are filming the whole embarrassing ordeal on their cell phones. (I guess I was wrong, of course there's a video camera.)

Just as we reach the finish, Elle pauses, and I glance over at her. Her face has gone sheet-white. Her eyes roll back, and her grip loosens on my waist. Before she actually starts to drop, I plant my foot on the ground to brace — pain radiates through my entire body— and tighten my arm around her shoulder, trying to slow her fall by sitting us both down onto the ground. Her head rolls onto my shoulder, and the crowd around us gasps. It's silent for a heartbeat.

Then everyone goes crazy.

It's a massive clamor and confusion for a solid minute after that, as both of our moms come sprinting towards us — and I thought we were supposed to be the ones racing — I realize I'm still clutching Elle, so I let the coaches separate us and put Elle's head onto a bunch of wadded up jackets. She's already moving again, and her eyes are fluttering.

"Did I faint?" she asks as she comes to, looking around wildly. Somehow in the confusion, our moms made it to us, and the EMTs as well. My mom is holding Elle's one wrist, checking her pulse, and her mom is on her other side. I'm still sitting back, and an ice pack is braced against my throbbing ankle. Who put it there?

I don't want to admit I'm worried, but I am freaked out.

"What did you eat this morning, honey?" my mom asks Elle, gently.

"An apple, some coffee..." she trails off.

"Did you drink any water or sports drink before your race, or have a snack?" my mom continues.

"Not really," Elle admits, looking down. My mom and Elle's mom glance at each other over her, but don't say anything.

"That's not like you," Elle's mom says. "You always eat at least a donut or danish for breakfast."

"I know, but I was nervous," Elle shrugs. "Sorry, everyone. I was just dizzy for a second. I'm fine now." She's sitting up now, glancing around warily. She doesn't notice it, but I can't help but be very, very aware of the fact that my mom has put her hand on Elle's mom's shoulder and they're having a very serious-but-intimate conversation. I don't know if it's about Elle or my mom is making a move, but either way, I don't want to encourage it.

I move to get up and pull Mom away, but my ankle is not having it and I let out a little yelp. Luckily, that also breaks the conversation up as Mom starts to help me up gently. "Do you want to take the bus home or do you want a ride?" she asks. The idea of suffering through a bouncing bus ride with a throbbing ankle and a knowledge that a) Elle and my stunt will be the talk of the bus, b) Jess will be there and I'll have to pretend to be happy when I'm feeling miserable, and c) the odds of another rendition of "Sweet Caroline" are quite high... is just not great.

"A ride would be excellent," I say. But before I can hobble to the car, Miss C is coming over with the EMTs. Perfect.

After a few painful pokes and prods, the one EMT declares it a roll, not a sprain or break, and wraps it in a bright yellow Ace bandage that absolutely does not go with my personal style.

"I know this hurts a lot right now," Miss C tells me as she helps me to the car, Mom on one side and her on the other. "If you just take it easy and rest it for a couple days, maybe ice it, you'll be back to running before you know it! And you were flying today — I think you're going to have a great season."

I nod weakly, though really all I want to do is go home and veg out and possibly never ever run again. And I notice that Jess is over chatting very intimately with Jenny, who must have won, and is completely unaware of what happened to me in the race. Or doesn't care.

I also spot Elle, who's now surrounded by what appears to be a gaggle of mean girls, all giving her sympathetic arm pats and shooting dirty looks in my direction, like I made her lose the damn race. I didn't ask for her help, I want to yell at them. She's just soaking in the attention, beaming at them and basking in the admiration.

Of course she is. This is so typical Elle — help someone who doesn't really need help, then take a ton of credit for it, making it seem like she saved the damn world.

When she walks past me with her flock of newfound followers, she gives me a sympathetic look that I assume is fake. "I hope you feel better," she says in a sickeningly sweet voice.

"Oh, screw off," I say under my breath, but not quite loud enough for her to hear. I just wave dismissively and look back at Mom. "Can we go now?"

We're pretty quiet in the car on the drive home. My ankle is throbbing, and Mom is quiet as well — plus, I'm not entirely interested in chatting with her, since I'm pretty sure she's been talking to Elle's mom more than she's been letting on.

Here's the thing. I don't mind that my mom is gay — she always has been, and that's always been part of my life. I just don't relish the idea of having to deal with her dating my ex-best-friend's mom. It's just plain weird. But they aren't dating (yet), they're just talking. Besides, Elle's mom was married before, I remind myself. She's straight. Stop panicking.

chapter
sixteen

Elle

WHEN I WAKE up the morning after the race, the first thing that I notice is that my phone is vibrating. Non-stop. And it's not my alarm — that's set to "All I Do is Win" by DJ Khaled in an attempt to get myself psyched up every morning.

Nothing is more terrifying than a phone that won't stop notifying you of notifications.

I roll over and grab it, and realize that the notifications are coming in from pretty much every single human that I know, and they're all saying the same thing: "Saw the video of you..." I keep scrolling, panicking, trying to puzzle out which video they're talking about. I don't think anyone would have been recording my last student council meeting, or the speech I gave in History the other day. Finally, one message has a link. I click through to YouTube and the first thing I notice is the number of views. 1,598,762.

The second thing that registers is the title: "Watch This Heart-warming Video of cross-country Racing Done Right: Two Girls Save Each Other."

Uh-oh.

I hit play, and there I am, sweating, red in the face, and dragging Krista across the finish line before — nooooo! — swooning. I had confused the tent at the finish line with the medical tent; I hadn't meant for us to actually finish the race. And I *really* didn't mean to faint. There are thousands of comments.

"OMG, Best friends!" reads one.

"GIRL POWER!" reads another.

"Ha, that faint is hilarious," reads yet another, and there are hundreds more below it. Some are kind and positive, but there are a few mean ones about my appearance, Krista's appearance, and how inept both of us are at running.

This is not how I wanted to become famous. I'm the girl who dragged her unwilling ex-best-friend across the finish line at a local race... And then fainted? You have got to be kidding me.

And Krista wasn't even thankful, though I don't know why I expected her to be — she's never going to change. Instead of coming over and talking to me and checking on how I was doing, she just glared from over in the medical tent while a bunch of nicer girls came up to tell me what I did was brave and self-sacrificing, giving up my race to help her. (I don't think it was, but they don't need to know how slow I was going even before I was helping Krista hobble.)

I'm still not feeling great, and this is making matters worse. I didn't want to eat dinner last night, but Mom picked up pizza on the way home, and since she was so excited about what happened, and so nervous about why I fainted (she even called the doctor to make an appointment, ugh), I didn't really have much choice other than to just deal with it and eat the pizza.

That fifth piece may have been a mistake though — after two days of finally managing to stick to my diet and eat under 500 calories, the huge amount of dough sitting in my stomach made me feel like I wanted to die. It still feels like there's a basketball in there, and I'm dreading getting out of bed because a) owww and b) ugh, some morbid part of my brain will want to scrutinize my midsection in the mirror and see if a food baby is a real thing.

A knock on my door is directly preceded by my mom waltzing in, looking sunnier than I've ever seen her. She's absolutely glowing, while I'm a step away from a whimper.

"You're on the local news!" she sing-songs, and practically pirouettes over to me.

"Go away," I mutter, trying to read all of the messages from friends, acquaintances, news anchors (!?!?!) and a bunch of other random people I don't know. I briefly wonder how Krista is feeling about all the attention, and wonder if her phone is going off too.

We've gone viral.

By the time Mom stops fluttering, I have just enough time to get ready for school. The only bright side is that among the flurry of texts, there's a series of messages from Jess. Result! He's asking if I'm okay, then mentioning the video, of course. Ever since he told me he missed me, I've thought he was sending me signals, looking at me a little too long in practice, high-fiving me after a set of intervals, but this is the first time he's texted since... well, since freshman year after Homecoming. This could finally be it — I'm actually going to win this time around! (Call me weak if you must, because I know I shouldn't go down this road again, but he's just so cute. And we have a history!)

There are even some heart emojis in his message, and it cheers me up immensely. I send him a mirror selfie of me in my PJs, a tank top and short-shorts, giving a thumbs-up to let him know that I'm okay (and that despite the pizza, I'm looking okay this morning... from certain angles!).

As soon as I send it, the three dots hover so I know he's seen it and he's writing back. Sure enough, he shoots back a picture of him... but he's not wearing a shirt, just his sweatpants slung low. Underneath, he wrote, "Send the same?"

I blush like crazy. I may have a huge crush on him, but I don't think I'm going to be sending him a topless photo anytime soon, so I make a quick fun Boomerang of me wagging my finger and shaking my head (with a flirty smile, so he doesn't think I'm mad) and send that instead.

He doesn't respond right away. Or in the next 15 minutes as I get ready for school, checking my phone every time it beeps a notification. But it's always just someone else saying that they saw the video and how cool it was that I'm 'famous.' And also, am I okay? That's getting annoying, so I don't answer any of them. My good mood from Jess's original text has completely evaporated, and I snap at my mom when she tries to talk to me again about a balanced breakfast. (I think Krista's mom must have given her some nutrition advice or something yesterday. SO annoying.)

Luckily, she's so busy buzzing around the kitchen talking and scanning her iPad as more stories about that video are popping up that she doesn't notice when I just grab a black coffee and bolt it down grumpily, staring at my phone. "Did you grab those hard-boiled eggs?" she absently asks, and I nod, not looking up.

"Absolutely," I say, which is true... sort of. I grabbed them, and snuck them into the trash can. Today is not the day that I want to show up at school feeling more bloated than I already do, so breakfast is a non-starter.

"I'll see you later today, after practice and debate," I say to mom quickly, slipping out of the kitchen before she can try to hook me up with an agent or a publicist or hug me again or something. You'd think I'd be excited that my mom suddenly has all the time in the world to talk to me, but it's actually bumming me out. When I wasn't all over the internet, we couldn't talk in the morning unless it was about my performance, and suddenly now we're best friends? Not into it... even though I wish I could believe it would last.

chapter
seventeen

Krista

EDITORIAL DRAFT #54: How It Really Happened

SEPTEMBER 24, 2021

Many of you reading this editorial may have seen a recent video posted of myself and a fellow student limping towards the finish line of a cross-country race. While that video makes it appear as though we were in perfect synchronicity, the truth is far from that. That moment in time, mortifyingly captured on video, was nothing more than that: a moment in time. And in that moment, this reporter was struggling to retain her composure, and thought it would be less embarrassing to accept help from an outside source rather than crawl back towards the finish on her own. Clearly, this reporter was wrong.

Oh god. This… isn't working.

Chapter Seventeen

Everyone is talking about the video when I get to school, hobbling with the cane that my mother thoughtfully provided. I covered it in black duct tape so it looks a little more punk-rock, and my cut-off black jeans go very nicely with the white bandage that's wrapping my rolled — not sprained or broken — ankle. I added little angry faces in black Sharpie to make it look a little edgier, and I'm wearing a crisp white button-up shirt with black horn-rimmed glasses and bright red lipstick so I look stylish with the cane, not pathetic.

As people gather around me wanting to hear the story — ugh, people who haven't talked to me in year, and for good reason (that reason: I personally dislike them) — I end up fleeing to the computer lab for first period, which is my free period anyway.

"As the school's editor-in-chief, you know you have to cover this," Miss C tells me as soon as I walk in. I groan—loud. I've been avoiding people talking to me about that damn video by blasting The Ramones on my headphones and putting on my firmest Resting Bitch Face, but I can't ignore my advisor.

"This is a huge chance for you — people are reading about you and watching this video and it could be your big ticket to NYU," she continues. "Going viral is a good thing, at least in this case."

I really hate it when she's right. And maybe I can think of an angle that doesn't make us sound like best friends *and* that doesn't make me seem like an ungrateful jerk. I don't care about the sprained ankle, though being known as an athlete (and a bad one!) is pretty damn humiliating too.

After an hour of sweating the syntax, I'm still no closer to making us seem like mortal enemies in a way that makes sense and makes her look bad while I look awesome. From every angle, we look like besties and it is infuriating. If I say anything that makes her seem less than amazing, I look like a jerk. My inbox for my high school email address is also packed, and while I'm floored by the emails I'm amassing from the media, from local papers to *Seventeen* magazine and *Refinery29* and a bunch of running magazines and websites, I'm not exactly thrilled at the reason why.

But any newspaper reporter knows, all press is good press, right? And at least now I have a bunch of the editor's emails, so I can hopefully turn those into contacts. Problem is, if I'm going to grow those relationships, I'm going to need to suck it up and respond to the interview requests, and talk about how Elle saved me during the race.

Just thinking about it makes my ankle throb even more. The school nurse (who, of course, saw the video) has already checked in with me this morning, declaring it a minor sprain at worst and saying that the cane and the brace the trainer gave me are enough to keep me moving around and that I can be back to running in a couple of weeks. Miss C, in addition to telling me I had to write something for the school paper, is clearly a total sadist and suggested that I take a couple of days off practice but then come back to start 'helping out' at practices, timing on the climbs and stuff like that.

'Sure, that sounds super fun, Miss C,' I think as I furiously work away at the post for the website. I'm trying to take a more objective newsy angle but it's turning out to be a Herculean task. I've started and stopped typing a dozen times already, and it's getting annoying.

Finally, I go full-on click-bait. "You have to see this video of two runners saving each other in a race!" as the headline, and just a video embed below. Not my best work and my journalistic integrity feels a little compromised, but I'm so over this.

Done with that, I don't leave. I stay in the newspaper lab way after hours, despite not having a ton to work on, just to avoid seeing anyone else for the rest of the day.

chapter
eighteen

Elle

I **THOUGHT** the story would die down after a day, but when I get home from school, my mom is actually waiting for me at the front door (weird) and she's looking almost electrified — that grin is Joker-level creepy.

"Guess what?" She practically shrieks as I walk up the stairs.

"What?" I ask, in zero mood to banter, even if suddenly Mom has looked up from her laptop to pay attention to me. Right now, I'm wishing she had a new, huge case to tackle. Today has been exhausting, and for once, I'm not really in the mood for her to start paying attention to me.

"*GMA* wants you and Krista to come on the show tomorrow!" she sing-songs, and my heart stops.

The biggest daytime talk show in the world wants us to be on, talking about how we're best friends and how we had this incredible moment together?

Shit.

Okay, this is good, I tell myself firmly. Being on *GMA*, getting to meet the host, Kendra, impressing her with my public speaking skills. That's got to help with my eventual career as a speech writer. All those hours spent working on the debate club will pay off. Colleges offer scholarships for debate, right? Well, they can start for me, anyway.

"Great," I say, my momentary panic now totally eclipsed with visions of myself in a crisp suit with gorgeous heels and a perfect blowout, striding onto set and having a casual, intelligent chat with Kendra about some intense topic — women's rights, maybe? — after we've quickly laughed at and dismissed the video before moving on. In this moment, Krista is nowhere in sight and I've lost about 15 pounds before walking onto the stage. And, is that an Armani suit I'm wearing? My imagination has great taste.

Okay, I think to myself. This is an opportunity. Maybe you won't be in a sleek suit or have dropped 15 pounds overnight, and Krista will obviously be there, but it's still a chance. You want to be a famous speech writer, and here you have one of the biggest stages in the country to show off your skills. Fantastic. This is your big break.

Inspired, I skip up to my room, but when I open my closet to sort out wardrobe, I catch myself in the mirror and freeze. The panic returns. Shit, what do you wear to be on *GMA* when you don't, you know, actually *own* an Armani suit? Specifically, what do I wear that won't make me look massive on TV?

Obviously, black is a no-go, since that's Krista's aesthetic and we don't want to look like weird goth-y twins, like Mary Kate and Ashley circa 2012. Do I go sporty? Or is that super corny since we'll be looking at a video of us in running clothes?

After what feels like hours of deliberation — okay, *is* hours of deliberation, it's 2AM when I make my choice despite our early departure in the morning — I lay out light brown suede booties with a medium heel (don't want to fall walking on stage), black tights and an oversized maroon cashmere sweater. It's Fall, it's cozy, and best of all, it hides my midsection. Sure, it's my go-to school uniform as well, but I think it'll work and not look like I tried too hard. Maybe they'll have wardrobe for us? I put that on the desk and lay out my makeup supplies and hair straightener, and set the alarm for 4AM. Luckily, I'm pretty good at under-eye concealer these days.

chapter
nineteen

Krista

OF COURSE OUR mothers have conspired to drive to *GMA* set together. And I'm sure Elle is absolutely thrilled to be going on national television. Me, not so much. I almost argued that I didn't want to go, but the idea of Elle telling the story without me and coming off as a hero? Ugh. Not a chance. Plus, it'll be good for my career—maybe I'll get an internship with the host, writing for the show! Kendra seems like she'd be fun to work for. But driving together feels excessive. Especially this early.

"It just makes sense," Mom is telling me as I groggily pour coffee into my thermos at 4:30 in the morning. I was dreading this already, and now that my mom has sprung a last minute road trip to NYC with the very person I loathe the most, I'm extra grumpy.

"Whatever," I grunt, and glance in the mirror. Understated-cool was my goal for today. I thought my go-to black button-up and black jeans would look too goth-y, so it was a bit of a shitshow picking what to wear.

I don't feel particularly inspired by what I settle on — dark blue wide leg jeans with combat boots and a tight black v-neck sweater plus a chunky rose gold watch — but it's the best I can do on minimal inspiration at the crack of dawn. It's only October, but the air is brisk so I toss a huge scarf around my neck as we head out the door. It'll work as a pillow so I can sleep and ignore Elle for the whole 90 minute drive to the city. Even though the show doesn't start until 10AM, we need to be there by seven to get prepped, so it's going to be a long day.

Mom gives me a side eye when I pop into the backseat of the SUV. "You'll be nice, right?" she asks-slash-warns me. I grumpily nod and slouch down in my seat, debating whether or not I should lecture Mom about not hitting on parents of my mortal enemies, but I'm afraid that might actually make the situation worse. Or spur a conversation about her dating life that I am definitely not ready to have yet.

Of course, Elle and her mom are waiting for us outside, coffee thermoses in hand, practically vibrating with morning-person energy. "Hi, ladies," Elle's mom chirps, and my mom practically swoons back a good morning of her own before handing Stephanie a pumpkin spice latte with an honest-to-God heart shape swirled on the top. Ugh. My mom is the worst. And just-call-me-Stephanie isn't much better, giving my mom's shoulder a squeeze and taking a sip before making a yummy noise that verges on creepy. Crap. She is still straight, right?

Luckily, Elle doesn't pick up on the vibes between our respective parents, or if she does, she's ignoring them entirely. Good.

"I'm super excited. Thanks for driving," she says to my mom before closing her door and nodding briefly at me. At least she's not trying to pretend to be my friend. She's actually sporting a travel pillow around her neck, so we both grumpily ignore each other and snooze for the rest of the drive. But as the city looms and traffic starts piling up, the tension in the car is growing by the minute.

It's getting closer to the time we're due at the studio. I can tell Mom is stressed by the cars on the road because I see her nervously looking at the clock. A quick look at the maps on my phone shows that we're going to be fine, but I understand why she's jittery. We both like to be moving forward at all times, so to be stuck in a gridlock is just frustrating. Elle's mom must feel the same, since she's started drumming her fingers on the window of the car like if she taps hard enough it'll magically make the traffic ahead of us disappear.

But finally, we're there and Mom lets the three of us out at the studio entrance while she rolls off to find a parking garage that will fit our SUV.

As we get out of the car, I have a moment of panic. We really should have prepared better for this. In fact, what if Elle did prepare something and she's ready to make me look like a complete idiot? I should have made more notes. I'm not a speech person, but Elle is. I need to take charge.

"We just have to act cool and get through this, right?" I mutter to her. I'm not happy about trying to make a parking-garage-truce, but I don't see any other option.

"Of course," she whispers back. "I don't want to look like a complete moron on TV. We'll be fine."

Easy for Miss Captain of Debate to say.

"This is huge, girls," Elle's mom says to both of us, and Elle nods, suddenly looking sort of terror-struck. This is the girl who fainted at the end of a race, so I guess I'm not surprised. "Make the most of it," she adds, almost snapping it, and this time we both nod emphatically. She is a little scary.

My phone buzzes as we walk in, and I glance at it. It's Jess.

We haven't really talked since the race, which I don't care about. I mean, I'm not about to go down this path again. Obviously. Definitely.

I still open the message though, because that's only polite. He's sent a super cute selfie of him without a shirt, and okay, I admit, he's not exactly the most ripped guy (he's a little scrawny, to be honest), but he is hot.

"Send me one?" he texted under it, with a winking face.

I know better than to send any kind of actually topless picture — I read the news! — but I do excuse myself and slip into the bathroom in the building's lobby, pull my sweater and bra strap to the side and take a fairly seductive picture highlighting my collarbone and an angle that makes it look like I have cleavage. Nothing too scandalous showing, just hinting.

He sends a smiley face back, but no text along with it. The three dot bubble indicating he's typing starts and stops a couple of times, finally disappearing, and I can't stall much longer. I don't really care about his approval, I tell myself sternly.

(I am clearly lying to myself.)

chapter
twenty

Elle

AS THE ELEVATOR whooshes up to the studio, I feel like I left my stomach on the ground floor. I focus on taking deep breaths, but subtle ones so it doesn't look like I'm freaking out. Out of the corner of my eye, I see Krista is doing pretty much the same thing (I think). She also looks paler than usual... though that might just be her foundation, because her skin looks flawless in addition to pale.

Mine is starting to feel blotchy because I'm getting hot and cold all over. My fingers feel a little numb, but my cheeks are burning. It's not a great look.

Mom nudges me with her elbow. "Feeling okay?" she asks, but it comes out more menacing than motherly.

Krista's mom looks over at me as well, and she looks more worried than my mom. She digs into her giant bag and pulls out a Lara bar and passes it to me. "Trust me, you'll feel better if you eat something," she says, and also pulls out a water bottle that she hands over. What is she, Mary Poppins?

"I love that you still have snacks for the girls," my mom says to her, and gives her a wink. "Remember that time they raided your bag and stole all of those cookies?"

"Two dozen incredibly expensive macarons that I was saving for myself!" Krista's mom laughs.

"We should find a bakery after this and pick some of those up—

there's a fantastic spot just a few blocks away," my mom says enthusiastically.

Weird. Mom doesn't really do the whole 'hanging out with other moms' thing. At least, not since Krista and I stopped being friends. Maybe my mom misses having a close friend in her life. It's not like Mom has a glittering social life either — she hasn't even dated since Dad left a freaking decade ago, and she never just goes out with other women to hang out, unless it's a work thing. Is that my fault? Did I turn my mom into a workaholic hermit?

The guilt threatens to make me do something stupid, like initiate a group hug, but luckily, we're at the 21st floor and the elevator dings open. Before we step out, a young-ish guy in funky glasses and an excellent cardigan is walking over to greet us, carrying a clipboard. He already knows our names, and in seconds, we're following him like ducks, guest passes on lanyards around our necks. They are efficient here!

We breeze through hair and makeup — just a bit of powder for both of us so we aren't shiny, but not the pancake makeup to cover my imperfections that I was hoping for, possibly with a hint of contour to give me cheekbones — as he chatters away. I'm internally freaking out and only catch the general idea of what's going to happen. We walk in, sit down, they'll play the clip from the race of us limping out of the woods and then me fainting (hooray...). We sit, smile, and watch, then answer a couple of questions for Kendra, and maybe she'll do some kind of goofy bit that we're just supposed to go along with. I wish we had more information than that, but it seems pretty basic.

After Chet — our guide, though I have a hard time believing that's his real name — abandons us in the waiting room by the studio, we all start talking at once: me to my mom, Krista to hers, and our moms to each other.

And we all fall silent at the same time, too. We have about 30 minutes before we're called to the stage, and Krista is slouched in her seat and pulling out her phone, so I do the same. Nothing from Jess. He hasn't messaged me since I wouldn't send him a sexy photo, and I'm starting to waver. We were just getting to a place where I knew he was about to ask me out.

Hopefully he's watching the show, at least. I take a few deep, slow breaths and try to remember all of the public speaking tips that we talk about in debate club, and the rules for myself that I created after a whole lot of mirror practice. Shoulders back, sit up nice and straight. Even a slight slouch looks super slouchy on camera. Make eye contact with Kendra and the camera, but don't make creepy eye contact with either. Smile slightly when not speaking in order to avoid Resting B-word Face. Nod or laugh silently when Kendra is being hilarious, but don't actually make noise — and, as Chet reminded us as he helped hook up our microphones, try not to move too much so our clothing isn't rustling into the mics. Short answers, but be funny and charming. Smile when speaking. Look at Krista, don't let on that we aren't friends.

Sure, no problems there.

But even as I worry about Krista and I playing off each other and coming off as charming teens, I'm feeling exhilarated. It's terrifying, sure, but I love the stage. I do well up there. And Krista has always had stage fright, even when we were kids performing for dolls, so it shouldn't be too hard for me to be the one in the spotlight directing the show.

chapter
twenty-one

Krista

WHILE WE WAIT, I try not to freak out. I really, really hate public speaking. That's why I'm a writer. I've been trying to run Joan Jett's "Bad Reputation" through my head to psych myself up, but it's not really helping. I know that in a few minutes, we're going to be out on that stage and millions of people are going to be watching.

My hands are shaking, and my palms are sweaty, which means Eminem's "Eight Mile" rap is competing with "Bad Reputation" in my head, and that is decidedly not making me feel more calm or badass. World's *corniest* mashup.

"You look like you're about to be sick," my mom says to me, looking concerned. "Do you need some crackers?" Trust the nutritionist to think to bring saltines for me. I silently take them when she pulls them out of her purse (seriously, what *doesn't* she have in there?!) and nibble.

Two crackers later, the clock is ticking down. Chet will be in here any minute to lead us to the stage, and I can feel sweat trickling down my back. Mom passes me a tissue to mop my forehead, which I'm sure is now super shiny thanks to me sweating off all of the powder.

And the door creaks open. Chet sticks his head in and with a perky grin, asks, "Ready?"

As though we have a choice at this point. Elle bounces up out of her seat, mirroring Chet's exuberant expression, and I slowly pull myself up, willing my legs to not give out. My ankle is feeling just fine now — so annoying to have all of this happen over a freaking rolled ankle! — but my nerves are making my entire body vibrate.

We follow Chet out as our moms whisper good luck and we avoid each other's eyes. And then, the lights are on us and we're walking out onto the stage and holy shit, there's Kendra. She looks smaller in real life than she does on TV, but her presence is exactly as large as it seems when you're watching at home. She gives off an aura, as my mom would say, that takes up the entire room. My vibrating intensifies, and Elle actually loops her arm through my elbow so we're walking arm in arm.

She's not doing it to be friendly, I realize as she digs her elbow into my ribs slightly, and when I glance at her, I see her smile a little wider. I think she's warning me to smile and make her look good. It's now actually sort of tempting to feign a faint just to get the spotlight on me and away from her. It would serve her right. But then, all eyes would be on me yet again.

So, I take the cue and smile and wave at the audience, glancing at the big screen on the wall opposite of Kendra that's got a picture of the two of us both lying on the ground, clasping hands like we've been best friends since birth. (Which is so close to being accurate while being so far from being the truth that it bums me out.)

We finally take our spots in the two chairs that are angled towards Kendra and the audience, and I give an internal sigh of relief. So far, so good.

"Can I just say, the two of you are so cute?" Kendra says, and Elle giggles and waves her hand, as if to say 'oh, you.' I just nod, like a dummy. (Literally, a dummy. Puppet-style.)

"Let's see what these two cross-country runners did at their last race," Kendra says, gesturing towards the big screen as the audience politely claps. And then, there it is, set to corny music, us hobbling out of the woods, the last few meters of the race, making it across the finish line and then, the collapse heard round the world, as Elle goes down and I make a grab and we sink versus topple. It looks more dramatic, like they've pumped up the colors and contrast, and the music makes it seem so much more epic. My face, looking freaked out, Elle lying there, me shaking her arm.

I hadn't watched the video until now, and hadn't seen it blown up to life-size, but there we are. And we really do look like best friends. I instantly hate it, and I realize that my face is saying exactly that — I can feel my nose starting to scrunch and I try to twist my mouth into something that reads more that I'm scrunching up because it's so darn cute, versus so darn nauseating to see myself like this.

Elle is smiling away, laughing as she looks at herself flop over. I know she's faking it — you don't spend years watching rom-coms with a girl without knowing what her real laugh sounds like, and this isn't it.

"That was a crazy moment for both of you, wasn't it?" Kendra asks. I'm thankful that she's just leading us to easy answers to start with, and we both nod.

"It was wild," Elle says, tossing her hair.

Now I feel like I need to say something. "I don't know what I would have done if Elle hadn't been there," I say smiling, but crossing my fingers in my lap. Of course I know what I would have done. Grabbed a branch, made a walking stick, literally anything other than hobble across the finish line with Elle.

"Have you two been friends forever?" Kendra asks us.

Shit.

"Yes, absolutely," Elle chirps. "Since we were in preschool! We've always been super close."

I'm not really sure what my response to that should be, but before I can do anything other than awkwardly smile, Joker-style, another image fills the screen — it's us, having a dance party in my living room. Except it's not recent — I remember we were maybe 10 at the time, and we're mugging for the camera while a guy in the background does a break-dance-y move on the floor. Of course, that guy is Jess.

Elle or Elle's mom must have given Kendra's assistant that photo, because I thought I had burned all of the ones I had of the three of us. I glance at Elle and she's looking as aghast as I am. Her mom, then. But Elle manages to quickly mask it with a smile and nod, and that makes me feel like my head is about to explode. I'm so sick of her pretending that everything is perfect and going great all the time. She's just so phony and plastic. This is why we're not friends. Maybe if she'd been willing to actually show some emotion, talk things over, but no. She just stopped speaking to me and started her campaign to be most popular most in-charge person in school, and hasn't stopped since.

"You two are so cute!" Kendra says enthusiastically. "I guess no one at school was surprised to see the two of you working together."

"Now, that, Kendra, is definitely not true," I hear someone say. And then I realize that the person who said that is me. I said that. Crap.

Elle is glaring at me, and even goes so far as to jam her elbow into my ribs, making it look like a friendly, giggling gesture, but I know she means business. "I think she means people were surprised that I was strong enough to carry Krista out of the woods," she says, trying to ad-lib and cover up for my stony expression.

"That's not what I meant," I retort.

Seriously, WHAT IS WRONG WITH ME? Why can I not keep my mouth shut?

Kendra looks confused, and then excited. "I think we're about to hear some juicy drama," she says to the audience before leaning closer. "So, are you two not still close?"

"That, Kendra, is an understatement," Elle says primly. Her debate team face is fixed back in place and clearly, she's ready to start taking control of the narrative.

Gulp. Words on paper are my thing, not words out of my mouth. This is why I hate public speaking: I always manage to say exactly the wrong thing.

"We haven't been friends for years, but I simply couldn't leave her alone in the woods," Elle continues, turning herself into a martyr for the crowd. "She was hurt."

"*Alone* is sort of pushing it, isn't it?" I sputter and stand up. "We weren't exactly at risk of being left alone on the course overnight. You just wanted to show off."

And there it is. I've officially lost my mind and confused Kendra for Jerry Springer. Elle looks furious, and I realize I've finally gotten under her skin.

"Show off? The way you did when you tried to steal Jess from me?!" she slams back, her voice starting to get shriller with each word.

Kendra looks thrilled. The audience is also apparently wondering if they've wandered onto the Jerry set, because they all do that "oOoooooo" sound. Perfect.

"I didn't steal him, you never had him," I spit out, and oh dear lord, we're fighting about a boy on national television.

"Skank!" she shoots back.

"Sore loser," I shout, and she shoves me.

"Umm, girls?" Kendra is suddenly between us and I realize that I'm *this* close to actually slapping Elle. My face is probably beet red, and I'm panting slightly. Elle, on the other hand, looks green and like she's about to faint (again). That'll look just perfect, her fainting away while I glare.

I try to reign it in, breathing deeply like Mom always says to do (though she was not referring to what to do on national television).

Kendra's hand is on my shoulder, her other one on Elle's, and while she has a concerned look on her face, I can see a little bit of glee in her eyes — she knows what this will do to the ratings, an already viral video going even more viral as the besties become brawlers. (Even in my head, I think in tabloid headlines. It's like a disease.)

I take a step back, and Elle does the same. We briefly make eye contact, and we both have the same look of horror. What have we done on live television? I see Elle, still panting a bit, make a move towards grabbing her phone, like she's about to text someone. Jess? Why would she be texting him? I don't know why my mind goes there, but I'm positive that's what she wants to do. She doesn't though, just leans back, like she can't get far enough away from me. Well, ditto.

"So, umm, that got a little Jerry-Springer-y," Kendra says, breaking our awkward silence.

We both laugh, as if to say, 'Yeah, we're hilarious like that' but I'm sure no one is buying it.

chapter
twenty-two

Elle

WELL, this is what hell must feel like. I feel tears well up but I blink furiously, trying to pull back some semblance of dignity. Fat chance of that. The cameras are still rolling, the audience looks hungry and Kendra looks delighted at this even-more-potentially-viral turn of events.

"I think that got a little out of hand," I say as beside me, Krista pulls back from her death glare face into some sort of mime-like apologetic rictus grin. It's not a good look on her; it makes her look like she's going to dress up like Margot Robbie as Harley Quinn for Halloween. Which, in this moment, is probably a good thing for me and I jump on it.

Hey, debate team taught me to go for the kill.

"We got a little emotional there, it's just been a really stressful couple of days in the spotlight," I blabber, as I grab for Krista's hand and grab it, squeezing hard. "When you've been friends as long as we have, it's hard to remember when to act professional and when to just fool around. And even though we haven't been close these last couple years, as you can see, a lot of tensions obviously came to the surface this week but really just cemented the fact that we do care about each other when push comes to shove... sometimes literally," I add, ending on a joke that has the crowd politely giggling.

Krista nods woodenly. I internally hive-five myself, because while we're still both going to be forever embarrassed by this moment, at least my damage control efforts aren't making things worse. My career isn't torpedoed yet—in fact, this might even play in my favor if I'm careful now.

Kendra is nodding thoughtfully.

"That's actually a great point, Elle," she says. "We see these videos go viral and expect the people in them to be able to handle the sudden spotlight, but it's not always easy."

"Exactly," I say confidently. "We're just students, and our idea of going viral is when the school paper publishes a semi-flattering picture of us!"

The audience is giggling and smiling now. I think we've turned it around! Well, I've turned it around, anyway. I beam extra hard at Krista, just to make her look even more grumpy than she already does.

I want to check my phone so bad — I can feel it vibrating in my pocket. Chet told us to leave everything in the green room, but of course I wasn't leaving my phone behind. I know that people have already seen us on the show and are trying to be the first to get in touch, and that just adds to my feeling of utter humiliation, no matter what spin I put on it. This was my chance and I blew it.

We both answer a few more questions — yes, I'm new to running, yes, it was really scary when I fainted, and yes, I was secretly a little glad to have a reason to walk all the way to the finish, thank you, Kendra — and our two minutes in the spotlight feels like it's over before it even started, and suddenly, I'm waving to the crowd and walking offstage next to Krista, who's lurching like a drunken sailor.

The second we're off camera, she beelines for a wastebasket and promptly throws up.

While she's vomiting in the waste bin, my mom storms up and grabs my arm, trying to drag me away while maintaining a "totally cool with everything that just happened" expression on her face for the people who are standing around and trying not to watch us, and I can see in her eyes that she is absolutely furious with me.

I've never wished for a different mom, but as I get pulled past the trash can where Krista is still hunched, I see her mom rushing over, looking concerned rather than angry, and she's already asking if Krista is okay, petting her back and holding her up.

But this is no time for a pity party. Reframe. 'That's why I'm tougher and could turn that around,' I tell myself firmly.

"What were you THINKING?" My mom hisses at me as soon as we're out of sight from everyone in the back room.

For a second, I think about pointing out that technically, Krista started it, but I know what Mom will say—that I should have immediately defused the situation, not added to the drama.

Instead, I go with "I ... wasn't?" I'm a little desperate to just get the lecture over and start working on damage control.

"I'd lecture you right now, but we don't have time for that. You need to get started on damage control," Mom tells me.

Yikes. We're even thinking alike now. This can't be good.

"First, you need to put out a post on Instagram, right now. Here, I'm Airdropping you a picture of you sitting on the couch before you went out of your goddamn mind," she says, tapping away at her phone angrily. Double yikes, Mom never curses.

My phone pings, and I dutifully open Instagram and start typing away. "Had a great time on *GMA* before things went a little sideways," I write, inserting a bunch of blushing emojis. "I guess we all have off-days and this was one of mine, hope you enjoyed the extra drama!" A bunch more emojis, a curt nod of approval from Mom, and I hit Post, sending it to Instagram, Facebook and Twitter.

"And now, do a quick Instagram Story, giving your side," Mom says, leaving no room for me to protest. So, I lift the camera up, fluff my hair, and hit Record.

"Sorry to anyone who tuned into *GMA* and ended up seeing a soap opera!" I say, smiling while blushing furiously. (I'll slap a filter on it to tone that down.) "Hope you enjoyed the show, but I promise, I'm back to your regularly scheduled programming now."

Mom nods approvingly as I give a thumbs up, hit the stop, switch to a paler filter to get rid of my red face, and hit Add to Story.

"That's a start, anyway," she says. "Maybe you can make this work for you."

In fact, already, I have 50 new followers, and the comments are stacking up. At a glance, it's 50-50, with some people being sympathetic and saying I'm just a kid, and the other half berating me and Krista for our unladylike behavior. At least people are following me?

I scan my messages while Mom is tapping on her phone, probably posting a similar post to her Instagram. Nothing from Jess, just stuff from literally every other person I've ever met.

"I can't believe you got in a cat fight on TV!" one reads.

(Ditto.)

"Totally on your side, Krista's a b-word," reads another.

(Truth.)

"You looked hot," says one, from a number I don't recognize.

(Charming.)

The unread tally keeps mounting, but still nothing coming in from Jess, so I click my phone off because it's just too stressful. Mom is already over by the elevator, and motioning for me. "Now, can you keep yourself together for the car ride home or do we need to get an Uber?" she asks.

Thanks, Mom. But also, fair enough.

"I can handle it," I assure her. After all, even if we screamed at each other the entire trip home, it can't be anywhere near as bad as what just happened. And if Krista's projectile vomiting is any indication, she feels just as drained as I do, so I'm betting it's going to be silent versus screaming match.

Mom nods and we're quiet the entire elevator ride down. When we get to the ground floor, she asks about a back entrance to the street, and the security guard points us down a side corridor. "Normally, I wouldn't let anyone do this, but you're so young, you shouldn't have to deal with the crowd out there," he says. Crap. I didn't even think about the fact that the show is shared on jumbotron at the studio and people stand outside watching.

So, we slip past the crowd so I can avoid further embarrassment, and huddle by the car waiting for Krista and her mom to get out. When they do slink into the parking garage, Krista looks like she's been crying (ahem, serious panda eyes from non-waterproof mascara) but her mom remains — as she always does — Zen AF.

"Every life well-lived has adventures like that, right?" she says, directing the question at my mom, who slides into her seat and scowls out the window and doesn't respond. Her knuckles are white.

"Mom," Krista groans from the backseat. "Can't we at least just suffer in silence and save the hippie bull for another day."

I'm expecting her mom to blow up at her, but she just laughs. I wonder what it would be like to have a mom like that?

chapter
twenty-three

Krista

I AM COMPLETELY and utterly humiliated. First, the word vomit. Then, the actual vomit. And, of course, the fact that Elle somehow managed to turn the entire situation around and come out looking thoughtful and intelligent while I looked demented.

Mom remains, as always, unfazed by what's happening, which is good considering the death glares Elle's mom is giving her. Bright side: this may just tank any budding romance my mom was trying to start.

I slouch in my seat and try to subtly check my phone to the side that isn't directly next to Elle, which involves more stretching than I anticipated. Nothing from Jess, but plenty from all of my too-cool-for-school (not literally) friends, who are blowing up my phone with "WTF" texts.

Jane messaged a string of WTF-esque emojis from her dorm room, along with a picture of her latest headline in the school paper about the pressure to fit in and stand out at the same time. At least someone is doing well. Ugh.

Opening Instagram, I see that Elle has already posted an almost-apology story and picture, making her seem sympathetic and subtly suggesting that I'm the crazy one. I curse myself inwardly, because I can't even blame her for doing that. As the writer, I should have been the one on top of these things.

I scroll through my photos to try to find a good one, and there's one my coach sent of the two of us hobbling towards the finish arm in arm.

Perfect. This will beat her saccharine 'all about me' post. I'll go apologetic TO her. Boom.

"Clearly, I should stick to print journalism," I type. "Hate that we had such a corny fight on national TV—so much for playing it cool under pressure! Thanks for always being my support even when times get tough @ElleBelle <3"

I hit send and hope that in the flurry of likes that I'm sure Elle is getting on her post, she doesn't notice being tagged in mine. Then, I pull on my massive black sunglasses and my oversized hoodie with the hood pulled up and tugged down my forehead, turn towards the window, and pretend to go to sleep. Hopefully she doesn't see it or bring it up to either mom.

The car ride is quiet, despite Mom making a couple of attempts to chat with Elle's mom. She answers pretty curtly, and I'm starting to think that our stunt might have been enough to overcome my mom's flirtiest lines.

But then I see Elle's mom reach over and pat my mom on the knee, and my heart sinks. With my luck, the reverse is happening and they'll be bonded and closer than ever.

I look over at Elle to see if she's noticed the handsiness happening in the front seat, but no surprise there, she's engrossed in her phone. So typical. Granted, that's probably for the best since I don't want her to notice this, but still. I need to have a serious talk with Mom. As the entire world just saw, there is no way that she can possibly think that her and Elle's mom hanging out more is a good idea, given that their daughters can't be in a room together without having a massive cat fight. Ohmygod, I had a cat fight on national television.

Maybe I can do a last-minute transfer to some kind of forest school where the students don't have internet access.

By the time we get home, the number of words spoken in the car hasn't gone over 100—this is the most silent I can remember Elle ever managing, honestly. As we pull up to our house, she doesn't acknowledge me at all, but says goodbye to my mom politely. Elle's mom says goodbye to both of us, but clearly she's still pissed at me. She's a little (a lot) scary in lawyer mode.

And again, I find myself almost sympathetic to what Elle is going to be facing once we're out of the car. Once we clear the door to our house, Mom is back to all sympathy. Sometimes, her level of hippie-like Zen even amazes me. It's one thing to be cool when there are people around judging her parental abilities, but to keep her chill even once we're behind closed doors? Next level.

"Want to have a turmeric latte and talk about it?" she asks, looking concerned.

"Yes to the latte, no to the talking," I say, though I'm already resigned to a deep discussion about our feelings.

As she pulls almond milk and turmeric and a bunch of other spices off the shelves and starts whisking them in a saucepan, she looks over her shoulder. "I thought you two had buried the hatchet," she says.

I slump onto a stool at the kitchen island. "Apparently, in an extremely shallow grave," I says, and Mom snorts.

"The original fight was over a boy, if I recall?" she asks, and I nod. "That Jess, right?"

"How do you keep track of all of this?" I ask, a little stressed about her encyclopedic knowledge of my life.

"Umm, mom superpowers?" she responds. I just bury my head in my hands.

"This couldn't be more embarrassing," I moan. "How am I supposed to explain this in college essays?"

"You're a journalist, aren't you?" Mom asks, in a tone that she rarely uses—it's almost brusque. I nod. "So, spin it into the story you want to tell," she says. "Think of this as a good emotional story to tell in your essays, and have a whole lesson you learned around it."

She may have a point: "The real cost of 15 minutes of fame," I say, thinking clearer now. "That's a good headline."

Mom sets my steaming mug in front of me, and I snatch it off the counter. "Thanks for the pep talk," I say, walking and talking. "I'll be in my study." By study, I mean my room. But still. It never hurts to try to think your way into an editorial mindset. So, I slam my door, boot up my laptop and start typing away, telling my side and spinning hard. I'm aiming to come across as sympathetic, admitting to being a little pathetic, definitely empathetic with Elle's plight and position, and most importantly, emphatically coming off as in the right. I don't know that this was exactly what Mom thought I was going to do. I'm sure she was thinking a bit more apology plus rainbows and sunshine, but the emotions come out with a lot more malice towards Elle than Mom would approve of.

By the time it's fully written, even I've forgotten exactly what happened, so I have to imagine the rest of the school will too. And without giving it a second look, I hit Publish onto the school's newspaper website and my blog.

chapter
twenty-four

Elle

WHEN MY PHONE pings with a message after remaining blissfully silent for a solid 30 minutes, I groan, very loud. But when I realize it might be Jess, I immediately grab for it. It's not—just a debate team buddy, sending me a link to the school's newspaper website. I click through, and immediately groan again. It's a screenshot of me and Krista slapping at each other with the headline: "Abusing my 15 minutes of fame."

And there's Krista's byline—and the minute I read her lead, I realize that suddenly, I've become the bad guy.

This is turning into a PR nightmare. And of course, I'm not the only one in the house that's seen it. I can hear Mom pounding up the stairs already, so I'm alert and facing the door when she practically slams it open. She's trying to keep her cool, sort of, but her eyes are looking a little bit scarier than usual (which is saying something!).

"Did you see what your former bestie wrote?" she asks, over-emphasizing 'bestie' as she strides into my room with her iPad in hand. What, does she have a Google alert on me now? (Probably.)

I nod.

"And what do you plan to do about it?" she asks, her voice going up a couple of octaves. "A thing like this could easily get picked up by a major publication, and very quickly, you're the one remembered as the bad guy. And how is that going to look to Columbia?"

I know that this is the moment when a smart person might opt to take the moral high ground, say nothing and deal with it in silence, just let it all fade away—this is high school, there will be a new drama the next time the it-couple of the week has a loud public breakup in the cafeteria. But all I feel is a pounding fury coursing through my blood. "I'm going to get her back," I say, as coldly as I can.

Mom nods, turns on her heel and leaves. I let out a breath, shaking slightly. For once, I feel like I have Mom's approval—granted, this wasn't exactly how I wanted it, but I'll take it where I can get it. It's game on. I sit down at my laptop and boot it up. I know revenge is a dish best served cold, but I don't have that kind of time.

What dirt do have on her? A brief semi-skanky friendship-ending blowup doesn't really apply, so I hit the usual channels first: Facebook, Instagram, and a deep-dive into her past articles and blogs, a minor stalking of that one guy she dated last year, and a blast to all my most gossipy acquaintances asking for the scoop.

After an hour, I'm forced to admit that she's stayed squeaky clean, though I do notice one interesting fact: Since the start of cross-country season, Jess has been liking every photo that she posts on Instagram. He hasn't even followed me, I realize — I hadn't noticed that before.

This deep dive is getting me nowhere, and I realize as I hit my fourth hour scrolling that maybe I need to do some undercover IRL work to really make this thing blow up. I'd laugh maniacally, but I just don't have the energy. Tomorrow at cross-country practice, the games begin.

I may not be the fastest girl on the team, I think — but that's just a matter of running faster, right? How hard can it be to just push a little harder? I can drop a few pounds and manage to get the guy all in this week. I just have to focus a little harder. I've been doing great so far with skipping breakfast, feeling lighter throughout the day and, okay, maybe a little lightheaded at practice, but in a good way. I just need to stop going crazy at dinner or at bedtime.

So, instead of snacking on the KitKat stash I have in my desk like I would love to, I start creating my plan of attack, starting with my wardrobe. I'm a serious runner, so I need some serious running gear.

"Mom!" I yell down the stairs. "I'm borrowing some running clothes!"

Chapter Twenty-Four

She grunts back up at me, but it sounds positive, so I take that as a go-ahead and start pawing through her pretty immense collection of workout apparel — all name-brand and way nicer than my stuff. Step one: show up looking sporty-but-gorgeous. A pair of velvety soft lululemon tights and matching sports bra in a soft purple, plus a tank top and hoodie from Athleta in slate gray looks both athletic and coordinated, and a matching gray ball cap that I can pull a ponytail through should make me look like a legit runner at practice tomorrow. And unlike a month ago, I feel like they almost fit now — in fact, I'm sure my legs are less sausage-like than they were a couple of weeks ago. That means I'm on the right track. I just need to take it to the next level. I stuff it all in one of mom's many empty gym bags and head to our den.

Next step: Getting run-ready. The den isn't really a cozy space where Mom and I curl up to watch movies and veg out—that's what the living room is for. Over the years, it sort of started to morph into a home gym, with a treadmill and free weights creeping in, then the couch being moved to make way for a yoga mat in front of the TV. Finally, a year ago, Mom hired a handyman to come in and rip out the carpet and take away the couch, putting down hardwood flooring that could handle the pounding of kettlebells, and installing an air filter and better windows so it's now a full-time exercise room, with no place to curl up.

I hate it and I really miss that couch, but right now, I'm happy we have the gym here. I do a few half-hearted stretches on the yoga mat before starting in on the real work: it's time to get ripped with one of the many, many workout DVDs that promise rock-hard abs.

Thirty minutes later, I'm stretched out on the mat gasping for air, possibly crying but I'm not sure. My abs aren't rock hard, they're just on fire. Not the same element at all. Even pushing myself up to sitting is hard after the last round of bicycle crunches, and I'm starting to ponder if crawling to my room would work, because even contemplating standing up on legs that did what may have been several hundred air squats makes my hamstrings start quivering.

When I do push myself out of my fetal position huddle—many, many minutes after the DVD has gone back to the main menu—there's a me-shaped sweat stain on the glossy hardwood floor where I rolled. It's like a snow angel, but a really depressing one.

Luckily, I'm already in a casual standing position, leaning against the weight rack (for support, not to act casual), when Mom breezes in, holding her iPad and wearing her most relaxed of workout gear: a t-shirt from her college softball league, and shorts that are more meant for pajama use than gym use. Her time in our home gym is the only time I really see her out of 'totally pulled together lawyer' character, and it's always a little bit of a shock. Even her hair is shoved up in a ratty bun like I would wear, and her mascara is a little panda-esque under her eyes, probably from rubbing them at her desk. This is actually my favorite way to see her, because it reminds me that she's still a normal human, even if most of the time she seems more like a combination of a robot and Wonder Woman.

"Were you doing the Iron Abs video?" she asks as she sets her iPad on the elliptical machine. She might not be dressed like a lawyer right now, but she'll still spend most of her workout reading briefs and making notes.

"Could you tell from the whimpering?" I respond, staggering towards the door.

"It gets easier the more you work at it," she says unsympathetically as she hops onto the elliptical and sets her workout speed and I lean in the doorframe. "It'll help your running."

"That's the plan," I say. "Goodnight, Mom."

Her headphones are already in and she gives me an absent wave as I head for the shower.

chapter
twenty-five

Krista

AT PRACTICE AFTER SCHOOL, I see Elle lurking outside of the group huddle and I choose to ignore her completely. Obviously. Meanwhile, Jess is hanging out right next to me and sending me pointed glances, though I have no idea what those glances are actually pointing at.

When Coach tells us it's time to do some intervals on the hilly trails a mile from school, I'm relieved—sure, hill intervals suck, but they're also so hard that there's no way I'll be able to keep thinking about how I slammed Elle in that editorial, or the slightly gnawing feeling of guilt that I haven't been able to shake.

Maybe it wasn't exactly fair of me to go after her for lying to Kendra on *GMA*, considering in the parking garage before the show, I was the one to suggest we try to make ourselves sound like friends. And maybe it wasn't exactly the truth that I was perfectly fine to get out of the woods on my own (though I still don't think she really *needed* to help me). And okay, it was a little mean to accuse her of only helping me because her race was going so pathetically that any reason to stop running was a good one, and she realized she could get more glory helping me than coming in last. So it was not my nicest moment. So what?

I give myself a good full-body shake to get out of my head, and to start warming up—the autumn air has gotten chillier, so my sleeveless Ramones shirt and black tights are a little cooler than I'd prefer when we're just standing around, and I pull my black sweatshirt on to stay cozier.

Miss C jogs over to me in her cute fleecy hoodie and purple tights, looking sporty and spry—neither of which I'm feeling right now—and lowers her voice when she asks me if everything is okay.

"Why wouldn't it be?" I ask, a little (a lot) defensively.

"Well, we didn't exactly talk about that article that you published yesterday," she says. "I would have preferred a chance to edit it before you posted."

Instantly, I feel chastened and a bit idiotic. "It was a spur-of-the-moment thing," I say. "You didn't get in trouble for it, did you?"

She shakes her head. "No, but it was a close one. Just... don't do it again, please?" she says, and pats my shoulder sympathetically.

I nod, and she smiles a little. She can't be too mad. "So, ankle is feeling better?" she asks, and we're back to normal.

"It's a little tender," I admit. "But I think I can run on it."

"Well, just take it easy on the hills today and slow down to walk if you feel it acting up—better to miss one practice than re-injure it and lose a week," she tells me.

As she walks away, she shouts back over her shoulder for me to start stretching, focusing on my calves and hamstrings, so I do a few half-hearted lunges and some leg swings. I admit, I might be getting into this running thing, but the actual pre-workout stretching? Not my jam. My mom's yoga class is more my speed, but standing in the middle of the field lunging around while the football bros watch? Mehh.

Out of the corner of my eye, I can see Jess is still watching me, and he shoots me a half-grin and a wink. Honestly, I'm not loving the idea of creating more drama with Elle, but at the same time, I find myself smirking back. Between all of my activities with newspaper and the lit mag, and the fact that I'm kind of a bit of a loner, I haven't dated a ton. So having a guy so clearly at least moderately into me? I'm digging it.

When Miss C gives us the day's workout—a mile warmup to the trails, then 10 hill repeats up the kicker hill that's about 30 seconds long, followed by a cool-down jog back to school—mostly everyone groans. It's a tough, grueling run and the hill she picked for today just plain sucks. I sneak a glance Elle's way and she's looking even more bummed than usual. Good.

Me, now that I've bounced around and warmed up? I'm feeling at the top of my game. Because what it comes down to, I remind myself sternly, is page views, not emotional twinges of guilt. All day, I've been getting sympathetic comments from fellow students, and page views are way up—even if Miss C is sort of pissed—and now that I've stretched, my ankle is feeling on fire... in a good way.

Coach shouts at us to get moving, and we all jog around the track and head towards the hole in the fence that takes us out onto the trails—some of us moving faster than others.

Even a week ago, I'd be jogging at the back of the pack, but today, I'm pushing my way to the front (casually) and running shoulder to shoulder with Jess. Not talking, just running like I only happen to be there. My ankle is tingling a bit from the sudden exertion, and my lungs are burning just a little bit at this pace, staying at the front. In fact, it's getting harder and harder to pull in a deep breath, which I'm trying to do subtly, rather than panting like I want to.

When Jess finally notices that I'm right next to him and says hi, I manage to eek out a 'Hey, how's it going?' without sputtering for air, though I use the 'going' to take an extra deep inhale. Running casually is a lot harder than it looks in the movies.

"Oh, you know—some weird looks, some questions about if we've ever had a three-way, the usual," he says, but he doesn't look perturbed—he actually winks as he says it, like it's a cute joke. My face, on the other hand, turns bright red at 'three-way.'

"Heh," I reply, smoothly. "Sorry about the whole thing."

Of course, as I get through my apology, I suck air down the wrong pipe and end up hacking and coughing while still trying to maintain my 'casual' pace next to him. Smoooooooth like butter.

But while my lungs are mildly cranky with the pace, it's my ankle that's the bigger problem. It's gone from feeling fire to *being* on fire, and my stride is starting to hitch a little bit as we crest the slight hill on the road and make the right-hander onto the trail, where the pace blissfully slows as everyone starts to prep for the actual interval session. I can almost hear my ankle sigh in gratitude as we slow to a full stop so everyone can hang their sweatshirts on the tree at the base of the hill before we get started.

I'm not normally the sexiest person on earth, but I make an attempt to pull off my sweatshirt without getting stuck in it or smacking Jess in the process. It pulls up my tank top with it, and while my head is still caught in the sweatshirt—DON'T PANIC KRISTA JUST BE COOL—I hear a whistle that I'm fairly certain is him. Mission accomplished.

When Coach blows his airhorn for the first interval, I charge up the hill feeling like I'm hovering above the ground. It feels so freaking good to be running fast again. I feel smooth, my arms pumping in perfect time with my feet, wind blowing in my face. Sure, I'm huffing like a steam engine, but I am mooooving.

I didn't really realize I liked running until my ankle went out and suddenly, I couldn't do it anymore. This feels free.

"Nice work," Coach says as I hit the crest of the hill and immediately let off the pace, my breath coming out in gasps. "Keep moving," he says as I try to stop to catch my breath, so I hobble forward a few yards before flipping to jog back down the hill for the next rep. Jess is jogging in place, and we fly down the hill together, side by side. Which sounds romantic, but I could have used a second to wipe my nose, since snot is dripping like I turned on a faucet.

And maybe it's the faster pace down the hill or maybe it's just a poorly placed stick on the ground, but I stomp in a weird way, and immediately my ankle lights up, shooting pain straight up through my hip and I let out a sharp yelp and grab for something to hang on to before collapsing in a puddle. Of course, that something is Jess's arm.

"You okay?" he asks, gripping my arm and pulling me back up. I grab onto a nearby tree so I can transfer my weight off of him, and grimace.

"Ankle is just flaring up," I say through my gritted teeth.

"Maybe take this next interval off, then?" he says, sympathetically. "I'll stay here with you."

I nod. Internally, I'm stoked. Maybe now we can have a few minutes to really talk, instead of just sending long looks and flirty texts that don't have a whole lot of content. Maybe we can talk about what to do about Elle being so unreasonable, maybe he'll ask me to homecoming again, maybe we can actually make something good happen out of this whole embarrassing debacle.

I reach down and rub my ankle, and he puts an arm out to help keep me steady. I'd sit, but the ground is still soggy and the last thing I need is a mud-soaked ass once I'm ready to run again.

Glancing back up at him, I start to open my mouth to ask what he thought of the article I wrote and published since clearly, he's not mad about it, but before I can get a word out, his mouth is on mine and suddenly, *boom*, we're making out.

For a half a second, it's romantic. The sunlight is hitting us and it feels warm, and for the first time in days, I can feel myself finally starting to relax a little.

And then, Jess's hand suddenly makes a move from my hip straight up my shirt. It happens so fast that I barely register what's happening, I just feel a huge sense of shock. And before I can move, he's grabbed my hand and is rubbing it against his shorts, where I can feel... well, everything. And then I snap out of my statue-state.

"Hey, back off!" I say, catching my breath and shoving him backwards. Hugely embarrassed—what if Miss C saw us—I tug my shirt back in place and shove him a second time, since he hasn't stepped back at all. "What is WRONG with you?"

He just smirks. "Like you didn't enjoy it," he says, and makes a grab for me again, but I jump back.

"Being pawed against a tree when a bunch of our teammates could run past any second? No, thanks," I say, furious and starting to shake. I turn on my heel and start to run, practically sprinting, back towards the school. I don't care if Coach thinks I've abandoned practice or I get in trouble for it, I just know that I need to get the hell out of there.

As I make the first turn back onto the main track, I'm trying to stay angry and ignore the tears that are starting to sting as I blink them away, but of course, the day gets even worse.

Standing just at the edge of the trail, with a perfect view of where I was just standing with Jess, is Elle. I'm not sure exactly what she saw but I'm guessing she saw enough, judging by the scowl on her face.

This feels like an odd deja-vu moment. But much worse.

chapter
twenty-six

Elle

AFTER THE FIRST HILL INTERVAL, I huff my way back down
and rather than heading right back up the hill, I walk back towards
where I dropped my jacket to grab my water bottle. I don't care that it
was only 30 seconds of running, I'm absolutely parched and needed a
place to catch my breath in private. You'd think I'd be getting better at
these hill interval things, but they just keep feeling worse and worse.

I jog my way into the trees where I left my stuff, and as I reach
down, I hear rustling. I look up, and almost scream. Jess and Krista are
pressed together against a tree, his hand straight up her shirt, and I taste
blood right before I taste bile in the back of my throat.

That *skank*!

The urge to run and puke is so strong, but I still grab by phone and
snap a photo. I'm not sure what my plan here is, but I need the photo-
graphic evidence to show myself that I didn't just imagine this, that
history is repeating itself exactly. And I know that this is entirely her
fault. Jess is into *me*. Not her.

Why else would he be texting me? We're so close to making a relationship work—and I already have a prom dress situation sorted out
that I almost fit in to and that would absolutely be just his style. (I mean
that he'd think it was hot, not he'd look good in it.)

But now, just like before, Krista is swooping in and trying to ruin
everything. Like she always does.

Chapter Twenty-Six

I stalk back to practice, rearranging my face into a smile so I look less murder-y and more like I just finished an interval and am feeling fresh as a daisy. Jess has jogged back too, and while I can't see Krista, I'm sure she's not far away. Probably had to compose herself—rearrange her shirt, fix her hair, perfect her red lipstick, the usual stuff you have to do after you're grinding up against a guy with a tree at your back. It's hell on hairdos. (Not that I would know.)

Jess looks casual and confident, as usual, and he even gives me a little private wave and meaningful look before he goes over to chat with Jenny. It's almost enough to convince myself that what I saw must have been Krista jumping him, and that the second I turned away, he pushed her off of him told her that he couldn't let things go any further because he really likes me.

The voice at the back of my head is shrieking at me to not be a moron and obviously he was into it, but I ignore that voice. What does she know?

The rest of the workout is sheer hell, but for once, I'm less focused on how much my legs hurt because I'm trying hard to keep from absolutely freaking out—torn between wanting to break down in tears, or hunt Krista down to punch her in the face, or to beg Jess to tell me that he isn't interested in her and that he really likes me. But I don't do any of those things, I just focus on making it through each interval.

For the first time, the running seems to actually help me: I can feel my emotions leveling out with each hard effort, like somehow all the power and force that I'm putting into each minute of running is letting steam out, like when you open the lid to a teakettle and all the steam rises up. By the time we get back to school at the end of practice, I'm feeling a lot calmer. Still angry, but the run has taken a lot of the intensity out of it and I'm feeling more balanced and ready to take on Krista as soon as I see her again.

chapter
twenty-seven

Krista

AFTER I SPRINTED OFF, I paused for a few minutes to cry into a tree, then walked the long way back to school, hoping to calm down. But as I'm getting changed in the locker room, I realize that I can't stop shaking. My hands are still trembling as I try to pull on my sweatshirt when Elle stalks over looking furious. I didn't realize practice had already ended. Was I crying against that tree for that long?

"He doesn't like you, you know," she whispers loudly as she yanks on her sweatpants.

I look over and realize she's panting slightly, red-faced and looking as furious as she did at Homecoming years ago. And I'm not just angry with her anymore: I'm scared *for* her, not of her. It makes no sense that she possibly thinks that I'm happy to have 'stolen' him again.

"Trust me, I don't care. And honestly—I'm not saying this because I want him. You should stay away from him," I tell her, but I know it doesn't sink in.

"Whatever, Krista," she says. "I know what you're doing and it's not going to work."

I take a deep breath. "Look, I don't want to get into this but it wasn't what it looked like," I say, and for a second, I wish we were still best friends because the voice in my head wants to scream, "I didn't want this, I didn't ask for him to touch me and I want to take it back and make it go away!" but I don't say that. I don't fling myself at her and end up in a best-friends-hug like I'm shocked to realize that I sorely want to.

"So, you weren't hooking up behind a tree at the bottom of the hill?" she asks me sarcastically.

I want to tell her how wrong she is, and how much I hate Jess and myself right now, but when I really look at her, she's just standing looking so smug that I can't bring myself to admit what happened. I'm ashamed of him, of me, and of how we've all screwed up this friendship. But more than that, I find myself getting more and more angry at her yet again. If she hadn't brought this whole thing up and re-started our old fight, none of this would be happening. I wouldn't feel this bad.

This is *her* fault.

"What can I say? He likes thin girls," I spit out instead of telling her the truth, and turn on my heel, slamming the door to the locker room as I leave.

But even as I head to where Mom is meeting me at the pickup spot, I feel even more ashamed than I did before, instead of righteous and angry. I see Elle out of the corner of my eye, standing in the bus line, looking absolutely devastated. She might think what happened with Jess and me wasn't a romantic we're-going-to-be-a-couple thing, but she still has no idea what it really was. And now, I've hurt her feelings by kicking her in the one place I knew would hurt just as much.

Great. I feel like double crap now.

And then, it gets worse. Jess struts out and heads towards the bike rack and I find myself shrinking away when he turns and gives me a wink, which makes me feel even dirtier than I already felt. And of course, Elle sees *that* too.

chapter
twenty-eight

Elle

I **AM DYING.** Emotionally and physically, I'm dragging around today like there's a 10-ton weight on my shoulders. Between the hill workout and the ab DVD, my body feels like it's been hit by a bus, and my mental state isn't great either. For the second time in our lives, Krista is stealing Jess away from me, but this time, I'm not going to make a scene. I'm going to be strong, understanding... and sexy.

Yesterday was hell. After Krista and I had our post-practice confrontation, I came home and, even though my legs felt like they were on fire, put in the fat-blasting DVD. It didn't give me a six-pack, just bad cramps.

The first moment I can, I whip out my phone and shoot a casually annoyed message to Jess. "Why do my muscles ache so much?"

The three dots pop up, go away, then pop back up.

"Yr still not used to running," he finally responds.

"Leg rub?" I send back with a wink at the end, hoping he catches the flirty tone and says something nice back.

"Love one thx" he sends back, which... wasn't exactly what I was hoping for, but it's not un-flirty?

But I'm not the one he's making out with right now, I remind myself. There's only one way I can catch up to Krista: Two can play with fire, and while I might not be as skinny as her, I have a whole lot more up top than she does. And I know that a picture is worth a thousand words. It's not a proud decision for me, and I feel awkward and uncomfortable, but I know this will catch his attention like nothing else will. So, I suck in my stomach and hold my breath.

Before I can think about it too much, I snap a picture—from the neck down. (As long as my face stays out of it, I should still be able to run for office even if it gets leaked.)

It takes a few tries to get one that's at just the right angle (boobs out, stomach in) but once I do, I send it before I can think too hard about it or panic.

He replies almost instantly with a smiley face, but that's it. No three dots to indicate he's typing a much longer, sexier reply, just a smile. I was hoping for a declaration of love, and this definitely isn't it.

When my mom pokes her head into my room to tell me that she's going out for the night, I shove my phone under a pile of papers on my desk, like somehow she has phone x-ray vision and will be able to see my recently sent (and already archived) messages.

"I might be back a little late, so don't wait up," she says cheerily, blowing me a kiss, and it's not until she's already left the room, trailing a cloud of perfume, that I realize she's pretty dressed up—I haven't seen my mom rocking a maxi dress in ages, the only time she dresses up is in a suit for court—and I also haven't seen her leaving the house at 8PM… ever, actually.

Something is up, but I have too much on my mind to focus on what my mom is doing in her spare time. Maybe she's finally dating again. Maybe that's why she's been so much happier lately. Or maybe I'm just more miserable and she seems perky by comparison.

I've been up for hours staring at the photo I took of Krista and Jess on my phone, trying to decide what to do with it. I'm still boiling with rage, but I haven't been able to hit Send to post it to my SnapChat. Partially because I know that people will screenshot it and it will be part of my permanent record of things I've done. Partially because it doesn't seem like enough.

So instead, I start by sending a few texts to friends telling them exactly what I saw, asking if they can believe how skanky she is. (Predictably, they 'literally cannot.' Which clearly means they do.)

That still doesn't feel satisfying enough, though.

Krista used the school paper to make me look like an idiot, I think. So why don't I do the same to her with my debate club? We have one of our bi-annual debates happening at the end of the week, and while I'd planned to talk about the issue of school sport participation and the pressures and demands students face from teachers and coaches (ahem) in order to get into a good school, maybe my platform can be around safe sex instead. A very specific platform around safe sex, in fact. One with real world examples.

If I was a supervillain, I'd be doing an evil laugh by now.

Muhahahaha.

chapter
twenty-nine

Krista

ENOUGH WHINING, enough feeling sorry for myself, enough being stressed. It's time to get back to feeling like myself. I'm not a runner, I'm a punk. And my favorite local band is playing at a coffeehouse tonight. I know that if I can just get back to feeling like *me* for a few hours, everything will be better.

And I clearly don't need Jess or Elle in my life or my brain anymore. I need loud music, I need to just escape in a crowd of people. And judging by the buzz going on in the band's online forum, a lot of people I know are going to be there.

So, I get ready, switching my usual more casual school attire for a full-out night on the town. Usually I don't get as dressed up for local shows as I would to go into the city, but it sounds like tonight is going to be a serious dance-fest with everyone going all-out on their looks. I pull out my favorite crinoline tutu and pull a black satin high-waisted skirt that flares out in an A-line over it, and put it on with my Converse low top black sneakers. A white tank top, black cardigan and subdued strand of pearls go on next, followed by blood-red lipstick and about 18 layers of mascara. I look like a 1940s housewife gone bad, which is the exact look I'm going for. Cabaret chic, without the lingerie (Mom would never let me out of the house!).

Tempting as it is to ride my bike over, it's a little challenging in the skirt, so I beg a ride from Mom to cover the three miles to the show and she easily agrees, though we have a minor skirmish over how late I can stay out on a school night. With 11 PM ("just this once") as the agreed-upon time, I've almost forgotten what I was so upset about by the time we get to the show and I hop out of the car. This is what I needed. A night with my people, not the normies from the team.

I pay the $10 cover and head in to the darkened coffee shop, the echo of music already bouncing off the walls as I head down the hallway to where the band will be set up in the back room. My confidence from the car begins to evaporate at an alarming rate as I get closer and closer. These shows always seem like a good idea, but then I arrive and I never know exactly where to start. I give a casual wave to the guys who are in the hall dutifully manning the merch tables and try to seem nonchalant.

Once I'm inside and sweating and jumping around and dancing, I'll be in my element, but the moments before, I always get hit with a wave of imposter syndrome, like I'm not cool enough to be here. Like I care too much. Like I have a sign that says 'loser' somehow stuck to my forehead, and I'm not getting it quite right.

Why do I do this to myself? One second, I'm confident and on top of the world. The next, I'm convinced everyone is laughing at me, or pitying me because I'm just not fitting in. And tonight, it feels more obvious than ever. I edge my way into the smoky room—not cigarette smoke of course, but the band uses a smoke machine for that same vibe —and survey the scene. All the kids I kind of hang out with when I have free time at school are there, standing watching the stage, slumped at tables, even sitting on the floor, exuding effortless cool.

Okay, Krista. Time to pull yourself up and get into the swing of things. Luckily, the band is warming up and strains of music are starting to make the crowd drift closer to the stage, so I'm able to let myself get swept away into the crowd. I edge my way into the center, and as conversations fade away and people start nodding along with the music as the warm up starts to shift to actual playing, not just feedback on the speakers, I feel a sense of calm that I haven't felt... well, since those few moments in the race when I was flying.

As the band begins to build up into their first actual song of the evening, my heart rate speeds up even as a feeling of calm envelops me, and for a few minutes, everything else fades away. I'm dancing along with the crowd, stamping my feet and shaking my fists, caught up in the music and the feeling of camaraderie. I lock hands with a guy I kind of recognize, and for a few moments, we do a clumsy waltz together as the band shifts into one of the danciest songs in their repertoire.

As we whirl around the floor—not gracefully, crashing into other dancers as we go—it feels almost surreal. For the moment, everything is perfect: I'm sweating, panting slightly, and my skirt is flaring out with every twirl. I feel hilariously, wildly beautiful. The boy I'm dancing with, in his too-big clearly-thrifted suit with sooty, smudged black eyeliner dripping down his face, looks eerily handsome.

We twirl around, bouncing into and off of other couples in a semi-waltz, semi-moshpit. It's wonderful and weird and wild, and it reminds me of who I really am. Maybe for a moment, I let myself get wrapped up in what it felt like to be popular, to be part of a normal sport, a normal group of people, and look where it got me: Feeling used and abused by both of my former friends. Jess can go to hell, I decide, letting myself be twirled around the dance floor. cross-country can go to hell. Elle can go to hell. This is where I belong.

And for a moment, that feels true.

After the music ends and the boy I danced with—I think he goes to the private high school across town—gives me a mock bow while I curtsy and we all cheer wildly, he fades back into the crowd and once again, I'm alone in the crowd. I try to shake it off and stay on the dance floor, jumping wildly to the next song, a fast, punkier number, but the moment has faded slightly.

And it fades even more as I glance around the room and see a few girls from school—the ones I used to hang out with before I realized I wanted to do more than smoke behind the bleachers after class and talk about the 'great art we'd make someday when we weren't stuck in these classes with these idiot teachers' (yeah, right)—whispering to each other and pointing at me. At least, it feels like they're pointing at me. I'm not positive, but my stomach drops and I feel sick again. What are they saying? Do they know what happened today? I don't know how they would, but I can't shake the feeling that they're talking about me, and whatever they're saying, it isn't good. Maybe I don't belong here anymore.

Suddenly, it feels too crowded, too tight in here. Rather than staying to find out if I was the topic of conversation, I push my way through the crowd and back into the fresh air outside, taking huge gulps, trying to regain my equilibrium. I have goosebumps, even though it's a warm night. I can't push away the feeling of dread, of feeling so outside of myself anymore. I have to go home. For a moment, I debate phoning Mom for a ride. She'd come get me, no questions asked. But I don't want to freak her out, so I start walking instead. Every step brings a new wave of emotion. I step with my right foot and feel used, dirty, alone. I step with my left and get a surge of anger. It feels like my thoughts are at war with each other. Am I righteous or depressed?

It seems like the walk home takes hours, but I get back just ahead of curfew and quietly let myself in. Mom is in the kitchen, pretending not to be waiting up for me, and softly calls out, "Did you have fun?"

I say yes with as much enthusiasm as I can muster, but quickly head up to my room before she can ask more questions. Right now, I just want to sleep.

chapter
thirty

Elle

AT HOME ALONE, as usual I can't help scrolling through Instagram Stories and seeing all the cool, alternative kids from school partying at the coffeehouse that's only a few blocks from where I'm sitting. They all look amazing in their funky outfits, so confident and sure of themselves, even though they're supposed to be the 'weird kids.' I think they're actually proud of that title—it's not an insult for them like it would be to me.

And of course, Krista is right in the mix—I spot her in a few videos, dancing madly with a really cute boy who looks surprisingly excellent in a three-piece suit. Of course, Krista looks skinny and ethereal in her funky 1940s outfit that I'd never pull off in a million years. She'll probably be making out with that guy by the end of the night too, I think sourly. And of course, I check my messages to make sure I haven't missed anything from Jess yet.

Nothing.

Meanwhile, Krista is out there having a blast, and I can just imagine Jess at home scrolling through her photos, seeing her having the best time. Is he jealous of the guy she's dancing with?

I throw my phone into the pillows on my bed and lean back in frustration. I'm torn between being so mad that I want to go downstairs and start breaking things, and depressed enough that I want to call my trusty delivery guy Jan and tell him to bring two of everything, immediately.

Between punching a wall or stuffing my face, I'm not sure which will do the most damage.

I could try to talk to my mom and get her opinion on the whole thing, but I know exactly what she'll say already: "If Krista and Jess want to get together, that's not your problem, it has nothing to do with you."

Then, she'll probably keep lecturing me about not making another public incident happen. She's still really, really mad about the whole *GMA* thing, even though she hasn't mentioned it in a bit. She doesn't have to: I can feel her disapproval whenever we're in the same room, and I don't know how I can convince her that none of it was my fault. And I definitely can't convince her that Jess and I belong together. Especially considering I'm not sure I'm entirely convinced anymore. If sending him that photo wasn't enough to keep his interest focused on me, I'm not sure what else I can do.

I can't even picture myself in the same scenario I caught him and Krista in. For one thing, I'd be way too out of breath and snot-covered to handle a mid-run makeout, but to be completely honest, even without the increased heart rate, that would be uncharted territory for me. I don't exactly date a lot, and when I do, it's been with the nerdy guys from debate team who's idea of sexy talk includes Powerpoint presentations about why we should be hooking up. It's not exactly a major turn-on, so I've never gotten further than an awkward goodnight kiss. Krista, on the other hand, seemed plenty experienced. And Jess... well, clearly that wasn't his first in-the-woods makeout.

So, in addition to feeling wildly depressed that Jess clearly is interested in Krista and furious that Krista is still interested in Jess, I get to be jealous and a little curious about what it would be like to make out with a guy in the woods.

Perfect. Just freaking perfect.

You know what? It's easier to just be plain old pissed.

chapter
thirty-one

Krista

EVEN THOUGH MOM made my favorite chai coconut milk latte with maple syrup and had it ready for me when I dragged myself to the door to head to school, I still feel like absolute crap. The show last night cleared my mind temporarily, but it was definitely not a solution. I waver at the door, debating if I should tell Mom what happened, and what her reaction would be.

It would be intense, I think, and I say nothing and head to school instead. I'm too embarrassed to tell her what happened. No one wants to talk to their mom about sex stuff, even—or maybe especially—stuff like this.

And when I get to school, it gets worse. I realize quickly that Jess isn't just acting like I was on board with the whole disgusting groping incident, he's actually told people that we 'hooked up.' I'm getting side-eyes from the other jocks and catcalls in the hallway. To say this has never happened to me before would be an understatement. Since our Homecoming incident a couple years ago, I haven't really dated anyone at school, much less hooked up with any of the guys in our grade.

It's exhausting, it's demeaning, it's... not who I am. I generally prefer to blend in, which is why I write the stories versus star in them, and why I joined cross-country instead of some other team-based sport. Even my "close" friends aren't that close—not since Elle and I stopped being friends. I don't want to say that I went into hiding after that, but I was never great at making friends and even the 'cool' punk kids I hang with at lunch or after school (well, that I used to hang out with before practices took over my only free time!) aren't that tight with me. I like them, but I also don't tell them about what's going on in my life or invite them over to have a *Buffy* marathon.

And I haven't minded, until today. Now, it turns out my so-called friends in my punk crew are giving me the cold shoulder because they think I've officially turned into a preppy jock now that Jess and I are some kind of 'item,' which we are absolutely not.

The worst, though, is Jess himself. He's swaggering around in the halls, winking at me when we cross paths, and even patted my butt between fifth and sixth period as I was making my way to the library. And of course, people saw. So the rumors about us are even more wild by the afternoon. I even heard one girl telling someone else that I didn't hurt my ankle while racing, I just collapsed because I was exhausted from my first trimester of pregnancy.

For the love of...

And even crappier than Jess thinking that he's a social god and that I should just be overjoyed that he basically molested me in the woods is that I feel guilty when I think about Elle. I feel gross when I think about Jess, so I'm trying really hard to not think about either of them, but the upshot is I can't stop thinking about both of them.

And it seems like Elle has done what she does best. *Hard reset.* It's this thing we came up with back in sixth grade, when either of us was in what our mothers referred to as 'a mood.' Basically, it's like when your phone freezes and you need to reboot it. You do the same with your feelings. It's not the best solution, since my mom would say talking things through is more important, but it does get you through the school day when you're feeling emotional. Judging by the way she's blinking her eyes and doing her warm-up stretches, Elle has hard reset regarding the incident.

I wish I didn't know her so well, so well that I know her post-practice plan may very well involve punching a pillow or crying into it. It's hell when your mortal enemy is your ex-best friend. You're far too aware of how they're feeling.

And it would be easier if I didn't feel so damn guilty about it. Intellectually, I'm aware enough to know I shouldn't feel bad, Jess is the bad guy here. And even if I had been an equal partner in that makeup session, I still shouldn't feel guilty, because it's not like she has any real claim on him.

Momentarily, I consider quitting the team to avoid the drama, but I don't know that NYU will accept 'boy problems' as a reason I didn't complete a single season of a sport. So I'm making sure I don't get caught alone again, and I can see Miss C giving me some concerned looks as I pound my way through intervals.

We do a set of ten 'one minute on, one minute off' intervals and I have a hard time hitting the 'off' moments because I'm just so nervous and twitchy that the whole thing feels like I'm moving in double time. So, I guess this has been good for my times but bad for literally everything else in my life.

In fact, practices are getting harder as we get closer and closer to the final race of the season, and even though my brain is constantly trying to calm down and figure out how it feels about the whole situation—Was it actually my fault? Should Elle be mad at me? Was it truly that bad?—I can't help but feel really excited to get out and compete again. I've been officially cleared for competition, and while I've missed a few races as my ankle healed, I can't wait to race again.

I know this vibe would ruin my too-cool-for-sport rep entirely. But it turns out that I crave speed, I thrive on that competition, and not finishing that first race has only left me wanting to do more and go faster. Miss C has gently told me—while I was doubled over and out of breath at the top of a hill—that I shouldn't expect to win this season. I should be happy with my progress, I'll get full participation credit despite the ankle rolling incident that's kept me from racing the requisite three meets, and I'm a strong runner. She added that I'm also very new to running and I'll be up against girls who've been racing since the third grade. I know all of that, but in the back of my brain, I do have a secret goal of finishing in the top five.

And to that end, I think Mom has picked up on the fact that a lot of stuff is going on for me. Even before this whole Jess thing, I haven't been hanging out with her as much and when I do sit down to watch *Buffy* with her, I'm sitting on a yoga mat practicing a few stretches Miss C taught me.

When I'm on the yoga mat, she's much less inclined to bother me for details of what's going on in my life.

The one bright spot in all of this is that Elle and my disastrous morning talk show incident has run its course at school. Sure, I'm still the hot gossip, but at least people aren't talking about an actual cat fight that I had on national television. A guy bragging about a hook up? At least that's normal high school stuff, even if it is super offensive because it didn't actually happen the way he says it did.

Of course, I'm also avoiding telling Mom because even if she believes me that nothing happened with Jess, which I think she will, it's going to prompt a whole heart-to-heart safe-sex discussion that I'd really rather just not have. Or she'll be furious and storm over to his house, berate his parents, and make it a whole thing.

In fact, after practice and during dinner, Mom asks if everything is all right with me. I know that tone of voice: She's onto me. So I play it off. "I'm just really nervous about the championship race," I say. "I feel good, but since I haven't gotten to finish a race yet, I don't have any idea how it'll go."

"Pre-pre-race jitters," she says knowingly. "I always hated the weeks leading up to a big race. It's hard to think about anything else, isn't it?"

I wish.

"I didn't think it was going to matter so much to me," I admit—though of course, it's not taking up quite as much emotional energy as she might think. "When I joined the team, I thought I'd just stick in the back and not really stress about how I was doing."

"What changed your mind?" Mom asks.

"Honestly?" I say. "I think it's that I'm actually good at it."

"That's the only reason?" she asks. "You sure you don't just... enjoy athletic stuff?"

"I mean, I'll admit it to you, but don't tell anyone else, okay?" I say. "I really do love the feeling of running."

"I knew it," Mom says, gloating a bit. "I knew if you just gave running a chance you would end up loving it."

"It took a while," I admit, and I mean it. Even though it got me into my current mess, it's also helping me deal with it emotionally. "But after a few practices, once it started to feel a little bit easier, it got really fun. Or, at least, less terrible. And then racing for that little bit before I rolled my ankle was just great. I've only ever felt like that when I had a great editorial come out!"

Mom looks so excited. I almost have the urge to spill everything else that's been going on, but I don't want to burst her bubble. So instead, I ask for some pre-race tips.

"I was always a huge fan of two things: death metal and meditation," she says.

I laugh. "Those are very, very different things," I say.

"Well, not at the same time, obviously," she says, rolling her eyes. "About twenty minutes before a race, I would find a quiet spot and sit where no one was watching, and spend a few minutes just deep breathing and counting to 10 over and over again. Like a mini-meditation. It helped get me calmed down after I'd finished with my warmup, because you want to be relaxed but also super aware. It really would work—my heart rate would be nice and low."

"And where does the death metal come in?" I ask.

"Well, with 10 minutes to go, once I was calmed down, I would want to get psyched back up, but in a positive, non-nervous kind of way," she says. "So I'd put on my cassette player..."

She pauses for me to make the obvious joke. "Yeah, you're old, blah blah blah," I say, smiling.

"And I'd rock out for five minutes to the loudest, fastest music I could find," she finishes. "That way when I walked to the start line, I was both calm and psyched—rather than nervous and keyed up. They sound similar but really, it's two very different feelings. You want to be excited and a little nervous about racing, but not shaking on the starting grid!"

"What did you do right before the start?" I ask.

"A few little leg swings, some shimmying around just to get the blood pumping, some little hops, but mostly, I would just touch each finger to my thumb over and over to distract myself," she says, and demonstrates.

"That's so weird!" I say.

She looks a little insulted.

"Sorry, I mean it's weird because I do that too!" I say and she shifts to looking pleased.

I want to keep chatting with Mom because we haven't had many nights like this lately and never related to sports, but it's getting late—and we have a big workout at practice tomorrow that I want to do well in. Every mile matters right now, not just for prep for the competition, but because it will determine how Coach lets us start and I really want to be out in front.

And on that bus ride, I'm going to sit as far away from Jess as I can.

Tomorrow, I realize, is also the big debate team thing that all of us seniors have to attend and Elle is going to have to do her big speech. A few years ago, I'd have felt very nervous for her. But now, I just feel angry because I just know she's going to try to subtly get in some kind of dig about the *GMA* and how she's learned such a valuable lesson and so on and so forth. It's going to be so annoying to listen to, and she's such a good speaker that I'm sure by the end, people are going to be back to remembering our fight with me as the bad guy.

chapter
thirty-two

Elle

Elle's Speech Notes

Seriously, no tears. That will make you seem emotionally unstable, possibly vindictive versus concerned.

Voice modulation. Keep it soothing, but persuasive.

Stay on message, don't deviate based on crowd response.

<u>Do not</u> wear the same thing you wore on TV

<u>Do not</u> think about the TV situation

<u>Do not</u> look to see where Krista is sitting.

One more time: <u>No. Tears.</u>

TODAY IS THE BIG DAY, the debate. Sure, it's only attended by students at our school, but I know Krista will be in the audience. Jess, on the other hand, won't be—he's in a different program, vocational tech for graphic design, so his first half of the school day is at the neighboring high school. This is a good thing: It means I can get through my whole speech without worrying that he'll be offended.

Not that I care.

Okay, I kind of care.

But I'm mad enough at Krista for—once again—swooping in and stealing *the same guy* from right under my nose for the second time that I can't get past that. I know that Jess is his own man and obviously wasn't hypnotized by her or anything, but I'm certain that she knew exactly what was going on with him and I. I've nearly convinced myself that she seduced him and since then, he's been wracked with guilt. That's why he's been out of touch.

So as I stand backstage, I'm a little shaky but I tell myself it's just a combination of righteous indignation and a little bit of light-headedness from skipping breakfast again. And lunch. Really, I should have thought that through a little better. Weight loss is the goal, yes, but passing out in front of the student body (again) would be extremely embarrassing.

I rummage around my bag and thankfully, my old self stashed a Snickers bar in there and I devour it in just two bites. I can actually feel the sugar hit my bloodstream and I'm more pumped than ever. And good thing, because it's my turn in under a minute—I can hear the person who's speaking before me starting to conclude her presentation.

Mine is written carefully on organized index cards, and even though I completely changed topics at the last minute, I'm still ready to go.

When Mary walks backstage looking shell-shocked and exhausted, I pat her on the back. "Great job," I tell her (insincerely, since I didn't really pay attention to a word she said), then I square my shoulders, think about walking tall and confident, like my mom walking into a courtroom, and I stride onto the stage. And then, I'm there. In front of the microphone, staring out at a sea of blank, bored faces.

I take a deep breath and count to three. It's a trick my mom taught me for public speaking—too many people rush into their talks only to have to pause just a couple seconds in because they've gotten too worked up, their heart rates have gone too high, and they need to catch their breath. Better to pause for dramatic effect before beginning than be forced to pause later.

"Today, I want to talk to you about sex," I begin, pausing deliberately after the word 'sex.' It's a guaranteed attention-grabber. "And how our generation is being entirely too casual about when, where and why we're doing it. Our hookup culture has gotten far too permissive."

I can't see Krista in the audience, but I imagine her shifting uncomfortably in her seat as I continue. "Suddenly, it's normal to steal a guy from another girl, to hook up during sports practices, to act like it doesn't mean anything," I continue. I know she knows I'm talking about her, and I'm pretty sure most of the other kids do as well—she's been the hot topic of gossip this week, and I've been listening and wanting to scream at people that Jess doesn't like her, he's with me.

As I continue with my talk, I notice that kids are paying less and less attention to me as it becomes clear that I'm *against* kids our age having sex. But I press on, pointing out teen pregnancy and STD statistics. I end on the importance of building friendships, especially female ones, during this time in our lives instead of relying on a romantic relationship to make us happy.

Only as I finish out the speech reminding everyone that relationships made in high school rarely last but friends can last forever, I feel a sharp tug of guilt. I still don't know where she's sitting in the crowd, but I can almost feel Krista's disgust with me, and I admit, I suddenly feel like a hypocrite. She may have stolen Jess from me—twice!—but I'm literally standing up on my pedestal condemning her for it, telling everyone female friends matter more than boys while I try to turn the school against her.

It's not a look I'm proud of now that I'm here, but I can't turn back now. I feel my face start to go flame-red, I trip over my conclusions, and I stumble off the stage to confused applause rather than the standing ovation I was picturing.

"Elle, can I speak with you for a second?" the debate team teacher, Mrs. Milton, says the second I leave the stage.

Crud. I didn't even think about her reaction. Not surprisingly, she is displeased. "Your speech on gun control was in perfect shape," she says as we sit down in a corner. "Why on earth did you change it to that half-baked mess?"

"A boy," I mutter, staring down at my hands. "And don't worry, I know I screwed up. It was a terrible speech."

I'm hoping that she'll soothe me a bit and say it wasn't as bad as I thought, but she nods. "Normally, I wouldn't say this, but you have such talent as a debater and this was nowhere near what you're capable of," she says. "I'm disappointed that you let whatever drama you're going through in real life mess with your academic life."

"I know," I say. I have the urge to scream at her that she shouldn't expect more from a teenager, but I know that she's totally right and I currently feel like enough of an idiot. I think she softens a little because I don't fight back, and she sighs.

"Well, you weren't the worst speech today," she says. "And your intro was excellent, very emotionally loaded. So if you can harness that emotion in something that's actually well-thought out, I think you can be a fantastic speaker or lawyer or whatever you want to do. But right now I'd say the main thing you need to do is figure out this situation that's messing with your head and get it straightened out. It's fine and normal to have the drama, but you can't let it impact your school work at this point."

"I will, Mrs. Milton, I promise," I say. I don't want to ask but I have to know. "So, this speech, it was a big chunk of our grade, right?"

She nods.

"Is there anything I can do for extra credit?" I ask.

"We'll see," she says. "Focus on getting your personal life straightened out in the next couple days and we'll talk again."

chapter
thirty-three

Krista

I'VE NEVER REALLY BEEN TEMPTED to get into a proper 'punch someone in the face' fight before today, but after Elle's little speech, I'm genuinely tempted to hunt her down and actually try to beat her up. I don't imagine it going super well, and I'm pretty sure that the last thing I need is a compilation video of our fighting, but... *What the hell?*

The worst thing about her speech—other than the fact that practically the whole school knows that she was talking about me and rumors are flying more than they already were—is that despite our many, many differences, I know her and I know that she actually believed she was doing the right thing up there. She honestly thinks that I'm conspiring to steal Jess from her and that he wants to be with her, but I'm blocking her way.

I'm scared for her.

But I'm not sure how to handle it, so I go through my day in robot mode—ahem, my version of a hard reset—ignoring any and all snide commentary, eating my lunch in the library hidden in a corner and buried in a book. When the final bell rings, I consider for the millionth time whether or not I should go to practice and I almost get on the bus before decided at the last second that I won't be scared away from practice by some obnoxious stunt, however hurt I am.

So I'm there stretching when Elle struts out, looking pleased with herself. She doesn't make eye contact and heads to the other side of the circle for her stretches, and I bide my time. When Coach tells us to do a warmup run and she hops up, I fall in line behind her as we jog out onto the kilometer-long loop we've been using for warmups in practice. She's still struggling with the pace of the warmup, so I wait just a couple of minutes until she's completely fallen behind the rest of the team before I surge around to her righthand side.

She looks slightly nervous and even jumps a bit, her eyes darting around nervously like she thinks I might actually hit her. (It's tempting.)

But doing The Right Thing™ prevails. "You know, you had no idea what you were talking about today," I say in a low voice.

She looks startled, then stubborn. "I know what I saw," she says in her primmest voice. "I don't think that what you were doing was appropriate and I feel very strongly about safe sex."

"If you feel so strongly about safe sex, did it ever occur to you that what you saw wasn't consensual?" I counter, and dodge around her quickly and stop on a dime, pivoting so she almost runs into me and we're nose to nose.

Forced to stop and look directly at me, she first looks like she's considering dodging around me or shouting for help, but she stands her ground and holds my gaze. "What, like you forcing yourself on Jess even though you know that he and I have a thing going?" she says.

I explode. "You don't have a thing going with him, he has a thing going with whoever will take him!" I shout. "You didn't stop to think for a second that maybe I didn't want him to touch me, that I didn't ask for that?"

"I know what I saw," she insists. "You were all over him."

"I was backed against a tree!" I nearly scream, my voice starting to crack as I choke up. I *hate* this, but I push through. "I didn't have anywhere to go and all of a sudden, boom, he's got his hand..." I trail off, my voice completely cut off.

Elle looks stricken.

"Seriously?" she says in almost a whisper, and I can see the shoe drop in that moment. She might hate me, but she knows I couldn't lie like this.

Chapter Thirty-Three

I nod, and look down so she can't see the tears that are filling the corners of my eyes and threatening to spill over.

"I told him to stop," I manage to get out.

"That bastard!" Elle curses, her mood completely transformed as she turns away and kicks the dirt.

"I don't know what to do," I say, and burst into tears.

As I'm crying, of course, that's when perfect track star Jenny perkily runs up, gives me a look up and down, and snidely says, "Your mascara is running."

"And if you could run too—preferably far, far away, that would be great," Elle snaps.

"Jeez, what's wrong with you two?" Jenny says, her voice suddenly dropping as she realizes she may have stumbled on something juicy. I don't think she cares, but she does love gossip. "Spill."

"Jess assaulted Krista," Elle says before I can tell her to keep her mouth shut. I wait for Jenny to say something along the lines of "I'm sure he wouldn't do that," or "Of course he didn't, Krista is a skank," but her face actually drains completely of all color.

"He didn't," she whispers.

I nod. "Nothing really happened but he tried," I say quietly, not looking at her or at Elle.

"Shit," Jenny says, her voice also dropping to a whisper.

"Why shit?" Elle asks. "Are you pissed that your crush is a total dick?"

"No, I'm pissed that I didn't say anything when he grabbed me during a practice last month," Jenny says, her face now going from ghost white to bright red. "He ripped my favorite singlet trying to grab my boobs."

"You're joking," Elle says. I can tell she's still holding out hope, but I'm not—I believe Jenny completely, instantly.

"I even told Coach but he told me to stop being such a girl about it," Jenny says, looking downcast. "Look, it doesn't matter. Forget it. I never said anything."

With that, she turns on her heel and sprints down the trail.

"You believe her?" Elle asks me, and I can tell she's hoping I'll say no, so that she can re-cast my incident with Jess as a one-time accidental thing, just an awkward misunderstanding we can all move past.

"I really, really do," I say, then wipe my eyes and turn in the other direction and jog down the trail, hoping she won't follow. When I look over my shoulder, she's still standing there like a statue.

Elle

WHEN WE WERE 12 years old, Krista and I had a brilliant idea: we would use Jess's huge backyard and in-ground pool to host an epic war between our friends — water guns, water balloons, buckets, whatever water weapons we could find were allowed.

It was soggy and it was awesome. It's one the happiest moments I can remember, hiding in an old tree fort with Krista, waiting patiently for one of the guys to walk under it so we could douse him with water.

Our *piece de resistance*? We added blue food coloring to our buckets.

Those were truly simpler times. I remember being mad at Krista that day for some small reason and, despite being on the same team, decking her with a water balloon to the face right at the end. She retaliated by pushing me into the pool, but I grabbed her hand and pulled her in with me. By the time we resurfaced, we were already best friends again and the blue food coloring washed off.

Now, we've both done permanent damage to each other and I don't know how to come back from it. Between the clips on *GMA* that will live forever on YouTube, the Instagram posts that have been screenshotted by who knows how many people, the editorial she wrote that's been archived, and the debate speech that was recorded, there are receipts scattered everywhere, leaving a messy trail of shitty behavior, betrayal and bad friendship.

When I lay it out like that, I find myself blinking back tears.

I acted like an idiot. Krista acted like an idiot. But... Jess didn't act like an idiot, he acted like a complete and total creep. I don't *want* to believe Krista that he'd made that move when she didn't want him to. I want to believe that he was interested in her because she was acting slutty and he was just taking advantage of that fact. But deep down, I know that's not right. She wouldn't lie like that. She couldn't lie like that, not to me.

I've read the papers, I've read the comments. I know we're supposed to believe the victim. It's just hard to do that when you don't like the victim, and you *really* like the guy who's being accused of something.

So, it's time to do what my mom would do if this was a case she was defending: look at all sides to figure out her arguments. But first, I have to define the questions.

chapter
thirty-five

Elle

FROM THE DESK OF ELLE

> *Does Jess like me?*
> *Did he assault Krista?*
> *What should I do about him, or about her?*
> *I hate even writing the word 'assault' in my journal. It seems so huge, but there isn't a more mild term for it if she's telling the truth. And there shouldn't be.*
> *If I believe her, then I don't know what to do. It would go beyond me just not being into Jess and giving up on that dream if she isn't lying. I don't know if I'm ready for that.*
> *My gut, though, is telling me to face these facts:*
>
> *1: Jess hasn't really acknowledged you in school, he hasn't asked you on a date, he hasn't acted in any way like he's going to be your boyfriend.*
> *2: Krista, while a huge pain in the ass, hasn't ever lied to you about anything—and if she wanted Jess for herself, why would she warn you away from him like that instead of just telling you that they were dating? It's not like she would see*

you as much of a threat, she just sees you as the preppy fat girl that made her look bad on TV and at school.

And with those two points, I believe her.

My gut still isn't telling me what to do, other than 'feel slightly sick and like I swallowed a soccer ball.' It's also growling at me, as if to say, 'I gave you information, could you please give me some damn food?'

This is where I know I should try to convince myself that a can of seltzer will make me feel full, but instead, I grab my phone and use the Postmates app to order a burrito bowl. Before I hit send, I pause and walk downstairs and knock on Mom's office door.

"Yes?" she says faintly, clearly annoyed at the interruption.

"Want dinner?" I ask. "I was going to order burritos."

She looks up from the computer. "Sure—I'll have a salad, no cheese or sour cream, extra veggies and with the chicken."

That's exactly what I should order for myself if I'm going to eat. I double it, and add a bag of chips. Hitting 'place order,' I confirm it and retreat to my room until the doorbell rings. My list is still sitting on the desk, where I've been staring at it for the full 30 minutes it took for the food to get here, but I'm no closer to a decision as far as what to do with the information in front of me.

When Mom grabs the food from the delivery guy, I expect her to call down to me, but she comes into my room with the bags instead, and plops them on the desk before settling down on the bed. "I need a break," she says dramatically. I've seen her like this before—she reads one self-help article and temporarily declares herself burned out before getting one decent night of sleep and waking up at 4AM feeling 'refreshed.' But at least on her 'overwhelmed' nights, she's fun to hang out with.

At least, she's fun until she spots my legal pad and snatches it up before I can hide it. "I love lists," she says enthusiastically. This is not sarcasm, this is how the women in my family operate. I make a grab for it but years of lawyering have made her amazing at speed reading and before I can get it away, she's seen enough.

She slowly sets it down. "What exactly did Jess do to Krista?" she asks in an spookily calm voice.

"It's nothing, Mom," I say, trying to grab the sheet back, but she's hanging on tight. She stares at me, giving me the interrogation look that I know for a fact she uses in the courtroom.

So, I try distraction. "What's the deal with you and Krista's mom, anyway?" I say, giving her the exact same look back. I can see us glaring at each other in the mirror in my peripheral vision and I have to admit, she is kicking my ass for fierceness.

"Answer the question, Elle," she says. "What did Jess do?"

"Krista says that he grabbed her during practice," I say, giving in. "She said he stuck his hand up her shirt before she had a chance to say no, and when she pushed him away he just laughed."

Mom's face is ghost-white. "She told you this, and you didn't tell *anyone*?"

"I didn't believe her," I admit. "But I do now, and I don't know what to do."

"You didn't believe your best friend?" Mom says incredulously.

"Former best friend," I correct automatically.

Her face goes from white to beet red in a millisecond, and for a second, I'm afraid she's going to explode. "Former has nothing to do with it!" she shouts. "Has she ever given you any reason to ever doubt her?"

I shake my head, completely ashamed. I knew I was wrong, but I didn't expect this level of anger from my mom, and certainly not directed at me.

"Elle, we're living in a time where it's no longer okay—it never should have been okay—to just assume that a woman is lying when she says that a man did something to her. I'm sad that you could even think something like that about a girl you grew up with."

I'm tempted to point out that I grew up with Jess too but I somehow don't think that would help the situation.

"I've been trying to let you figure your stuff out with her for the last couple of months, but clearly, I've been missing a lot of things about your life," Mom continues. "Your teacher emailed me about your debate speech, you're fainting at meets, you're skipping breakfast, you're up later than I am most nights, and you're taking the word of some snotty little jock that already ruined your friendship once over the word of the best friend you've ever had?"

That list, when she slams out each item like a bullet point, sets me off.

"Maybe none of this would be happening if you paid more attention!" I yell back. I don't know if that's true—honestly, I don't even know why I'm saying it, I just know that I don't want to keep being blamed for every damn thing.

But instead of getting madder, Mom nods and her fierceness droops slightly. "I know I've been distracted lately," she says.

"Lately?" I say back, sarcasm dripping. "You barely talk to me, you haven't in a few years! And I have no idea what's going on in your life other than the fact that you're always working!"

She glares. "I have a lot going on between running a law practice and trying to keep this house together," she says. "And that's not an excuse, but you're just shifting the argument to avoid talking to me about Krista right now."

Damn lawyers.

"You don't even make time to talk to me anymore," I say, my voice starting to crack. "I even joined the team and started losing all this weight so that you would be proud of me and want to make more time for me."

She looks shocked. "You don't need to do any of those things for me," she says. "And I didn't know you wanted to lose weight."

"Of course I want to lose weight, look at me!" I say, tears starting to roll down my cheeks. "Krista said it before, no wonder Jess doesn't like me, I'm fat."

"Honey," Mom says, then pauses like she forgot what point she wanted to make. "Krista was probably just saying that because she was mad at you and knew exactly how to get under your skin, and looking at this list, I don't really know why you want Jess to like you anyway. Besides, didn't you all get in that big fight because he was mean to you back then? What made you think he changed?"

"He started texting me and talking to me again," I say. And then, my face flushes. Crap. I almost forgot that in addition to all of the actual real life drama going on with him, he also happens to be in possession of a topless photo of me. Just perfect. A perverted dick has access to a photo of my boobs, one that I elected to send him. I've never felt more stupid, or more used.

Mom raises an eyebrow like she knows something else is up but thankfully, she doesn't probe on that any further.

"Yeah, he's still a jerk," I say quickly. "I guess, all this time he's been texting me and stuff, he still hasn't been talking to me in front of people, and he did that to Krista and who knows what else. I think he did the same thing to Jenny from the team too. I feel stupid, okay?"

She nods. "But you know aren't," she says briskly. "So, break it down for me, debate-style."

This, I can do. "Well, texting me without talking to me in real life or wanting to be seen with me around his friends is mean, but it's not actually wrong," I say. "But him pushing Krista into going farther than she wanted, even if she was kissing him, that wasn't just emotions, that was him being a predator," I add.

I don't want to tell her about the asking for nudes thing because I think that one might be sitting directly on the jerk-versus-predator line and that's a bridge too far for this conversation right now.

Mom nods. "So, what are you going to do?"

"I don't know! What should I do?" I ask helplessly. This is where I'm getting stuck.

"For starters, I think you have a best friend—excuse me, *former* best friend—to call," she says. "Tell her you believe her, because that's the most important thing you can do right now and the first thing you can fix. We'll talk more soon, but I need to take a minute to think about who I should be talking to about Jess and this whole situation. And frankly, I'm so damn pissed at him that I can't think straight."

I nod. I was afraid she'd say that, but also hoping that she would, so I wouldn't have a choice.

"And about me and Krista's mom?" Mom says, as she walks out the door. "I'm not ready to talk about it. I'll tell you when I am." With that, she shuts the door—not too gently—and leaves me sitting alone, still clutching my list.

chapter
thirty-six

Krista

WHEN I SEE a text from Elle asking me to meet her before lunch the next day, I almost don't show up. I've had enough emotional drama to last me until at least graduation. And I mean college graduation at this point. But then, another text comes through from her:

> Talked to a couple other girls on the team. One said Jess tried the same thing on her earlier this season. Another said he asked for nudes and then sent them to his friends when she sent them. We have to do something.

And so, here we are. The band is back together. Sort of. Elle and I are standing outside of Coach's office, debating what we're going to say to him. "It's simple," Elle says. "We say Jess is harassing and assaulting girls on the team."

"Why do you care so much, anyway?" I ask. "You know he's a creep, you don't like him anymore, so why should you be here? It's not your problem."

"Because," she says, looking awkwardly at the ground. "I also sent him naked pictures when he pushed for them."

I'm actually stunned speechless—perfect Elle sending nudes? Huh.

"So we're united on this?" she says, clearing her throat. I nod. She knocks on the door.

"What do you want?" Coach barks from inside.

"We need to talk to you," Elle says, opening the door. For once, I'm thankful for her take-charge vibes.

We go into his dark cave of an office, where his desk is piled high with random papers and books, and there's a whiff of *eau de* sweat sock in the air. He gestures at the two padded chairs for us to sit down, but one look at the stains on the chairs is enough to keep us standing.

"We need to talk to you about Jess," Elle says. "There are a few girls on the team who've had problems with him harassing them this season, including Krista and..."

"I'm going to stop you right there," Coach says, cutting Elle off mid-sentence. "I've had just about enough of this BS girl drama from you two."

"I believe you mean BS everyone-in-high-school drama," I say dryly, stepping up. "Seeing as this is because one of your top guys seems to enjoy messing with all the girls on the team."

"Are you saying that girl drama—in this case, sexual assault— doesn't matter?" Elle says angrily.

We exchange a look with each other, and suddenly, we're completely in sync. After a whole season of hearing his patronizing "ladies" and "stop acting like girls" to the guys when they're going a little slower, it's nice to finally fight back, even if it was a little unexpected to have Elle as an ally.

"Really, you should be more careful with your phrasing," she adds, and smirks a little in my direction. "My mom is a lawyer and she loooooooves to talk about equality."

"And I think that would make a great quote for a profile on you in the school paper," I say, shooting a full-on grin in Elle's direction.

Coach gets just a little bit pale. "No need for any of that," he says, and slowly starts edging away from us and out of the room, like we might explode at any moment.

But before he can get too far—out of his own office!—I'm following after him, Elle at my side. "Do you have any idea what Jess has been doing to the girls on this team?" I ask.

"Actually, we know you know, because at least one girl has told you before. But you didn't do anything about it," Elle says. This is new information to me, but I don't blink. It's not surprising, sadly.

"Girls accuse boys like Jess of stuff all the time because they're upset when he dumps them," Coach says. "He would never do anything other than break a few hearts." He smirks.

"That's not true," I say, and I'm terrified to realize that my voice is starting to shake.

"He assaulted Krista at practice," Elle says, putting her arm around me. "And he pressured me to send him naked pictures."

Now, Coach looks like his eyes are going to bug out of his head. I don't know if he believes us, but it's sinking in that something isn't right.

"He ripped Jenny's shirt the last time he grabbed her, why didn't you believe her when she came to you then?" Elle presses.

"She's a drama queen," Coach says, swallowing hard. "She was just upset because her race didn't go well and Jess's did. She was jealous."

"But she came to you and you didn't tell anyone else? You just ignored it?" I ask, loudly.

Coach snarls. "If I took the complaint of every girl on the team seriously, we wouldn't have a team left," he says.

"Hear that, Miss C," I say even louder. Coach whirls around and—amazing dramatic timing—there's Miss C in her office doorway. I saw her hovering there as I was trying to blink back tears a few seconds ago, and the look on her face showed that she had heard everything.

She walks into the hall, and Coach's face turns from pale to purple. "These girls are just trying to cause trouble," he says desperately.

"Sounded more like you were trying to cover up trouble," she says calmly. "Why don't we take this up with Principal Harden."

"I don't have time for this," Coach says and turns and starts jogging down the hall like he plans to run far, far away and never come back. I look over at Elle, who looks like she's frozen in place. I'm shaking with a combination of rage and nerves, not sure what to do with this energy that's pumping through my veins.

"Girls, we're going to the office and having a very long talk with Harden," Miss C says briskly. "I'm just going to grab my bag—and I'm sorry I didn't know about this before." She walks back into her office, giving us a moment standing alone together in the hall.

And then it hits me—there's a very real chance we've been wasting a lot of this energy being crappy to each other when really, we've both done mean things, and the one common denominator, the one things causing this, is a guy who doesn't want to make up his mind, and doesn't seem to really care about either of us.

"I guess we get along when we have someone else to get mad at," I say, and Elle snaps to attention.

"I guess so," she says, and pauses (for dramatic effect). "So, want to get mad at Jess?"

"I think it's about time we did," I respond, and it feels like a weight has been completely lifted off of my shoulders. "He is the one who's trying to play us both, right?"

"Exactly," Elle says, and looks down. "Can I ask you something?"

"Sure," I say, feeling charitable. "But... I still don't like you very much."

"Ditto," she says, surprising me again. "But that doesn't mean we can't be friends, right?"

I just stare.

"Look," she says, "I get that we're not actually friends anymore, but let's be real: We're going to be on the team for the end of this season, right? We're both stuck?"

She makes a point that I can't really argue with, much as I wish I could. "I suppose," I admit.

"Wouldn't be it easier if we didn't, you know, hate each other?"

Again, fair point.

"Okay, fine," I say. "Truce. And in the spirit of a truce, can I make a suggestion?"

She nods.

"Whatever problems we have with each other, we stand by each other when we're talking to Harden," I say. "This isn't about us, this is about all the girls Jess has hurt."

"You know, he was our best friend," Elle says, suddenly looking devastated.

"And now he's not the guy that we knew back then," I say, trying to look firm and implacable, but I feel the same way that Elle looks. It's bad enough knowing what he did to both of us—individually, and the fact that he was playing us both at the same time. But knowing that we're not even the first girls that he's pushed into hooking up or sending him photos or who knows what else? That's pushed him far beyond 'an ex-friend who's kind of a jerk.'

"Okay, girls, ready?" Miss C says, walking back towards us with her messenger bag slung over her shoulder.

We nod.

"Let's go kick some ass," she says, her mouth set in a grim line as we walk down towards the office.

chapter
thirty-seven

Elle

IT DOESN'T TAKE a lot of convincing to get my mom to bring me over to Krista's for a serious sit-down with Krista and her mom. She *did* take a bit of pushing to get her out of the house, but only because she kept trying to fiddle with her makeup and she changed her shirt three times. Finally, though, we're all sitting at the big counter in Krista's kitchen, where her mom already pushed a green smoothie into my hand and one into Krista's, stuck a glass of my mom's favorite white wine into her hand, and poured herself a whiskey on the rocks.

Krista's mom might seem like kind of hippie, but she's actually pretty badass.

"We've been talking," Krista's mom says, gesturing towards my mom. (They have?) "And we think that while we're tempted to go to the administration with this whole Jess business and try to get him suspended, we don't want to do anything without you two on board."

"We want to," my mom says, looking fierce. "But Nancy and I thought about it, and you two are nearly 18—old enough to make decisions for yourselves. We want you to talk to your coach or go to the principal and tell him about Jess's actions, but we think it should be your decisions to make."

This feels a little like a war council, because, well, it kind of is.

Krista and I look at each other. "Good news, mom," she says. "We already talked to the coach."

"Bad news," I add. "He was kind of a huge dick about it and isn't going to do anything."

"Good news," Krista says. "Miss C overheard the whole thing, and I think she's going to be doing a whole lot."

"When did this happen?" my mom asks, her face breaking into a slightly scary, slightly proud smile.

"This afternoon," I say, and we tell the whole story, from Coach admitting he'd already heard from other girls to Miss C's perfect entrance to how tired and sad Principal Harden looked when we told him everything. He promised to make things right, and was already on the phone before we even left the office.

"We're not sure exactly what's going to happen," Krista says, "But he said Coach was going to have to answer for not speaking up, and that he was going to deal with Jess himself."

"I feel kind of bad for Jess," I admit, and wilt a bit as all three women glare at me. "I can't help it!"

Krista's mom actually is the first to say something, and she pats my hand. "It's a lot harder to deal with someone you know and cared about not being who you thought he was," she says. "I know he meant a lot to both of you, and I remember him as a kid too."

"I never liked him," my mom interjects.

"Oh, stop," says Krista's mom, patting my mom's hand the same way she patted mine. "You never had a bad feeling about him back then either."

Mom looks like she wants to argue but she just sighs and puts her head in her hands. "I just can't believe a boy we let run wild in our houses would grow up to be this kind of man," she sighs.

"I know what you mean," Krista's mom says sympathetically. "But people change."

My mom gives a half laugh. "Now, that is definitely true," she says, and the two of them look at each other for a beat too long. Which leads to Krista and I doing the same, only our look is more horror-stricken than happy. Yep, we're on the same page here and it is not a good one.

"Mom, shouldn't we be heading home to dinner?" I ask, getting up to go.

"I made enough grilled chicken and salad for everyone," Nancy says.

"I just need to put on a little more quinoa, but we'll be ready to eat in 20 minutes."

"Sounds delicious," Mom says, clearly lying through her teeth. Mom hates quinoa ("it's pretentious" is her exact quote).

"Why don't you girls go and civilly watch some TV or something for a bit while we get dinner on the table?" Nancy says, as she started adding quinoa and water into a rice cooker.

We both hang our heads like we're in a Charlie Brown cartoon and sulk our way into the living room. Of course I remember where her TV is. I spent most of my weekends sprawled on the living room carpet watching *Friends* with her when we were kids, and when I walk in and nothing has changed, the nostalgia almost overwhelms me.

"I've been watching *Buffy* again," Krista says in a monotone as she flicks on Netflix.

No. Way.

"Which season?" I ask, like I could care less.

"I'm up to season 5," she tells me as she clicks 'play next episode,' and I can't help but laugh.

"I'm on season 6," I say.

She smiles just a tiny bit. "Still team Angel?" she asks—remembering my undying (like him!) alliance to Buffy's first boyfriend.

"Always," I say loyally. "Let me guess—you still looooooove Spike."

"Have you seen a picture of that actor lately?" she says. "Yikes."

For a second, I can see all too clearly how we could have been if we hadn't chosen to change. If we hadn't let Jess come between us, if we hadn't decided that 'growing up' meant dissociating from anyone that didn't fit our new identities.

It wasn't just Homecoming that torched our friendship—it had been coming for a long time before that, from day one of high school when I showed up in pastels and Krista showed up in all black with a scowl on her face and a notebook of angsty poetry. Clearly, this wasn't a friendship that was going to survive the high school years. We picked our lanes and let them keep getting more and more divided—and I guess the Homecoming situation was never the real issue. It was just easier to fight and call it a day on our friendship. But that never should have meant that I should have doubted her about something like this.

"I'm sorry," I say, staring carefully at the screen, as Buffy battles a herd (gaggle? pack?) of vampires on screen.

"Why?" Krista asks, and sounds more curious than forgiving.

"Honestly, I don't even really know which thing I'm apologizing for," I say, still not making eye contact. "I didn't believe you. I didn't invite you to my Sweet 16. I said mean stuff about you after Homecoming. I didn't know how to stay friends. I didn't want to."

I sneak a glance over and she looks wary, like she thinks I'm still plotting something. Which, to be fair, is a pretty reasonable reaction. But if I remember her right, she also looks like she wants to cry, just a little.

"I'm sorry, too," she says finally. "And if it makes a difference now, I did feel really bad about Homecoming. I just liked Jess so much back then, but never wanted to tell you since I knew you felt the same way. And when I had the chance to go for it, I did and I didn't think about you. And I'm *really* sorry I called you fat. You're not, you know."

And right there is the reason that I miss her so damn much. Because of all the shit that's gone on, the showdown on *GMA*, the debate team, the editorial in the paper, all that stuff, even the Homecoming thing—she knows that she hurt me the most with that stupid, off-the-cuff insult, because she *knows* me. No one else in my circle of friends now would have any idea that a quick comment like that would crush me, but she knows.

"Elle, can you come in here a second?" Krista's mom yells from the kitchen.

I look at Krista quizzically. "No clue," she says, before looking back to her laptop.

When I go in the kitchen, I'm expecting my mom to be at the counter, but it's just Nancy. "Your mom ran out to pick up some more wine," she says. "But I wanted to talk to you for a minute before dinner."

I'm terrified that she's going to yell at me for the debate club incident or for not believing Krista at first, but instead, she turns back to the skillet where she's tossing veggies and chicken in some kind of delicious-smelling tangy sauce. It's enough to make my mouth water.

"What did you have for lunch?" she asks, casually.

I know how I'm supposed to answer this: a balanced meal, maybe a salad with some rice and a protein source, plus plenty of water. I'm about to lie, but when she turns and looks at me directly, I end up stuttering, "A can of seltzer water."

"And breakfast?"

"Coffee," I say. I'm not sure what's making me want to tell her the truth, but I'm just so damn tired of trying to pretend that everything is okay. "I've been trying to lose 15 pounds," I add. "But it's not coming off and I think I'm gaining even more weight!"

"First of all, you absolutely don't need to lose weight. I'm actually a licensed expert and I can tell you with certainty that you're well within the healthy range," she says reasonably. "But I also know how it feels to be a teenage girl who isn't happy in her body. So I get it, but I think your issue might be more about nutrition rather than weight loss. Your mom tells me that when you do eat together, it's usually fast food, right?"

I nod. "And I eat way too much of it," I admit. "I can't help it, when she brings home that stuff and we have a few minutes to sit together and I'm so hungry, I just can't control it. But I don't make myself throw up or anything," I add quickly, because I can guess that's her next question. I might not be great at losing weight, but I've read plenty of the literature around eating disorders and I know that purging would be the natural next question when someone admits to binging.

She looks a little skeptical, but sighs. "And how long have you been trying to diet?" she asks.

"Only since cross-country started," I say. "I didn't really notice how much weight I'd gained until I was at practice with all the other girls and running wasn't easy."

"Well, good news: Running is hard for everyone, especially at first," she responds. "But I know how hard it can be to feel like you don't have the right kind of body for something."

It's my turn to look skeptical, since she's one of the fittest moms that I know. "Come on," I say. "I'm jealous of you and you're my mom's age!"

She looks a little sad, and pauses before she says, "I know it might not look like it, but I had to learn to live with my body too."

"When?" I ask. I'm both curious and a little willing to challenge her on this—I can't imagine her having a day of insecurity in her life. Krista's mom has maybe the best genetics I've ever seen: She almost never wears makeup but looks like she could be in a photoshoot with Heidi Klum if she wanted to be. I actually can't imagine what it would have been like for Krista these last couple years, living with someone who just looks flawless.

"When I realized I couldn't have kids," she says.

I stammer. "I didn't realize…"

"I tried IVF before I started looking into adoption," she tells me. "But I found out that I actually couldn't have a baby."

"What did you do?" I'm both so sad and fascinated. I never realized she would have even considered wanting to actually give birth.

"I started looking into adoption, and when I found Krista, I realized that things worked out that way for a reason," Nancy says, smiling again. "But even then, I was still so mad at my body for not doing what I wanted it to do and not being what I wanted it to be."

I suddenly feel stupid making my weight gain seem as important as something like that, but before I can say as much, she continues. "We all have things that seem like the end of the world, but they so rarely are."

I nod.

"And you don't need to be focused on losing weight," she adds briskly, turning to stir the veggies on the stove. "But if you do want to focus on eating healthier to actually fuel for your running, I can help you."

"Seriously?" I ask. "That would be great! Could you maybe help me learn to cook a few things? Mom isn't exactly Martha Stewart."

Nancy gives a cackling laugh. "That is definitely true, and I'd be happy to. And I just wanted to tell you: I'm proud of you, Elle. You could have dropped off the team, or just hung back and gotten the participation credit, but you're really trying. And I know you and Krista might not be best friends anymore and you've both done some pretty dumb stuff lately, but neither of you can fool me into thinking you hate each other. You still have each other's backs when shit gets real."

I love a mom who can drop a curse word into casual conversation.

"All right," she says. "If you want to learn about cooking, come over here and you can watch the veggies and chicken in this stir fry and keep moving them so they don't stick."

"What's in here?" I ask as I walk around the counter.

"It's just frozen stir fry veggie mix with a little soy sauce, some ginger, and some boneless, skinless chicken thighs," she says. "Don't get the pre-made sauces, you don't need all the extra junk that's in them."

She reaches in the fridge and pulls out a bunch of kale, which frankly, looks intimidatingly healthy. Next to my frying pan, there's a rice cooker that's bubbling away and looks like it could blow up any second.

"A rice cooker is your best friend," she says, following my gaze. "We're doing quinoa in it right now: just use the one to two ratio of rice or whatever grain you want with water and click it on and you're good to go. Perfect for dorm rooms."

I nod, then ask what the hell she's doing with the kale, since she's quickly shredded it and is now rubbing avocado oil on it and beating it up with her hands. "I'm massaging it," she explains. "It tastes less bitter and it's easier to digest this way. You just need a drizzle of oil and you're good to go."

Next, she grates some carrots and beets over top of it and tosses it all together before dividing it onto four plates, then topping each with a scoop of quinoa. She takes the frying pan from me and scoops the veggie and chicken mix on top, sprinkles a little sea salt and slices a few chunks of avocado onto each. She does it so quickly and efficiently that I can barely keep track of what she's doing. And instead of grabbing some cans of diet soda out of the fridge, she grabs a jug of water with cucumber slices floating in it, and gestures to the cabinets. "Grab glasses and some forks," she says, as she grabs four of the plates and brings them to the kitchen table before coming back to swoop up the water and the final plate.

"You can do that any night, and it only takes a few minutes of actual prep time," she tells me.

"This is awesome!" I say, and snap a picture. In my head, I'm doing the calorie count, but compared to the burritos or Chinese takeout we usually have on weeknights, this is way less scary.

Nancy looks over at me like she knows what I'm thinking. "Do me a favor," she says. "For the next few days, try to think about the nutrients you're eating instead of the calories. So, what do you see when you see this plate?"

"Chicken, vegetables and quinoa," I say.

"Or, is it a protein from the chicken, some fiber from the veggies, some carbs from the quinoa and some fat from the avocado?" she says. "That's what a plate should have on it—and of course, there's always room for a little treat, so we have cookies I baked last week for dessert."

"Looks great," my mom says as she walks into the kitchen, and does a double-take when she sees me holding the frying pan about to put it in the sink. "Did you cook, Elle?" she says with no little level of surprise.

"She did great," Nancy says. "I'm going to give her a few pointers, if you don't mind." She winks at my mom and again, that sneaking suspicion hits me again, but before I can ask some pointed questions, Krista strolls in too.

"I'm starving," she says, plunking down in her chair and instantly digging in.

Suddenly, my stomach is growling too—I guess I'm hungrier than I thought.

Dinner goes smoother than I would have expected. We actually all end up in a *Buffy* discussion that tackles the important topics like which season was the best, which boyfriend Buffy had that we hated to most, and favorite moments. When my mom mentions Willow and Tara and being choked up when they finally got together and Nancy nods her head in agreement, I internally groan, but Krista just argues back that Willow's ex was way more right for her.

We don't talk about the team, or what happened in the principal's office, or mention Jess at all.

Mom and I finally take off after a couple of cookies and small cups of decaf espresso—so fancy for a normal night!—and when we get in the van to drive home, she pats my hand. "I think you and Krista are going to be fine," she says.

Then, she shocks me when she adds, "I know a lot of this is my fault."

Ugh, I hate when someone beats me to the accusatory punch. It feels so much less satisfying.

"Why did you make such a big deal about the whole *GMA* thing anyway?" I ask instead of instantly just agreeing and letting her off the hook.

"I honestly don't know," she says. "I've just gotten so used to winning over the years that in a situation like this, I don't know how to turn it off, so when there were chances for you to take over the story and come out on top, I wanted that for you."

I nod.

"But I never would have condoned the debate team situation if I had been told about it in advance," she adds, looking at me sharply. "You left quite a few things out when you were telling me all the stuff that was happening."

I nod again. But on the other hand... "Mom, you're a lawyer. Haven't you kind of spent your entire life teaching me how to craft an argument and make sure that I win?" I ask.

She grins a little bit. "You got me there," she says. "But in serious situations like this, I need to know I can count on you to tell me the whole truth,"

"And nothing but the truth," we finish together. It might be a thing that you say in court, but it's also our household mantra. "I will, though hopefully there won't be another incident like this," I add.

"Fingers crossed," Mom says grimly.

chapter
thirty-eight

Krista

ONCE WE'VE CLEANED up dinner, Mom seems exhausted, though she promises that we'll have a big talk tomorrow (so very much looking forward to that). She thankfully lets me retreat to my room so she can do the same. Once I'm settled in bed with my headphones on and Kindle out to finally do some relaxed reading for the first time in a couple of days, though, my phone buzzes with a text.

Fingers crossed that it's a wrong number. Instead, it's one that hasn't popped up in a long, long time.

ELLE

Can we meet up before school tomorrow?

I knew I should have blocked this number.
But I respond.

Fine. But I need to do a run, so meet me at the track and we'll hit the trail. 7AM.

I don't offer any other option. I'm mostly expecting her to say 'nevermind,' but she just sends a thumbs up. Switching my phone onto Airplane so she can't keep messaging, I try to get back into the novel I've been reading but I can't concentrate. I wonder what she wants.

It's hard to fall asleep, but 7AM isn't that far away.

In the morning, I put my regular clothes—black jeans, black hoodie —in my messenger bag and pull on tights and a long-sleeved running top with a vest stolen from my mom's closet. I grab my coffee thermos that Mom has ready, another pumpkin spiced latte laced with protein powder and coconut milk to pack in pre- and post-workout calories, and hop on my bike to pedal to the school. By the time I lock my bike, stash my bag and jog out to the track, Elle is already there doing stretches, much to my surprise. I figured she'd bail at the last minute.

I nod and start walking quickly towards the trail to warm up. She pulls herself up and trots after me. "I thought we could talk," she says. "You know, now that we're on the same side."

"Remember, I still don't like you," I say over my shoulder, though it feels a little mean and I don't like how it sounds.

"Ditto," she says, but she's smiling, which makes my mouth curve up a little too. "However, we have a bigger issue to deal with. Fallout."

As usual, she's not wrong, though I wish that she was. "What exactly do you mean?" I ask.

"Best case scenario for us, Jess is kicked off the team and suspended," she says. "In that case, we're going to piss off a lot of the guys who were counting on points from him to keep the team in the top three ranking. It helps them with college applications. Not only that, they clearly worship him and may tell people we're lying."

Crud. "I hadn't thought of that," I admit. "I just assumed people would be on our side. Why did I assume that? I *hate* people."

"Well, despite us being entirely in the right here, other people will be thinking about that, and it's not just us who will be or have been hurt by Jess. It's going to effect the guys on the team and they might not be psyched about it. Added to that, Jess was also clearly scamming on a couple of other girls on the team, and I'm sure some of them will be relieved or upset when they hear what happened, but a few might be pissed. And I bet even a few of them will assume that we're both lying or were asking for it or are just trying to screw him over to be vindictive."

Double crud. "I definitely hadn't thought of that," I say. "Why do people suck?"

"The patriarchy," Elle says, but she huffs as she says it and I let out a snort. I almost forget that she can be kind of sardonic and hilarious when she wants to be.

"Well, we probably can't solve that problem today, but what can we do?" I ask as I turn onto the trails. I can hear her breath hitch behind me, so I slow down slightly. I don't want to ruin my training run, but I also don't want to kill her.

"The same way we were trying to wreck each other—we get ahead of the story," Elle pants. "I've been thinking about it all night. Between my student council meeting at the end of the week and your newspaper editor-ness, we should be able to put together a really great set of stuff around sexual assault and harassment in high school and all the different forms it can take. If we package it really well, it could be really great for us for college applications and getting the word out. Either way, it helps us."

"Social justice plus a great resume builder," I say in a dry voice, though I have to admit, it does sound compelling. "I hate to say it, but that's pretty smart."

"And even if people on the team are still pissed, if we make the story big enough, they'll either have to see where we were coming from and understand, or if they're actually gross enough that they think Jess is still in the right or that Coach isn't the worst, if we tell our story and make it public enough, then they can't do anything about it. Or if they do, they'll come off as psychopaths."

On one hand, it feels like we're planning something illicit and sneaky and maybe we should just chill out and let it blow over.

On the other... as soon as that thought runs through my head, I trip a little on a root and curse myself. "What is wrong with me?"

"Let me guess—you're wondering if we're the ones doing something wrong if we do this?" Elle says behind me.

I nod.

"I felt the same way last night and did some research."

Of course she did.

"It turns out, that's super common in anyone who's dealt with any kind of assault or harassment, Krista," she says gently. I've slowed to a walk to let my root-kicked toe stop throbbing, and she sounds less out of breath.

"It's normal to feel guilty and like you're wondering if you're wrecking someone else's life. But you're not. Jess and Coach are the ones who screwed up here, not you. And as far as using this as a resume builder, it's not like that, or at least, not entirely. You're telling an important story, and who knows how many other girls will have their own stories to tell after it, or how many guys will rethink how they're acting?"

"All right," I say after taking a pause. "Let's do it."

"Great," Elle replies. "Meet me in the library after lunch? I'll email you the outline I started of how we can package this so it gets the most attention."

"You're the expert on attention," I say somewhat sarcastically. "And nice work."

"What do you mean?" she asks.

"You just ran four miles without stopping," I say as we hit the school's driveway.

"Holy crap," she says, before we head off in separate directions.

chapter
thirty-nine

Elle

MY LEGS ARE BURNING but so is my righteous indignation, so it's a pretty good combination as I sit through math and biology classes this morning. Rather than pay close attention like I normally would, I have a sheet of blank paper in front of me as I try to work through the best way to share our stories with the entire student body.

I look around at the other students in the room. Some are intently following along with the teacher in bio, two are napping, three are doodling, and two are whispering in the back. How many of them have stories to share? How many of them have been coerced into sending 'sexy' photos, how many of them have been pushed to go farther than they wanted, how many have dealt with even worse?

I write down that thought, because it might make for a strong opening. It's not just us, that much I'm sure of—just look at Jenny. But how many? Jess has always been considered a nice guy. How many other 'nice guys' are getting away with doing whatever they want?

It makes me wonder: would other girls share their stories? And then, a brilliant idea hits me. We can create an outlet for those stories to be shared, anonymously or with full recognition. Take this outside of just what's happening to us. Will anyone else respond? I think so.

Either way, I think it's worth a shot, and I bet Krista will love the idea too.

"I don't hate it," she says when I tell her about it in hushed tones at the library an hour later.

"You love it," I say, needling her a little. I know I'm right.

She smiles a little. "It is a good idea," she admits. "I can set up a contact form on the newspaper site for people to write in and share experiences anonymously or with their name."

Krista nods and scribbles a few notes to herself. "Another thing I was thinking—I'll work on a few stories that talk to counselors and psychologists about what victims can do," she adds. "I think that's going to be an important thing to think about for after."

"Great point," I say. Then, I take a deep breath. "I know you probably think I sound really Machiavellian here, like I'm trying to make this work for me, but I promise you, I want to do this the right way and help other girls and give them a voice. I acted like a dumbass because of some boy, and I was lucky that it didn't go any farther than it did. But other girls might not be as lucky, or have a friend like you to tell them what's really going on."

Krista looks away when I say 'friend' but I barrel on, since I already put it out there. "I know friend is pushing it, but you didn't have to say anything, you could have just let me keep making a fool out of myself and letting Jess take advantage of me. You helped me and you didn't have to."

"Friend is still a little strong," she says, but I don't think her heart is in it. So I just smile and snuggle into my beanbag chair and keep scribbling notes in my old-school composition book. Krista, wearing basically the opposite outfit of me—black leggings and an oversized black hoodie to my light jeans and pale yellow boat-neck t-shirt—is writing away as well. In her old-school composition book.

chapter
forty

Krista

~~Elle and Krista's Game Plan~~
~~Krista and Elle's Game Plan~~
The Game Plan

1. ~~Make appointment with counselor~~ (voice recorder app?)
2. Look up statistics, make sure they're from good source
3. Put out call for stories – find way to upload (email? form?)
4. Krista to write article
5. Elle to create presentation—need to let secretary know RE AV equipment
6. Article goes live on school site at same time Elle starts talking in presentation – set on schedule?
7. Krista needs to practice public speaking (seriously)
8. What to wear??? Serious, but not absurd. No suits.

9. Set appointment with principal for after presentation ahead of time? Damage control? Have Elle mom at the ready to show up threateningly if needed.
10. Tell Miss C what's going on?

Chapter Forty

MAKING an appointment with the guidance counselor is easy. It's the 'going to the appointment and being vulnerable' that's hard. But between Miss C, my mom and my plan with Elle, it's necessary. I'm doing my finger taps—tapping each finger to my thumb in slow rhythm, just like Mom does—to stay calm in the waiting room during my free period, but the only thing that's really keeping me from panicking is knowing that if I need to default to interviewing her, I can and I have a good reason. I might be the story, but I'm definitely not alone.

In fact, I'm guessing that our story is going to make more waves than I realized as two girls come out of the office with tear-streaked cheeks. Maybe I shouldn't have waited until it happened to me to do something. I don't know what happened to them, obviously, but it could be the same thing.

The counselor comes out and smiles at me. "Krista?"

I nod, and she motions for me to follow her into her office.

I want to say that the next 30 minutes is productive. But I'd be lying. Which, by the way, is more or less what the counselor accuses me of. When I sit down and start to tell her about how Jess was pushing Elle to send him naked pictures at the same time he was trying to hook up with me, she basically tells me that it's just typical teenage drama. Then, when I tell her about him mauling me during practice, she doesn't quite say that I was asking for it, but she kind of implies it.

Finally, after a few of the most painful moments of my life, I bite back a scream and say that I'm sorry for wasting her time and mine, and exit the office, careful to blink back tears and keep a straight face.

Instead of going to my next class, I slip into the newspaper office and start to write down what just happened, and how I'm feeling now. Alone, lost, and starting to wonder if I am the one who's wrong, even though my gut is screaming at me that I didn't do anything.

As I write, though, I stop feeling quite as helpless. It's like everything that I tried to say in the guidance counselor's office and the words I was stumbling over suddenly click into place, and when I re-read them in black and white, I realize even more firmly that I'm not crazy.

By the time I finish the writeup, the school day has ended, and I'm so drained that I'm tempted to blow off cross-country practice. But while my brain feels a little emotionally empty, I realize that my legs are feeling good. In fact, my feet have started tapping their own rhythm like they can't wait to get out on the trails. I don't want to see anyone else, though. Well, not just anyone else, and certainly not Jess.

When Miss C walks into the newspaper room a minute later and looks at me still sitting at a computer, she asks, "Still planning on coming to practice?" I'm sure she knows what I've been working on—she has access to all of our drafts, and the concerned look on her face kind of gives her away.

"I was thinking of doing my own trail run, if that's okay," I say. I'm as surprised by those words as she is. It's one thing for me to get my competitive juices flowing, but another to hit the trails casually, like it's for fun.

"Sure," she says, and smiles. "I knew you'd become a runner."

"I am not!" I say, offended. That's not quite as bad as 'jock,' but it's not far off.

"But you have to take a buddy. What about Elle?"

I groan.

"She could use the extra practice with you, and she's having just as hard a time with the team as you are," she says gently, again, telling me what I already know.

"Fine, fine," I say and pull out my phone to text her. If she says no, and I hope she will, I'm off the hook.

Trail run in ten? I type.

Instantly, three dots pop up. Crap. She saw it.

"Meet by the fence," she types back.

"Well, looks like we're running together," I tell Miss C, who nods approvingly.

"Don't forget to warm up!" she says as I push back from my desk and head to the locker room.

Ten minutes later, some cursory stretches done, we're walking to the trailhead yet again, me in my black tights and dark gray hoodie, Elle in her purple tights and baby blue zip-up jacket.

When we hit the trails, I take a long, deep inhale and tentatively jog a few paces. It feels good, like I'm getting cleansed of all of the crap that I was just writing about. My face, which felt oily as I went to change to run, suddenly feels like it's glowing, vibrant. My mom always says that running makes her feel more invigorated, instead of more exhausted, and I think I finally understand what she means.

I'd speed up more, but I can hear Elle panting behind me, and I slow down to accommodate her slightly less brisk pace. But while I expect to feel annoyed that she's throwing me off my game, a few minutes at her pace—easy for me, I realize—leaves me feeling even better. I feel light, and I'm feeling a whole lot more inclined to like Elle suddenly.

"Your mom is pretty cool," I say, rather than telling her all about the therapy session from hell. I consider mentioning Jess and asking how her side of the scheme is going, but I realized as it was about to come out of my mouth that I genuinely wanted to talk about anything else with her.

"She is, yeah. When she's talking to me," Elle says glumly, only gasping a little between sentences. "She's always busy with work, unless there's something drastic happening like right now."

"But she has really important cases, right?" I ask. Elle's mom, even when we were kids, intimidated the crap out of me, but at the same time, I admired her so much. Secretly, I wished my mom was more like Elle's—more ambitious, more career-driven, more of a badass. I love my mom, but her hippie-nutrition all-natural-everything is sometimes a little too soft for me.

(Even thinking that makes me feel guilty, like I'm complaining about not having a more masculine figure in my life. I'm not, and my mom is a badass in her own way. But Elle's mom? You know she has a five-year plan and vision boards but has also made a grown man cry in court after he made some kind of dumb comment and you know she rocks the hell out of a perfectly tailored suit. Now that's just plain cool.)

"She does," Elle says. "And I guess she's the reason why I'm on the debate team and student council, so it's definitely pushed me to be more of a leader. But I don't think I really am one."

I guess it's confession time all around.

"You obviously are a leader," I say. "How else did you end up leading the debate team or sitting on student council since we were like, five years old?"

We're still holding a solid pace, and something about being on the trail is making me feel a whole lot kinder than I normally feel towards

Elle. That must be it—the crisp fall air is what's making me soft, I'm not starting to actually want to be friends with her again. At all.

"Sure, but I can't make the hard decisions or big impact statements," she huffs as we hit a slight uphill.

"You didn't seem to have a problem with inflammatory statements about high school skanks the other day," I point out dryly. I'm feeling kinder towards her, sure, but not forgiving entirely.

"Yeah, but that was only because I was so angry at you," she says, her face turning redder than it already was.

"So maybe your mom does the same with all of her cases—and maybe that's why she's so preoccupied and takes them so seriously?" I say, feeling a little smug with my psychological read on her mom.

She stops dead in her tracks. "You think every single case gets my mom that emotional?" she asks, and puts her hands on her knees while she catches her breath.

"Walk it off," I say, slowing my pace. "Yeah, I think she does. How else would she be such a good lawyer? Maybe you should think about that next time you're heading into a debate, as long as it's not about me next time."

"Well, it will be about you next time," she says, getting back up to speed. "And me, and any other girl who's been assaulted by some jackass jock their junior year."

"Solid alliteration," I say. "But we should probably head back now, we're already two miles in and we have to go back the way we came. And we already ran this morning."

She looks appalled. "I have to run two miles back?"

"Race ya!" I say, before tearing off down the trail. I hear her strangled laugh and her feet start thudding behind me—I'll slow down in a couple minutes, but I want to make her really work for it first.

By the time we get back to school, we're both drenched with sweat, and not in a sexy way. My bangs are sticking out in different directions thanks to the headwind on the way back, and Elle's face refuses to turn a lighter shade of red even after we've cooled down.

Naturally, that's the moment Jess picks to stroll by us on his way to his car. "Lookin' hot, ladies," he smirks as he saunters past.

"Dick," Elle mutters under her breath, while I'm a bit more forward and shoot up my middle finger. Of course, he doesn't bother to glance back so my effort is wasted, but at least I tried.

"Seriously, are you okay with what happened to you?" Elle asks, looking subdued.

"Honestly?" I say. "I'm not okay, but I feel like I'm actually getting there. That run helped. And knowing that you're in my corner and believe me. I'm not sure that the guidance counselor did."

Elle looks appalled. "We should tell someone else!" she says. "She can't do that to you, that's victim blaming."

"Let's tackle one thing at a time," I say. "I get the feeling that once my editorial and article go out and you do your speech, she's going to be dealing with a whole lot of trouble coming her way without us specifically ratting her out."

"If she doesn't, she will soon," Elle promises ominously. "Remember, I'm the one with the scary lawyer mom and I'm not afraid to use her."

chapter
forty-one

Elle

OF COURSE, all of my talk with Krista during our run was great, and it added fuel to my fire, but that doesn't mean speech writing is easy. But since running seemed to help before, I take my notebook and laptop to Mom's home gym and pop onto the elliptical. For the first time, I'm not using it to think about calories burned, I'm using it to help clear my head while I outline. I set the pace to easy while I think through my speech.

It's hard to write a speech that's meant to sound natural and like it's coming from the heart (which it is) but is laid out in a way that will sound right is slow-going. The facts are there: Jess assaulted Krista, he pressured me into sending him nudes, we've heard he's done it to other girls, and to top it off, he's bragging about his exploits and acting like we're both still interested in him. Add to that a coach and a guidance counselor who've been informed of his actions and aren't taking any steps and my anger practically flies off the page.

My thesis? Simple: This can't keep happening. It is a big deal. It's not just 'bullcrap teenage drama,' as Coach put it. It's sexual assault and harassment and it's not okay.

As far as intros go, that isn't too shabby. I look up some statistics on my phone: 1 in 16 women's first sexual experience wasn't consensual. A study found 3.3 million women who's first time having sex was rape. When I see the number, my stomach drops and my fists clench.

Chapter Forty-One

That's when Mom walks in and sees over my shoulder. "It's unimaginable, isn't it?" she asks—but I know she means that rhetorically, since she deals with those victims every day at work, and she knows that it happens.

"It really is," I say.

"I'm not sure what you and Krista have in mind," Mom says, "But for what it's worth, her mom and I are both behind you one hundred percent—but only if you promise to let us know if you need help or if you feel like you want us to get involved. Promise?"

I nod.

"Kick his ass," Mom says, before she shuts the door.

Fueled by the statistics—and a sip from the water bottle that Mom thoughtfully stuck next to me before she left—I message the study I found to Krista. She sends back a barrage of angry faces so fast that I know she must also be sitting on her computer working away.

And I know I'm still not her favorite person to hang out with, but I still find myself typing: "Want to come over and work on this together?"

The three dots pop up almost immediately and I hold my breath. Was that too much? Did I push the friendship angle a little too far?

"I definitely still don't like you," her next message reads, and my heart sinks. But then, "I'll be over in 10" pops up immediately after, and I laugh out loud.

"Mom, Krista's on her way over!" I yell.

She grunts a generally positive sound in my direction, which I take to mean she's back at work as well.

And ten minutes later, the doorbell rings and the door opens. Krista aims right for the kitchen, where she pops open the cupboards and rummages for forks. "Mom sent apple crumble," she says by way of a greeting. "Can you make tea?"

Lulled into domestic bliss—and the delicious smell of apple wafting through the kitchen now—I hop off the elliptical and make the tea, only a little sweaty.

"She also said to tell you that you ran a lot today and to make sure you had some protein plus this apple crisp," Krista says over her shoulder. "Is she your new nutritionist?"

"She's just giving me some advice," I mutter. "I was having trouble with figuring out how to eat for running." (Kind of true.)

"Maybe she'll stop giving me so much advice as she starts working with you more," Krista says. "There's a bright side to everything."

"Isn't that supposed to be my line, Miss Emo About Everything?" I ask.

She smirks, but then her face drops a bit. "This is pretty heavy stuff we're dealing with," she says, gesturing to her laptop and my notebook. "The more I read about it, the more freaked out I'm getting."

"Same," I admit. "But I'm feeling more and more like we're doing the right thing."

"I think so," she says, digging into the apple crumble. "I just hope it's enough."

"It will be," I promise, but I know we're both thinking the same thing. It's high school, which means attention spans are short and it's much less fun to think about the star athlete being a sex predator than a total stud.

"Okay, what's your plan?" Krista asks, settling down with her computer.

I flip open my notebook. "I keep thinking about how guys like Jess have been getting away with stuff like this for ages," I say. "We're definitely not the first girls at school to get harassed by a guy, and not even the first to get mauled by Jess."

Krista nods. "I've been kind of thinking the same thing," she says. "What if, instead of thinking about individual speeches and editorials that are just our voice... what if we asked other girls to share their *voices*, not just their stories?"

"You think that many girls would be willing to get on stage and talk about getting harassed?" I say, a little skeptical. "Considering what a big deal it is for you or I to do something about it in venues we're already super comfortable with, I can't really picture it."

"That's why I'm thinking voices, but anonymous," Krista says triumphantly.

"Huh?" I'm completely baffled.

"Here's what I'm thinking," she says, looking like she's coming up with the idea on the spot. You can pretty much see the lightbulb coming on over her head. "What if we make an online voicemail box that girls can phone into and leave their stories? We talked about doing it as a write-in, but voices would be so much more powerful to play during your speech."

"What would we do with them, and how would we spread the word?" I ask.

"Spreading the word is easy—your mom can make us copies, right? So, we'll make a flyer with the info and stick copies of it all over school, and I'll post the links on the website in my first story in the series, listing those statistics and then asking girls to share anonymously."

I nod. "It could be brilliant... But sounds like it's more your project than anything to do with my speech."

"That's where you're wrong," Krista says. Then, she fills me in on her—I have to admit—completely brilliant plan.

chapter
forty-two

Krista

Attention all female students!

1 IN 16 women's first sexual experience isn't consensual.

3.3 million women in the US report that their first time having sex was rape.

And many of us have experienced some form of harassment or assault while at this school.

Let's stand up for ourselves and say NO MORE!

If you have a story you want to share but have been too afraid to speak up, now is the time.

Call in to our anonymous hotline at 833-867-5309 and share your story. Or go to bit.-ly/shareyourstoryHRHS and write your story. Either way, it's time to speak up for ourselves!

Chapter Forty-Two

I hit publish, then hit print and make 100 copies to plaster in the girls restrooms and locker rooms, and take a huge breath. Holy crap.

Miss C looks over my shoulder. "That's a big move," she says. "Are you sure you're okay with what you're starting here?"

I look at her in shock. "I thought you'd be on my side," I say softly, feeling completely let down.

She does a bit of a double take. "No, that's not what I mean at all," she says, sitting down next to me. "I just mean that you're taking on a lot of actual work *and* emotional work by asking for this. And I know you already have a lot on your plate as it is."

I nod. "I know what I'm doing."

"I think you do to," she says. "And for what it's worth, I think it's a great idea. I just..."

She doesn't burst into tears, but her eyes well up.

"What's wrong?" I ask. I don't really know how to handle a teacher crying.

She pauses, like she's debating if she should say something or keep it to herself. "I... Well, I'm frustrated and upset. Harden agreed to suspend Jess and he says he's debating what to do about Coach, but he's not willing to make any kind of announcements or talk about sexual assault in the student body and he's just going to sweep this all under the rug," she says in a rush.

I know I should be shocked and upset, but I'm not exactly surprised. Spineless is the word I'd use to describe our principal.

"Maybe this article and what comes out of it will convince him," I say instead of cursing and raging about what a jerk he is.

"I hope you're right," she says, and takes a few deep breaths. "Whatever happens, I'm proud of you and I'm behind you."

She walks away and I roll my shoulders back a couple of times and crack my knuckles. Just a couple things left to do before I sneak in my training run for the day, and I admit, I'm kind of craving the idea of getting outside at this point. Putting this online, making it real, has made me twitchy, like I have all this energy crackling under my skin and need to release it somewhere. And normally, I would have just kept writing, but now, I just want to get outside in the stinging cold air and run as fast as I can. It's not just because with my ankle healed and the meet coming up, I want to be in ultra-fast shape. I just need to move. It's weird, having this feeling—but I like it.

But before I do, I send a few emails to trauma and sexual assault experts and counselors—not the school counselor obviously. For her, I send a complaint to the school board from my official school email. I am no longer in the mood for this crap.

By the time I'm done, I feel righteous, and ready for anything. As I go to turn off the computer and get ready to go outside, though, my email dings, notifying me of a new voicemail. And a new response to my form.

"It's really working," I say under my breath before pulling off my sweatshirt, logging out of the school's system and stowing my bag behind Miss C's desk. I jam my headphones on, pick my favorite Clash album, and jog down the hall heading for the trails.

A few minutes later, I can see my breath in front of me, and I finally feel like I've calmed down, like I've worked a venti triple-shot latte out of my system. The feeling of overwhelm is still there, and my mental checklists are going crazy. I still need to get in interviews with experts, get more statistics, do the actual editing assuming we do get enough stories, figure out the accompanying article or audio file or video (and learn how to edit video), plus normal homework, plus getting ready for this race. I'm tempted to turn back towards school and put in another hour in the library instead of pounding out another 30 minutes on the trail.

After all, I didn't even want to be on a sports team anyway, so why should this race really matter? Isn't it more important to share my story, share Elle's story, share the stories of all the girls who've been dealing with guys walking all over them?

But I keep running.

Because yes, that's all so important. The most important thing I'll do in school. But I want this too, I realize.

chapter
forty-three

Elle

WHEN I GET HOME, I have the shock of my life when I walk into the kitchen and Krista is perched on a high stool chatting away with my mom. "What are you doing here?" I ask, trying to not sound accusatory or at all offended that Krista seems to be having a more in-depth talk with my mom than I have in years.

"I wanted to show you this in person," she says. "In some ways, I'm super happy—but on the flip side, holy shit, I wish the voicemail was empty."

She swivels the computer so I can see and I gasp sharply. I instantly know what she means: calls have started coming in with girls sharing their stories. There are 25 files in already, and the article just went live this afternoon. "There are a few more written ones too," she adds, and clicks one of the MP3s at random.

A girl's trembling voice fills the kitchen. "We were out bowling with some friends and he said he forgot something in my car, and when we went out to get it..." Her voice trails off and breaks, and the line goes almost silent before she finishes, practically whispering.

I can barely listen to it, let alone imagine how she must have felt. It makes me realize just how sheltered I've been, but also, how easily what Jess tried on Krista and I could have been so much worse. Krista looks up at me, her eyes shining—she's as close to tears as I am.

"So many of them are like that," she says.

My mom doesn't say anything, just glares off in the distance, biting her lip.

"The rest are like that too?" I ask, because I can't believe it. I don't want to.

"Some are less scary, some are worse," Krista says, choking on the words.

"What exactly are you girls planning to do with this?" Mom asks. Not accusatory, just interested. Like she finally cares about something I'm doing that isn't winning or getting some kind of honor or grade.

"Well, we were going to make an audio montage to play at the debate, and then post it online on the school's newspaper, with these files and one of us reading the write-ins," I say. "That's going to be the introduction to my address to the student body this Friday. Then, I'm going to talk about our story and the statistics and what girls can do to protect themselves and what to do after something happens."

Mom nods. "That's a great idea, but can I offer one suggestion?"

We both nod.

"First, that you put my information in your presentation and articles, if any of the girls do decide to pursue legal action. I'll take their cases pro bono. And second, you may want to distort the voices slightly in the audio files—I can show you how to do that—so that way the girls stay anonymous. Voices are easy to identify," she says. "I have to do this in court pretty often."

My mom is kind of a genius sometimes.

"Show me," Krista says, eagerly handing Mom her laptop. Minutes later, we have an audio program installed and Mom is showing us how to tweak the voices. It's hard to listen to each one a few times, but we'll have to hear them more as we prep, and Mom is absolutely right: I can identify a few of the voices of girls I know, which makes it even sadder. The couple that I do know are all strong, tough, cool girls who I never would guess had bad things happen to them. But then again, I wouldn't have expected it for me and Krista, either.

It's late when Krista's mom arrives to pick her up, and even later when they actually leave our house. When she realizes that none of us have eaten dinner, she scolds all three of us and whips up some veggie-packed omelets with limp peppers, half an onion, a handful of cherry tomatoes and some freezer-burned frozen spinach she finds in the fridge. It's surprisingly not horrible, especially with some sourdough toast on the side. ("Thank goodness I stopped at the bakery earlier!" Krista's mom says as she goes to bring it in from her car.)

We don't play the audio for her tonight—I don't think any of us, even Mom, are up for it right now. We just shift gears as best we can and talk about running. Krista's latest revelation—that she doesn't hate it—causes both of our moms to burst out laughing. "Told you," her mom says, hip-checking her gently.

"Yeah, yeah," she says, and reaches for her phone. "Crap, it's past 10! Mom, we gotta get home. I need to run tomorrow morning before school, we have too much to do to get to practice later."

"Do you want a pick-up, Elle?" her mom asks before she can object. "You two can do your early run together, it'll make me feel a lot less nervous if I know Krista's running with someone."

Looks like once again, we're stuck together, since the only thing I can really do is say yes. (Also, crap, now I have another morning run? Like this wasn't brutal enough already.)

chapter
forty-four

Krista

ELLE IS PROMPT, I'll give her that. When Mom drives up to her house at 6:15, she's already outside with her backpack in hand, wearing fuchsia tights with a plain black jacket and a cap pulled over her hair.

She actually looks like a legit runner, I realize. In fact, barring the fact that my tights are dark gray, we're essentially dressed alike, and I feel more like myself in running gear than I have before. Maybe my style is starting to shift, though I shudder a bit at the thought of it shifting to a wardrobe packed with spandex. (Flip side: it is comfy.)

"Four miles with a few hills work for you?" I ask as she pops into the backseat.

"Ugh," she mutters, and I detect a hint of eye roll.

"Hey, this wasn't my idea," I say defensively. "You agreed to come."

"I know, I know," she says, and smiles wide and creepy. "I'm so pumped!" she says in her perkiest student body president voice. "Better?"

"Ugh. Go back to grumbling," I say, but it does make me smile.

We hop out of the car and stash our backpacks under the bleachers in the field, where no one else likely to visit until school is finished for the day. A few half-hearted stretches for both of us, and we're heading towards the trails as the sun is just starting to poke over the trees.

"I hate early runs, but I kind of love them," Elle says.

"I completely know what you mean," I say, wholeheartedly. In some ways, the idea of getting going when dawn is just breaking seems entirely too early but at the same time... There's just something magical about getting the run done this early in the day and starting with something that feels so positive. (Ugh, I'm starting to sound like Mom.)

We break into an easy trot, though I can tell even this pace is still a bit hard for Elle so I try to ease up. The last thing I need is for her to suddenly give herself some kind of asthma attack before we even hit the hill.

As we warm up more and start to pick up the pace a bit more, we don't talk, which works for me since the cold is forcing me to focus much harder to stay comfortable. I can see my breath when I huff out, and it makes me realize that it's going to be pretty damn cold soon—and I might need to start thinking about asking Mom to get me some winter running gear. If I'm sticking with it—*since* I'm sticking with it—I guess I'll need it.

When we get to the base of the hill and pause. I set my stopwatch app to zero and explain the workout. "Miss C says we have to do five thirty-second intervals with two minutes of rest in between," I say and Elle nods.

I pause dramatically, then shout "GO!" as I hit the Record button, and we both thunder up the hill.

My breath comes in shorter spurts—the first few seconds feel like flying, but after a few long strides, my quads start to burn. Good.

chapter
forty-five

Elle

JUST. Keep. Running.

I repeat those words over and over in my head as we run for the longest thirty seconds of my life.

When Krista finally yells stop and we jog back downhill, I catch my breath. I truly hate intervals, but at least in the back of my mind, there's a tiny voice reminding me that the fastest way to get I shape isn't by food alone—especially now that Krista's mom seems to keep popping up at mealtimes and making sure I have healthy food to eat.

Calorie restricting is getting harder and harder, especially since a) her food tastes delicious. Even today, when she picked us up, as she dropped us at school, she casually handed me a thermos with chili in it and a piece of baguette and an apple so I had a lunch. I can't *not* eat homemade chili, especially since I know by lunchtime my stomach will be growling since we're starting the day with our run.

Also, and harder to grasp, is that b) she sent me a bunch of information on how it's better to focus on eating enough food to fuel the work that I'm doing—and getting plenty of veggies, fruit and protein throughout the day—instead of diet *anything*, and explained how my body will eventually come to the right shape and size for me if I'm eating healthy and moving enough.

She also explained to me that the way that I see my body probably isn't how other people see it, or how it actually looks. Apparently, a lot of teen girls have this thing called body dysmorphia, where we think we look a lot different than we actually do.

When she said that, it sort of hit a nerve with me. So, I looked back at a few random photos on my phone of me this year, especially in group shots, and thinking about what she said, I guess she's not wrong. I'm not really any bigger than most of the girls and guys in any of the photos, but when I stand next to them in real life, I feel like a giant.

And I have to admit, since we had our talk and I've tried eating more consistently and following some of her recipes and meal suggestions, I've started feeling a lot better. I have more energy and running actually sucks less these days. The acne that was starting to cover my face has even calmed down now that I'm not sneaking downstairs for candy at night because I'm so damn hungry. And while I don't think I've lost weight, I don't think I've gained any either.

I'm still definitely far from perfect, but it finally feels like progress. And maybe rather than losing weight, feeling fit is a smarter goal.

It's funny, isn't it? When it seems like you're taking charge of one thing in your life, it's easier for the other things to fall into place. With the Jess situation, it was easy to start getting freaked out about my weight and want to do something drastic. But now that Krista and I are —well, we're not friends, but colleagues?—and working together again *and* it feels like we're doing something positive, it's a little easier to think about wanting what's actually best for me. And that doesn't mean looking a certain way or wanting everyone to like me. Me losing ten pounds wouldn't have made Jess treat me differently and it wouldn't have made me not make an ass of myself on *GMA*. In fact, if anything, me not eating was what made me make an ass of myself on *GMA*.

(Maybe not entirely. But I'm thinking that my blood sugar dropping may have had something to do with me acting like a complete idiot. That, and the fact that I acted like a complete idiot.)

At the bottom of the downhill, I remember the problem with downhills. Once you hit flat ground again, suddenly, even running on a flat feels hard and slow compared to the lovely flowing feeling of bombing down a hill. Especially since I'm finally getting better at not 'hitting the brakes,' as Miss C calls it, making my muscles scream in pain by actually trying to slow down on descents. Now, I lean into them and let myself just get carried away. Almost, anyway.

As we jog along heading back to the school, I do end up glancing over at Krista and internally cursing her just a teensy bit. It still doesn't seem quite fair that she's naturally a good runner and I'm just not. It's also not exactly fair that she and my mother seem to have more to chat about than my mom does with me.

In fact... "Why are you and my mom suddenly so chummy?" I find myself huffing out.

Krista looks over in surprise. "I told you—I think she's basically Wonder Woman, but with better clothes. I love hearing her talk about work, and she seems to not mind me asking about it. Why? Did she complain about me?" She looks distressed—more distressed than she did at the end of the interval, honestly.

"No, nothing like that," I say. "Though jeez, like it should matter if she did say something? But no—I just was wondering how you get her to stop working and talk to you, when she barely makes time to talk to me."

"Oh," Krista says. "I didn't realize you didn't talk to your mom a lot. You two always seem super close."

"That's just because she has to drive me everywhere since my dad isn't around," I say flatly. "It has nothing to do with her liking me."

"She definitely likes you," says Krista. "But she is pretty tough and not the most emotive—she's nothing like my mom, and that's maybe what I like the best about her. She's all business, and she doesn't ask me about how stuff is making me feel, the way my mom does."

I barely notice that we've slowed to a walk because I'm so captivated. "But that's what's so great about your mom!" I say. "I love that she wants to know how I'm feeling about stuff."

"Try living with her," Krista responds, rolling her eyes. "Trust me, it's not all it's cracked up to be."

"I bet it's great," I say.

"Well, the food is," Krista admits. "But I do love that your mom doesn't stress about getting takeout like my mom does. That's just annoying. Sometimes I need my General Tso's, you know?"

"Oh, I know," I say, in a way that is completely heartfelt. I don't want to live in a world where that's off the table.

Back at school, we go our separate ways, heading to class. We didn't even discuss the fact that today is The Day and our whole world could get turned upside down. But I think that's because we both realize that this isn't the time to be stressed about what will happen after our presentation, because we both know that it's the right thing to do.

As I get ready in the school locker room, I pull out my power outfit that Mom picked out for me earlier this year when we were back to school shopping. A loose-fitting blazer, a simple white button down with black buttons, and dark blue skinny jeans with an awesome set of ankle boots with a thick heel. It's an ass-kicking outfit, but a comfy one as well.

I debated if I should wear a bright or dark lipstick, but that's more Krista's thing, so I don't want to make it seem like we're twinning, since I'm already opting for her monochrome aesthetic for my clothes. So I stick with keeping it light, and skip mascara altogether because the last thing I need is a panda-esque look heading into the presentation, and I can already feel tears welling up behind my eyes as I look in the mirror.

"You've got this," I tell myself and head to class before the bell rings.

I have no idea what we learned during the first three periods of the day, and my jeans are starting to feel damp from how many times I've wiped my sweaty palms on them. When the bell goes off to signal the end of third period and the start of fourth, I head for the gym, along with half of the student body.

Today sounds like it's going to be a boring high school speech day, because usually it is—just generic announcements. Only Krista, Miss C and I know what's going to happen, so when I see people grumbling about wasting a lunch period or study hall in assembly, I don't blame them. They have no clue what we're going to talk about.

Backstage, I meet up with Krista and Miss C, who agreed to run our PowerPoint and play the audio portion when we give the signal. We decided, after a lot of back and forth, that instead of any photos or major amounts of text on each slide, we wanted it black and white, stark with huge numbers relating some of the statistics we found. It makes more of a statement than a jumble of text—that was Krista's argument and I think she was dead-on. It's a lot sharper looking than any of the presentations I've given to student council over the years.

But even knowing that we've nailed the presentation design doesn't stop my knees from shaking slightly as the countdown begins. Great, I'm an Eminem cliche with my sweaty palms and weak knees. And Krista, who's sitting on a folding chair and panting slightly, looks paler than ever (and I was 100 percent right about skipping the lipstick, since she's wearing a dark red color that looks great against her black button-up and black skinny jeans).

Miss C is holding a paper bag anxiously, like she's wondering if she should hand it to Krista or use it for herself for a breathing exercise. While I know we're doing the right thing from a moral standpoint, I'm just now realizing that Miss C has really put herself and her career on the line, or at least, in front of a potentially messy battle. I'm pretty sure legally, she's covered (a very important thing my mom makes me think about regularly!) but I know that she could really piss off the administration, who probably won't take kindly to the fact that we're about to point out that they've ignored a super-serious problem, and in the case of some like Coach and Krista's guidance counselor, they've actively encouraged ignoring or covering stuff up.

"Five minutes," the school secretary informs me, and gives me a little thumbs up. She's always liked me, and hopefully today won't change that.

"You ready?" I ask Krista.

She nods, though she looks a little bit vomit-y.

"Just follow my lead," I say, trying to sound more confident than I actually am. "You're going to do great."

She nods again.

"Umm, can I just sound-check your voice?" I say, going for a joking tone but a tiny bit serious.

She swallows. "Testing, one, two, three?" she says, her voice wavering a little bit, but she's smiling slightly.

"We're good. Don't forget—this isn't just for us. This is for all of those girls," I say, and gesture out at the audience. At last count, we'd gotten 50 audio messages and another couple dozen emails from girls detailing their terrifying stories. Even this morning, there were more coming in. And our school isn't even that big! Krista will have to do another part in the online series, which should be going live any second now. We timed it so that the kids who weren't in this assembly would be able to immediately hear what was going on, so there couldn't be any clamp-down on information, or when the game of telephone starts up, people can easily go see and hear the cold hard facts.

Krista checks her phone, looks at the time, and refreshes the school website. There it is, in huge letters splashed on the front page: "Sexual Assault and Harassment Rampant at Union High." Her byline is there, but my name is right under hers.

We lock eyes, and for a second, we're 12 years old again and best friends, heading into battle.

"Let's do this," I say, and she gets up and we walk out towards the stage, where the secretary waves us onto the stage and to the podium that we're speaking from. We're hoping that us together makes an interesting enough statement to quiet the crowd.

As we stand together looking out over the audience, despite the blinding bright lights (honestly, this is a high school, do we really need such an intense lighting setup?), I somehow hone in on exactly where Jess is sitting: off to the side, surrounded by his buddies and smirking towards the stage as he gestures and whispers something to his friend on his right, who hoots with laughter. I look over and see that Krista has spotted him as well.

"Don't think about him," I whisper, making sure that my hand is blocking the microphone, just in case it's turned on already. The last thing we need is another awkward public speaking situation...

And of course, someone in the front row starts a "Fight, Fight, Fight!" chant, a charming callback to our *GMA* incident.

You know, I should have seen that coming, but I somehow did not predict it.

Fortunately, the school secretary steps up and grabs the mic, admonishing them to quiet down and listen. She introduces me—student council president, debate team, honors student... and then she realizes she has no idea who Krista is, and pauses awkwardly.

I seize the mic and thank her, and she gratefully steps down. It's my show now. Our show.

"For those of you who didn't see our 15-minutes of fame, this is Krista," I begin. "Editor-in-chief of the school newspaper, super-fast runner, and someone who I deeply, deeply underestimated and hurt."

Krista looks at me in surprise. This wasn't exactly what we had rehearsed, but I'd planned it.

"I started a mean rumor about Krista—I won't say what it was, though I'm sure some of you remember." I see a few people nod, a couple more snicker. Krista's ears are bright red. "I shouldn't have done that, for a few reasons. The first is that it was just a crappy thing to do to someone, regardless of the truth. The second reason is because what I saw wasn't something that she should have been ashamed of, or something that she should be gossiped about because of. It was something she should have been helped through. I misinterpreted a situation, I hurt my friend, and I made the same mistake that we're here to talk about today. I not only blamed the victim, I shamed the victim."

Krista steps up to the podium, and to my surprise, she squeezes my hand before she takes the mic.

"I'm not much for public speaking," she says, looking right at our public speaking teacher. She nods, but gives the thumbs up. "So I'll let Elle do most of the talking here. But before she starts our presentation, I wanted to say that I do forgive her, because I understand how easy it is to go with the explanation that doesn't involve pain for anyone. It's easier to think that a girl is acting a certain way instead of thinking that a guy assaulted her or forced her to do something she didn't want to do. Because at least then, sure, it's a mean story or a vicious rumor, but it's not a big deal. But it is a big deal—and after I put out the article asking for some of you to share your stories about sexual assault, we got over 75 responses as of this morning. I want you to hear a few now before I turn the mic back to Elle."

She nods towards the audio booth where Miss C is sitting, and the lights dim as the voices come up. We worked really hard to edit the voices so they're unrecognizable as certain students, but still sound like people, and we knit them together so that the words start to stumble over each other and speed up as it goes on.

"I didn't know where we were going until he pulled off onto this deserted road..."

Chapter Forty-Five

"He hit lock on the doors and I couldn't open them..."

"I thought he was just kidding around..."

"I tried to say no but he wouldn't listen..."

The voices keep coming, and after 45 seconds, the file stops on an echo of the word *No*, from so many different voices. There's so much pain and anger in each. But there's a power rising too.

When the lights come on, I realize that my eyes are wet and so are Krista's, but we're not the only ones: Looking out in front of us, there are girls through the audience with tears streaming down their cheeks, guys looking angry—some glaring at us, but some glaring at other guys and looking protectively at their female friends. Jess shifts in his seat and suddenly looks uncomfortable. And the teachers in the audience look shell-shocked.

I pause and force myself to slowly count to 10 before I pick the microphone back up, and gesture to Miss C to put the presentation on behind me, starting with 3.3 million.

The bold block lettering glares out at the audience—we decided to write it out with all the zeroes for maximum impact so it reads 33,000,000.

forty-six

Krista

<u>**33,000,000**</u>

THANK God Elle loves public speaking. That's all I can think as I stand there, completely terrified at the sea of students staring at us. I stumbled through my opening remark and I know I have more to say before we're done, but I'm so glad that she's taken the reins and is willing to do the hardest part of our talk.

"I know when you came here today, you expected some kind of generic school announcement or debate, like if we should have school start an hour later," she says.

One kid in the crowd lets out a 'hell yeah,' but I can see the people around him shushing him.

"But after a lot of reflection, I—no, we—realized that this platform may seem small, but it can have a real, wide impact. It's not a national talk show, but in some ways, it might be better than that because you can't change the channel. You know that the voices you just heard are your classmates, your siblings, your friends, your girlfriends, even your enemies. And no one would even wish that on their enemies, right?"

Looking around, I see heads shaking. She's captured their attention perfectly.

"In the US alone, 3.3 million women report that their first time having sex was rape," Elle says in a loud, clear voice. "And one in 16 women's first sexual experience isn't consensual."

"Every 73 seconds, an American is sexually assaulted."

She pauses.

"Sexual assault isn't just rape—it doesn't 'not count' if you're 'just fooling around,' or you 'didn't think' she wasn't into it," Elle continues, adding air quotes for emphasis. "It can include bullying or pressuring someone into doing something that they're not ready for, and using intimidation or violence to get what you want. That's scary enough, but what I recently learned is that there's a category of harassment that may not be legally wrong, but it definitely is *ethically* wrong. I don't expect you to raise your hands, but how many of you have felt pressured to send a nude photo or have phone sex or let a guy stick his hand up your shirt?"

I can see girls in the audience whispering to each other, nodding along slightly, and a few even raise their hands in the air.

"And after you do, if you do, give in to that, how many of you have had that guy show the photo to his friends?"

More nods.

"It's not as uncommon as I thought it was," Elle says. "And I'll be honest, it happened to me recently. I thought a guy would only like me if I gave him what he asked for, and shocker, when I did, I felt like absolute shit... sorry," she says, looking at the secretary, who's looking perturbed, but that may just be the topic, not the profanity. Either way, she doesn't seem like she's going to stop us.

"And guess what? He didn't magically fall madly in love with me. Nothing changed, other than the fact that I'd given up this power I had and gave him something to hold over my head. He could send it all over school if he wanted, print it and put it on a flyer, or show all his buddies. Luckily, he hasn't, and luckily, I was at least smart enough to sort of protect my identity. But what I didn't expect was how violated I would feel, how ashamed I felt of myself. I didn't feel liberated or sexy, I felt like I had let myself down. I felt dirty, I felt like I would deserve it if he did show the whole school."

"And that is absolute bullshit, by the way," she adds, vehemently. "Sorry again. But that's a huge part of why so many assaults go unreported and I'm sick of feeling like I'm the one who did something wrong. Something kind of dumb? Absolutely. But wrong? What he did, pushing over and over for the photos, *that* was the wrong thing."

A few girls in the middle of the crowd start applauding wildly as Elle pauses to gulp in air, her face looking a little redder under the lights, partially from exertion, partially emotion, and I'm sure a little embarrassment at that admission. I know how hard it was for her to talk about and we considered not bringing it up, but we decided it was a huge part of our talk. It's not just the big things: the little moments like that can destroy someone's self-esteem and really mess them up. We wanted to let girls know that no matter how trivial something like that feels, it matters. They matter.

And that's my cue.

"One out of every six women in the US has been the victim of an attempted or completed rape in her lifetime," I say as Miss C clicks to the next slide that just reads '1 in 6.'

"Many of us are leaving for college next year, and the statistics for rape on campuses are even scarier," I say, trying to control the shaking in my voice and focusing my eyes on the very back of the auditorium while simultaneously trying to look like I'm scanning the crowd and making eye contact, as per our public speaking teacher's advice. It's not going so well, so I pause for a split second to refocus, opting to look towards the back only.

"But just as scary are the new pressures that we face every day, the decisions that are often taken out of our hands. Most of you heard rumors about me in the past couple of weeks. The rumors are true—sort of. I did get caught hooking up with a guy in the woods, but it wasn't consensual. Would I call it assault? Probably not, since when I shoved him away, he didn't push back. But I never said yes, I wasn't asking for it, I wasn't part of the decision. And that lack of a yes—guys, take note—is a no."

"Only 20 percent of female victims report the assault to law enforcement, so even these terrifying statistics are heavily flawed," I add. "Of the 75 call-ins we got, only two said that they told an adult what happened. And those other 73 are the girls who are brave enough to come forward at all—there are more. So many more."

I step back from the mic. That was my major piece and I'm so relieved that it's over that I almost turn and walk off stage before remembering that I'm stuck there while we conclude.

"It shouldn't be our job as women to be the only ones standing up for ourselves," Elle says, smoothly slotting in as the next slide flashes to read '4X.' From the age of 16 to 19, women are four times more likely to be victims of sexual assault compared to any other time in their life. Those victims are four times more likely to have problems with drug abuse, and are four times more likely to have PTSD as a result. Think about that happening to the girls in your class, on your team, in your own household."

"How can you help?" she asks the crowd. I have to say, they're riveted—guys included. "You can stop laughing and joking about a girl being a 'slut,' in fact, you can stop calling girls 'sluts' altogether. You can tell your friend who's showing off naked photos that that's not cool.

You can take no for an answer. You can help the girls who are speaking out by believing them."

"You, every single one of you, has the chance to do the right thing—legally, morally, ethically. I hope you're up to the challenge."

Elle doesn't drop the mic but she might as well have.

It's a solid finish and even I'm impressed with her delivery. She punched the words just right. There's utter silence for a few painfully slow beats, and then the applause starts. The crowd doesn't go wild, but they do stand up and cheer for us. There are a few students and teachers who don't stand up, but even most of them grudgingly do after almost everyone else has stood. And thankfully, the bell rings at that moment, allowing the auditorium to quickly empty before the secretary or a teacher can come in with any final words that would make our presentation feel less powerful, or cut the mood.

"They'll be talking about this all day," Elle says to me, and I grin.

"Let them."

chapter
forty-seven

Elle

MY BODY WAITS until we're off the stage to start completely breaking down in a shaking fit, and next to me, Krista looks just about as exhausted and frazzled.

Miss C comes rushing up to us backstage. "You did a great job," she says—not in a super-enthusiastic way. She seems really subdued. But she shakes both of our hands like we're actual adults, and tells us she's proud.

"So, what should we do next?" Krista asks as we gather our stuff to leave the auditorium. It's hard to believe we still have a couple of periods of class left to go, though mine are all study halls and open times today.

"Wanna blow off the rest of the day and go for another run?" I ask, unsure of why those words decided to come out of my mouth. "I'd rather be in the woods then dealing with stares for the rest of the day, I'm tired. And also wired, though. Like I chugged espresso."

"Same," Krista says. "Let's do it."

Five minutes later, we've both made the switch into spandex and slipped out the doors and to the trailhead.

"I can't believe you're the one who thought we should cut class, and go for a run," Krista says as we start padding down the trail.

"I know, who would have thought?" I say, already feeling breathless. My heart rate still hasn't come down from the speech and I hoped that would be a good warm up. It wasn't. "I just had all this nervous energy and if we didn't run, I think I was going to explode."

"I know that feeling," Krista says. "I still can't believe we did that."

"You did great," I say. "Let's be honest, we are both seriously brave, tough women."

She smiles. "True. Now we just need to not get suspended for inappropriate language and topics, or for posting to the school newspaper website without permission, and we need to crush it at the big running meet. So, business as usual."

I laugh. "I think you mean *you* need to crush it at the meet. Personally, I will be happy with just finishing, not having to drag your ass across the line."

"I think we're both hoping for that," she says dryly. "I never thought I would want to be competitive at anything, but I just really want to crush this race."

"You're competitive at the paper," I say, and she looks confused.

"How do you mean?"

"You're editor-in-chief and you write most of the articles and you have your column," I point out. "Tell me you didn't have to apply and argue for that position? Just because you chose an avenue that doesn't have rankings or a voting system like a sport or student council doesn't mean you're not competitive. It just means you prefer being kind of sneaky about how competitive you are."

She smirks at me. "I guess that's true, I just never thought about it like that," she muses. "If I could crush my deputy editor in the application process, I should be able to be competitive in a race... on purpose this time."

We spend the next 45 minutes running mostly in silence, as I marvel about the fact that I'm actually running for more than a few minutes at a time, winding around sections of trail that are so full of twists and turns that normally, one of us would be tripping over a root or running into a tree, but we're flowing nearly flawlessly and it feels beautiful.

By the time we make it back to the school, classes are done for the day and the parking lot has emptied out. "Want a ride home?" Krista asks, checking her watch. "My mom should be here in a few minutes."

"That would be great," I say. I don't really want to ask at the risk of sounding mushy or making something more dramatic than it needs to be, but I can't help it. "We can still train together and stuff, right? Like, after this is all over?" I realized as we got back that really, our work together is done. There will be some aftermath with the school, I'm sure, but for the most part, we can go our separate ways. But I don't think I want to.

"I guess," Krista says casually. But I think I know her well enough to know when she's happy about something—or, at least, not unhappy about something. And she's definitely okay with this.

chapter
forty-eight

Krista

KRISTA'S RACE DAY PLANNER

9:00PM Pack bag. Shoes, water bottle, extra clothes, snacks, hair tie, big headphones, outfit for post-race podium ceremony, hair brush for same.

9:15PM Bedtime.

5:30AM Alarm set. (Ramones)

5:45AM Eat breakfast. Coffee (duh), bagel with peanut butter and jam. Read something relaxing or watch *Buffy*.

6:15AM Get dressed. Shorts + sports bra, sweats and hoodie over. Comfy shoes.

. . .

6:20AM Poop.

6:30AM Leave house with Mom, head to race.

7:15AM Arrive, time to hit bathroom, get number, say hi to Miss C, get warmed up, race. DO NOT ENGAGE WITH COACH OR TALK ABOUT JESS TO ANYONE. WEAR BIG HEADPHONES.

Warm up: 3 Sex Pistols songs, easy jog with 5 sets of 20-second pickups, ending with Anarchy in the UK as walk-up-to-line music (in head obviously, weird if played out loud), hand off headphones to Mom then.

9:00AM Race. Win? Try.

When I wake up the morning after our speech, it's well before the alarm goes off, but I can't sleep. At the same time, I feel like I've been run over by a truck. It's like I have the emotional flu. I've never put so much out in the open, never had to deal with so much staring and whispering from everyone when we came back from our run to pick up our backpacks. And in a weird way, the assholes who snarled at Elle and I and said they didn't believe us and we were liars were the easier ones to deal with. They're just wrong. The ones who felt bad for us and seemed sympathetic were much harder to deal with. I assumed Elle would bask in that, but she seemed just as uncomfortable as me. And to make things even worse, at the end of the day, we came back from our run only to get bustled into a meeting with the principal, where Miss C, the guidance counselor and the principal were all sitting looking serious.

If it hadn't been for Miss C standing up for us as much as she did, the conference would have been more like a witch hunt, I'm sure of it—I could tell immediately that the guidance counselor was on edge since she ignored me when I tried to talk to her, and the principal was playing extreme defense, trying to avoid a potential scandal for the school. But Miss C refused to let either of them steamroll over Elle or I, and as we both told our stories for the second time that day, I didn't feel angry or sad or upset, I just started to feel numb.

But by the end of the talk, I think we turned the tide—the principal looked grim and told the guidance counselor that they would speak about it later and dismissed her, and then thanked us for our honesty and willingness to come forward with our stories. (You could tell that there was a bit of an unspoken 'but God, I wish you hadn't done it so publicly' behind it but to give him credit, he didn't voice that opinion.) And he nodded when Miss C called us brave.

I don't think they were happy, or even understood why we did it. Harden might be pissed at Miss C, but he can't exactly fire her—and if he did, between Elle's mom and our new media contacts who love us after that running video that started this whole cascade of events, I don't think she'd be out of her job for too long.

But Elle and I still both sort of stumbled out of his office after, feeling a little shell-shocked and frankly, disappointed because it feels like not a lot has changed other than the fact that we've upset a lot of people and made ourselves a combination of unpopular or, even worse, pitiable.

When I got home and Mom asked how it went, I just mumbled that it was fine and we could talk about it later, and for once, she didn't pry and pepper me with questions, just let me go to bed and crash. I never knew putting yourself out there emotionally would be as draining as doing a race.

And speaking of races, in just a few days, I'll be back in competition. As I haul myself out of bed, I also get hit with the realization that things on the team are going to change. Will Jess get kicked off? If he does, what happens to the team standings? What will racing be like without the ridiculous triangle that he created between Elle and I? And now that Elle and I made our statements, what happens to us? Are we supposed to go back to being enemies or besties? Do we still run together in practice or do I go out with the fast kids?

Suddenly, there are a lot more questions. I thought standing up for myself would be more fun and more liberating than this.

It certainly hasn't made me faster, that's for sure. So instead of sitting around and sulking, I pull on my tights and a sweatshirt and head out for an extremely early morning jog around the neighborhood—thankfully, our little development of townhouses is super-well-lit at night and loops around in an almost perfect one-kilometer loop, so I can do a few loops without the stress of running in the dark.

"Mom, I'm heading out for a run," I yell in the direction of her room as I tug on my sneakers, and I'm out the door before she can offer to go with me. With the sun still down, it's a little chillier out than I expected, but it's kind of a welcome change, a nice bracing wind to make me forget about the day, the week, the month and focus on one thing: this run. My feet pound nice and steadily on the pavement, my breathe comes out quickly but evenly, and I can see it in the air. It's crisp, and my hands are chilly, my nose is cold, but I feel wide awake and after the first loop, I can feel the cobwebs flying out of my brain.

Then, it's all business. I do one loop hard—hitting a four-minute kilometer and breathing like a locomotive—then I do one easy, one hard, one easy, one hard, and then a final cooldown lap. By the time I'm back to my door, I've done seven kilometers—around four miles—and

I'm sweating profusely but I feel fantastic. I don't know why I didn't start running years ago, because after that, I feel a little more refreshed and ready for the day.

Practices have been okay and racing has been fun, but I realize that solo runs in the dark might be the most appealing to my extremely introverted personality. I'm definitely going to work these into my regular training routine, I think to myself as I hit the shower to get ready for the day.

Chapter Forty-Eight

You probably heard us talking in the assembly yesterday, or if you didn't, you almost certainly heard about it. And if you're one of the people who's come up and told myself or my colleague just how sorry you are, thank you. We appreciate it. But here's the thing: We didn't do this for the sympathy.

We did this because we want change.

The only way we'll get it is if you help us. It's not enough to just tell us you're sorry or tell us your story. That's a start, it's a great first step, but it has to go beyond us. We want you to tell your counselor or teacher or the principal if something has happened to you. We want you to start petitions for better education on consent in health class. We want you to stand up for your friend who's too scared to speak up. We want you to take an action beyond just saying you're sorry that something happened.

If you don't, something will continue happening. You'll just keep saying sorry.

chapter
forty-nine

Elle

WHEN I WALK INTO SCHOOL, I'm expecting everything to be different. For some reason, I assumed they'd be replacing all of the anti-drug posters with anti-nudes posters, but that might have just been a really weird dream I had last night when I was tossing and turning. Which was most of the night, because it was pretty darn hard to relax after that whole debacle.

My mom was super proud though, so that's a plus. The minus, of course, is that she wanted to go to our favorite pizza place to celebrate, and finish off the night with a half-gallon of chocolate chip cookie dough ice cream, my absolute favorite.

At first, I didn't want to have a big meal—but then I remembered what Krista's mom said about making sure I fuel the work I'm doing, and I do plan on going to practice whether or not Jess is there. But over dinner, I told Mom that I wanted to start working with a therapist and a dietitian to figure out how to eat healthy, and she said she'd make some calls. She seemed proud about that too.

And yes, Jess is still in school. I guess the principal is stuck reviewing his case before he can actively suspend him, according to my mom. Jess's parents have already gotten him a lawyer, so it may get messy—a fact that Mom warned me about as I tried to drink a relaxing cup of tea to boost my spirits this morning. Come to think of it, I really should relay that message to Krista as well, since Mom seemed to think that it was going to mean we both had to talk to the principal *again*. So I text her to meet me by my locker, and predictably, she quickly texts back, 'Why?'

"I want to borrow your makeup," I type back.

I pause for a second before adding under it, "Jess stuff. Duh."

Three dots appear, then "two min" pops up, so I start hustling towards my locker.

She beats me there. "What is it?" she asks, looking around like she's afraid someone will notice us together, though I'm not sure if she's embarrassed about the Jess stuff or if she's just embarrassed to be seen with me for style reasons. It's probably a little of both, since I'm in a preppy chambray button down and nice dark blue jeans. It sounds a little Canadian tuxedo-y, but it looks stylish, I swear!

"Jess's parents hired a lawyer," I say before she can make any snide remarks about my outfit.

"Seriously?" she says, her face contorting into an angrier sneer than normal. "That little shit! What does he think they'll be able to do?"

"Probably avoid suspension," I say. "At least, that's what Mom said."

"Perfect. So what did we do all of this for, anyway?" she rants. "Some asshole lawyer is just going to habeas corpus that all away?"

"Umm, I don't think that's a thing," I say, but she's already on a tangent before I can add that he may just avoid suspension, but it's not like he can erase the collective minds of everyone in the school.

Still, it sucks. I interrupt her mid-stream of expletives, though, to divert her attention to something a bit more pressing. "Look, this sucks, but it's sort of out of our hands for the moment since we don't even know what he's going to do or what a lawyer will advise him," I say. "My mom says a smart lawyer will keep him away from suspension to look over the case, then advise that he take the week and the counseling and detention and just let it go. It's too hard to argue and he'll look like an even bigger dick if he did end up in court with us."

I almost don't say us and say 'you,' since technically, my sending him naked selfies is just as much my problem as it is his, legally speaking —a fact that Mom grimly explained to me last night, in one of the most awkward conversations ever. But I wouldn't let Krista have to face him in court alone if it came to that, embarrassment be damned. Besides, we've already fought over him on national television once, what does it matter if we do it again, just on the same side this time?

"Okay, I'll withhold freakout for a little while longer," she says, catching her breath. "I need to focus on the meet this weekend. And so do you," she says with a little grin.

Crap, the meet this weekend? I kind of forgot that I'd have to race again—in shorts and a tank top, ugh—in an even bigger race. At least last time I competed, I had a perfect excuse for sucking (Krista's ankle was my blessing in disguise). This time, it's going to just be me as a party of one at the back, huffing my way into the finish line. Fan-freaking-tastic.

As though she can read my mind, Krista grabs my shoulders and gives me a shake. "You're going to be fine," she says determinedly. "We are not going to let that idiot have the satisfaction of throwing either of us off of our racing game."

She says it with such conviction that for a second, I almost believe that I have racing game, until I remember who I am. Not a runner.

"Come on," she says. "You kept up with me on that run yesterday. And if you can give a speech like you did this week to the entire school, you can have lungs burning and aching legs for a couple of miles."

She's right. I gulp in a deep breath. "Well, I guess that means I can't skip practice today," I say, and admit that I was going to spend a couple of hours chilling in the library and avoiding people instead.

"I can't believe I'm even saying this, but we'll run together again today," Krista says. "I'll tell Miss C we're doing solo practice again, she'll absolutely be okay with it." With that, she stalks off to class, yelling over her shoulder to meet her at the trailhead 10 minutes after the bell.

The rest of the day flies by in a blur. Girls keep coming up to me and telling me stories that make me want to break down in sobs, while some guys give me dirty looks and a couple make snide comments. But for the most part, guys are either ignoring me or actually going out of their way to be polite, and not in an obnoxious way. A few even tell me that they were impressed by my speech, one admits that it didn't occur to him that asking someone to send nudes could be as hurtful as it was, and another actually told me that he was pressured to do some stuff he wasn't ready for.

Jan — that's right, our Chinese food delivery guy — even told me a horror story about a drunk woman who tried to grope him when he delivered her dinner. I couldn't believe when he sat down to tell me about it. We didn't say much after that, but I told him I was around if he wanted to talk, no egg roll drop-off required. He laughed about that and said maybe he would message me sometime, whatever that means.

Jenny whispered a thank you to both of us in the hall, but I don't think she was one of the girls who called in. I think she appreciated what we did though.

All of that doesn't exactly make it easy to get through the day without stressing, but I do what I can to stay calm. Funny enough, though, I don't really start feeling relaxed until Krista and I are a few minutes down the trail in the woods together, me huffing a bit to stay on her heels, neither of us saying anything.

It's still not easy, and I can feel my legs and lungs starting to protest, but for the first time in the day, my brain has shut off and I actually feel good. For 45 minutes, we just run along at a steady pace (fine, I run along at a steady pace, Krista attacks hills like they stole something from her and then jogs back down to finish them with me). By the time we loop back to school, I feel like a whole new woman, and we haven't even said a word to each other.

I feel stronger, sweatier and more determined than ever, but I don't tell Krista that. Instead, I say a quick thanks and that I'll see her later before heading towards my locker to grab my backpack, texting Mom that I'll be heading home on the late bus in a minute. I grab my backpack, throw on a sweatshirt and rush to jump on the bus right before it closes. A few of my friends from student council huddle in the back giggling, and I'm tempted to join them, but I want to get some thoughts down in my journal before I forget them.

After the first hill on the run, when I wanted to stop and walk, a phrase kept running through my brain:

Quiet determination.

I didn't want to complain, I didn't want to crack a joke about how much I hate hills or how much I suck at them. I didn't want to get in a conversation about the right way or wrong way to run up. I just wanted to get to the top, my own way.

I think I might have a new mantra.

Chapter Forty-Nine

Elle's Race Day Planner

2 days before: Pack bag. Sneakers, water bottle, granola bar, purple tights with maroon zip up for after race, extra scrunchies, AirPods, hair brush, puffy coat, soothing playlist and boring podcast downloaded as well as pump-up playlist.

10PM Bedtime.

5:30AM Alarm set. (Taylor Swift)

6:15AM Get dressed. Shorts + sports bra, sweats and hoodie over. Comfy shoes.

6:30AM Leave house with Mom, head to race. Eat breakfast in the car—half a bagel, lots of water.

7:15AM Arrive. Get number, warm up. Remember what Krista says: <u>Do not</u> engage with Coach or talk about Jess to anyone.
Warm up: 10 min light jog, few speedy moments.

9:00AM Survive.

chapter
fifty

Krista

THE WEEKEND ROLLED ENTIRELY TOO QUICKLY for me—one minute, I was walking around school and feeling like a zombie, trying to ignore my classmates whispering, *definitely* ignoring the comments on the school blog, trying to just go through the motions.

The saving grace has been that since that first day when Jess made his surprise appearance at school, he either hasn't been back or he's managed to stay out of my way. I heard a rumor that a couple of other girls talked to the guidance counselor about him and that this time, she actually listened. (Or was mandated to by the school board.) But I'm not sure, because they didn't come to me. Not that I expected them to or would have wanted them to. I know Elle and I are closer because of all of this, but that doesn't mean I want to be the ringleader of a support group or a lynch mob against Jess. I just want to go back to what I do best: writing. Or, in today's case, running.

Even though it's Saturday and I should be getting to sleep in, my alarm blares ridiculously early. If Mom has taught me one thing, it's that you don't want to eat breakfast too close to race time, so here I am, up before it's light out, sitting in the kitchen in my baggy sweats and chowing down on my bagel. It's delicious but annoying.

Thankfully, Mom is doing enough talking for both of us and wisely doesn't comment on my decision/desperation to have a second cup of coffee with a sprinkle of cinnamon and nutmeg in it, basic-B commentary about pumpkin spice be damned. Mom is running through the day's schedule, offering suggestions for what I should wear over my shorts and singlet for warm up, ways to mobilize my ankle before the start, what my early race strategy should be and where she should stand on the course. It's in a park she used to run in a lot more when we lived on the other side of town, so she knows it pretty well, and after a vicious debate with herself, she decides that the best vantage point will be around mile 1 so that she'll have plenty of time to cheer for me before running back to the finish line so she can be there when I come through after three miles.

It's a good plan, but I think all of her concern is stressing me out more, so I subtly try to ignore her in favor of re-reading *The Devil Wears Prada*, my de-stressing book despite the incredibly stressful scenarios presented in it. Honestly, after this year, Miranda Priestly doesn't scare me at all. And yes, I know I'm supposed to be too cool to want to read about high fashion. But high fashion, when you really look at what's on the runways, is super alternative. It's fascinating—and while I see myself running an edgier fashion and music magazine in 10 years, I know I'll have to pay my dues at some of the more generic publications if I want to make a name for myself.

It's only 6:30 when we head out of the house with huge duffel bags with enough clothes for a week, even though we'll be home before dinner. I'm already wearing my racing outfit, but with my big sweatpants and a hoodie over top—it's chilly out this morning. But by 9, the temperatures should be over 45 degrees, which means I'll still race in sleeveless and shorts. It's a bold move, since a lot of people elect to wear long sleeves and tights if it's under 60 degrees, but I think I'll be faster if I'm a little chilly to start, and my kit makes me feel more like a real runner than my tights do.

Mom is quiet on the drive, but that's only because she's made me a pump-up playlist of some of her favorite Riot Grrrl bands from the mid to late 90s, plus some more generic Spice Girls and Britney Spears. It's a weird mix but time flies and by the time we're rolling into the park, we're both singing "Spice Up Your Life" at the top of our lungs, completely un-ironically. It's the least cool moment I've ever had and I love it.

The cool fall air when I step out of the car makes it a little hard to catch my breath and my enthusiasm starts to fade into a bit of pre-race panic. I want to do well in this race so bad that I can taste it, and even though my ankle has felt great for a while now, there's almost a phantom pain in place, like a ghost of injuries' past warning me that maybe I'm not ready for this. I shake my head, and then do a full body shiver, mentally warning myself to relax and reset.

I plug in my earbuds and wave goodbye to Mom. I told her I'd see her at the start line but that I wanted to do my own thing pre-race. It's too distracting having her hover. She didn't seem to mind and mumbled something about meeting up with Elle's mom. I gave her the evil eye at that, but she gave me the most innocent look she could muster.

And of course, as my mom hunts down my (mostly former) arch-nemesis's mother to hang out with/hit on, I end up nearly running smack into Elle as she turns a corner heading towards race registration. We have to pick up our own bib numbers this week unless we came with the team, and since both of us decided we had no interest in riding the bus with teammates who may or may not hate our guts since our star runner has been suspended from the team thanks to Miss C pushing the issue, we both opted to be driven to the race. And now, we seem to be back in each other's path. Elle looks so lost and confused that I can't help but offer an olive branch.

"Are you warming up yet?" I ask, looking at my watch—about an hour until race start, a good time to start moving around and thinking about racing.

She shakes her head, and for once, doesn't have a ton to contribute to the non-conversation that we're having. I'm about to turn and start jogging away, but my conscience gives me a kick and I find myself saying, "Do you want to jog around a bit?"

"Okay," she says, a little robotically. It's like she has serious stage fright all of a sudden, which seems ridiculous for someone who just stood up in front of the entire student body confidently, telling a story that could have been more embarrassing for her than it was for Jess.

Chapter Fifty

But then again, even the thought of doing public speaking gives me the jitters, while the start line at this race is just making me feel more excited by the minute, so I guess everyone just has their different capabilities. I start walking over towards the 1-kilometer trail that's been designated as the warm-up loop to try to keep kids off the actual race course, swinging my arms a bit more than usual to try to get some blood flowing into them. I'm a little stiff from the car ride and the biting cold (and a little bit of nerves of my own too), but after a couple minutes of walking together with Elle in silence, I can feel my system start to warm up.

When we hit the trail, I break into a very slow jog—no sprints or random drills quite yet. Elle huffs along next to me, our breath making little fog clouds that we're running into. We both have headphones on, and while I assume she's rocking out to Taylor Swift now, since she looks a bit happier and calmer, I'm jamming to River City Rebels, one of the corny ska bands that my mom used to listen to.

One lap down, Elle taps my shoulder. "We're done warming up, right?" she asks, looking nervously at her watch. "We only have 35 minutes until race start, shouldn't we head over there?"

"One more lap," I tell her. "We only need to be there 15 minutes beforehand, so we'll do a few sprints, then jog over. My mom can take your stuff at the line if you need her to."

Taking gear at the line is usually Miss C's job—she grabs all the team's sweatshirts and jackets so we don't have to leave them sitting on the grass while we race. But today, with how many students are here and the disorganization that's happened since Coach, along with Jess, isn't at the race... Well, I just figured I might be better fending for myself and not relying on school spirit to make today a success. Honestly, I don't know why I'm offering my mom's help, but I know how much Elle likes her, and I'm hoping that calms her down. (I'm telling myself that I don't care that she's calm so much as her freaked out demeanor is throwing me off. So if I can keep her calm, I'll stay calm too. It's not about being nice.)

"Thanks," she says. "Mom said she'd be there but it's good to have backup."

We do one more loop and my legs are feeling great—the three quick sprints we do feel effortless, like I'm flying on the trail. I know better than to start feeling over-confident, considering that's how we ended up on a national talk show embarrassing the hell out of ourselves last time, but I do feel pretty darn good and ready to put up a fight.

Before we head to the start line, we detour at the park's bathroom to pee one more time. I do a quick check in the mirror. I know it's not traditional, but I wanted to feel more like me on the start line today, so I'm wearing super-long-lasting dark red lipstick and tons of waterproof black mascara, and my hair is looking brighter white than ever since I used waterproof eyebrow powder to darken my brows to almost black. And instead of pigtail braids, I had mom help French braid my hair into more of a crown around my head, like an alternative Heidi. Basically, I look like a goth-y cartoon from the neck up and I love it.

I don't want to blend in this time. I want to stand out.

We make our way to the start line, and both of our moms are already there, looking nervous. We still have 15 minutes until the start, but this is the point in the race day where it starts to get a bit hectic and the girls start casually inching their way towards the front row. There aren't call-ups in the race, with the exception that each school gets to put one student in the front row.

Unfortunately, that is not going to be me thanks to my lack of racing. Jenny will get that spot. So I need to be ready to slide into the second row if I want to have a good start.

The front row is called to staging. The crowd gets thicker, and I can see girls giving each other slightly violent looks. My mom catches my eye. "Elbows out," she mouths. Mom might be a bit of a hippie in some aspects, but she's also a hardcore racer and a former punk who spent a lot of time getting punched in mosh pits. It's a weird dichotomy, because while normally she looks like she could be leading a meditation retreat, right now, she looks like she wants to start throwing punches at the other moms and possibly the runners, then jump into the starting grid herself. Elle's mom looks similarly intense. (*Elle must be panicking*, I think for a moment. I've lost sight of her in the crowd. But I shake my head, hard. No time for that now.)

As I slot in right behind Jenny in the front row, she actually turns around and says good luck to me. I say it back, and mean it. I still want to kick her ass though.

I feel a nudge at my side. Great, the elbows out have started already. But then I realize it's like Elle materialized out of thin air just because I thought about her. "Crush it," she says in a low voice. We lock eyes and I nod. She fades back a bit into the crowd, probably because she's scared of getting trampled as everyone surges at the start.

In a small way, doing well in this race feels like it would be payback to Jess. It would send a message to our team that he wasn't the only important runner—he might have been holding the girl's team back, honestly. Jenny's potential without boy drama alone could push our team to some serious wins. I know that's what Elle is thinking. But I only care about that so much: I want to crush this race for myself, because I think I might actually love this sport.

So, I stay firm in my spot in the second row, which is easier said than done since there are about 40 of us jockeying for a 10-woman-wide section of grass. We're so crammed in that I feel like when the gun goes off, if I just hop up a bit, I'll be carried forward along the grass without running a single step.

When the ref shouts that it's two minutes to the start, I make eye contact with my mom, who looks a bit green now. My heart rate, which had been reasonable until this point, starts to spike and I can feel the nerves moving up from my stomach and into my throat. My head feels like it's buzzing a little. All I can think is, 'Can we please get moving?'

This is easily the worst part of any race. Tom Petty was right: the waiting *is* the hardest part.

"30 seconds," the ref yells, removing the tape from across the start line. Everyone tenses, shifting their weight onto their front feet and adjusting their elbows to be primed to go. It's that Eye of the Tiger moment. Now, I just have to deliver, I think—and try to set my feet properly. I look around one last time. I'm definitely the outlier in this group, a punk among normies, but that doesn't matter now. What matters is how fast I can get my feet to turnover when the gun goes off.

And then it does. It blares and suddenly, we're on the move.

The start happens so fast that I don't have time to think about what's happening, I'm just running like my life depends on it, hanging on the heels of the girls who started in the front row. It feels like I'm going all out, like there's no way I can hold this pace, but I do—for the first 10 seconds, then another 10, and another. And mercifully, I'm still in the lead pack after the first 30 seconds and the pace slows just enough that I can stay in it. I should have prepared better for this, I should have remembered what the race starts felt like—my internal dialogue is going into overdrive thinking back to all of our practices, and how I could have focused on starts a little more. I'm gasping for air.

Then, the pace relaxes even more and I realize that I'm still with the leaders, still hurting but not feeling as bad as I was a few seconds ago. And my internal voice is still running different training scenarios in my head, things I could be doing better. Abruptly, I shake my head—which makes the girl sprinting along next to me look sideways at me. "Get a grip," I tell myself sternly. "You're right where you're supposed to be."

I knew that this could happen: my thoughts would start catastrophizing and assuming the worst, but really, no one could have felt good in that start. I risk a glance over my shoulder as we crest the first small hill on the course and see that the group of ten of us has a small gap to the next runners. We seem to collectively agree on our next move and punch it into an even higher gear on the slight downhill and again, my breathing and heart rate are sent into a frenzy. But I try to control my thoughts.

This time, my internal monologue manages to stay excited for me, and I feel inspired by the little voice in my head screaming GO instead of freaked out.

At the one mile mark, Mom is waiting where she promised to be and bursts into a huge round of cheers as we sail by. I want to look at her, smile or wave, but all I can focus on is the fact that snot and drool are dripping down my face and I'm sweating. I don't know how the girls who opted for tights and long sleeves are surviving.

When we hit the next corner, I realize that our group has gone from 10 girls to a couple less, maybe eight. I can't get a perfect count, but I don't see Jenny or the other fast girl from our school in the pack anymore. My mind goes into mean girl mode for a second as I think how much I want to be the top girl from our school, beating out the one girl who I overheard tell some of our other teammates that Elle and

I were lying, jealous skanks (her words, not mine). So yeah, victory over her would be sweet. I wouldn't mind beating Jenny, either, come to think of it. But I also know we have just under three kilometers left to run and a lot can happen in that time, meaning we very well might meet again.

Eyes straight ahead. I almost let the girl in front of me open a gap as she neatly sails over a branch that's down in the middle of the trail, and my stumble over it is far from graceful, but I speed up for a couple of seconds and regain contact. (Mom told me the best thing to do in any race is to maintain that contact—it's apparently in-race suicide to let yourself get gapped, because once you do, it's super hard to get back up in the field.)

We're barely at the halfway point when I feel my legs start to protest almost as loudly as my lungs. It was right around this point where I stumbled and twisted my ankle in the first race of the season, so I know that I'm entering uncharted racing territory for me, and being in the lead group makes that feel all the more obvious. I'm surrounded by only those few girls and they're all looking fierce and comfortable at the front. By comparison, I'm almost having an out-of-body experience and imagining exactly how weird I must look loping along with them, snot and drool running down my face, looking like I belong mid-pack or back with the other kids who didn't really give a crap about actually doing a school sport. For a moment, I feel like putting on the brakes and going back to another, easier group. Why do I care about this sport anyway?

Thankfully, just as I'm about to pull the plug and let myself fall back to catch my breath, we hit another downhill and the pace eases up—or, at least, the effort level eases up while the pace stays high. I risk another glance over my shoulder and see that we're far enough ahead that the group behind us still hasn't hit the descent. I can't drop back now.

There are only six of us still in this group, I count, and now we only have two kilometers to go. I'm surprisingly able to focus on faces, and realize with a shock that Jenny hasn't come back to this main group. I thought she would have made connection by now. At the pace we're running, there's under eight minutes of sheer pain left in the race, and the fact that I'm able to do the math tells me that I can and should keep pushing. I'm not quite seeing red yet, but there's orange haze in my peripheral vision. Volunteers are cheering for us at the next corner and we all hit it aggressively.

Too aggressively, I realize, and I actually nearly take myself out as I run a little too tight to the inside line and almost fall into the ditch. The stumble forces me off the trail and into the brush, and I can feel thorns pricking into my ankles as I leap my way back up onto the course, thankfully not losing contact with the last girl in the pack.

As I run next to her—we're lined up in twos now, on the thin doubletrack straight that will take us to the lakeside where we'll know we're only 500 meters from the finish—I realize she's breathing just as hard as I am. I feel a bit of wetness hit my cheek and realize it's snot from the girl in front of me and I almost gag, but can't quite feel any anger about it. If I was in front of her, she'd be in a rainstorm of snot. It's not personal.

Seconds pass. The group keeps holding the pace now. Earlier, we had some experimental surges of speed but now, the six of us realize we're close enough to the finish that burning a sprinting match now would torpedo chances for the win. I didn't realize just how much I wanted to be the winner until this moment—and the lake hovers into view.

The pace picks up for a second as we all spot it, but slows again. It's not time to go all-out yet. 500 meters doesn't sound like much but it's still four football fields. Anything could happen.

We hit the hardpacked sand, and the blond with the streaming braid's shoulders snap back and she bolts off. Instantly, the girl with the black hair neatly tied in a ponytail is on her heels, and the rest of us surge abruptly to stay with them. Ponytail falls back—her attack failed, but she's not out of the game yet.

My heart is pounding like we already crossed the finish line, and I know it's far from over. My legs and lungs feel like they might explode. I can hear cheering, and it's like the exertion and effort has made me laser-focused so that I can hear my mom, I can hear Miss C, and I can hear our entire team screaming my name.

This is my chance. I abruptly pull out of our two-by-two-by-two formation and blaze up the side, going so fast that I can feel the sand giving way and kicking up behind me. I catch the group unaware—maybe they never thought I'd still be with them, maybe the girls at the front assumed I'd already fallen behind. But suddenly, I have a gap. It's probably not even a full second and I still have 300 meters to go but I'm sprinting with all I have and despite the blood rushing in my ears, I can hear the shrieking of the crowd as I make my charge for the finish line.

chapter
fifty-one

Elle

SO, I wasn't going to win. I mean, no one thinks that would happen, so it's not really shocking anyone to admit that at the start. But I did want to try. Honestly, when I lined up at the start, I didn't feel like an imposter on the line.

I felt like a runner.

When the gun went off and the group surged forward, I was right there in the mix, pounding up the hill, feeling my lungs expand and contract painfully as I stomped my way up, slip-sliding on the dew-covered grass.

I don't know why I thought that this race would go any differently than the first, but I actually tried to sprint along with the group, letting their collective energy carry me through the first couple of hills. As girls dropped back behind me, I almost couldn't believe it. I wasn't sitting in last.

As I hit the one mile marker, Krista's mom shouts for me and jumps up and down, and I feel a rush of happiness. At least someone will be proud of me for simply finishing. And for once, I don't feel like I'm the out of shape, pudgy one embarrassing the team. I actually feel like I'm running a race, not looking for an excuse (or an injured teammate/frenemy) to help me avoid having to schlub my way across the finish line. My shoulders have pulled back and my head is held high—and I feel like I'm actually racing.

It isn't pretty. By the first mile, I had snot dripping from my nose like someone had turned a faucet on, and could barely swallow because I was gasping for air so hard. But I was freaking *moving*.

Up the trail, I can see the group of just a few runners pulling away from the rest of us, and I think I spot Krista in the group. I'm a little jealous of her, but since I never actually anticipated having a chance of winning, I'm not exactly feeling too stressed about it. I'm more just thrilled that I'm still running after a few minutes. And I have her to thank, mostly, so I'm cheering her on silently.

I want to say that the race goes by in a blur, but that's not exactly the case. It goes by in a fairly painful haze of exhaustion though, which is sort of the same thing. My mom is at kilometer three, screaming at me to go harder. I think she means it in a nice, helpful way, even if it sounds a little too angry for my personal preference.

A minute after we hit the four kilometer mark, there's a wide opening at the top of the hill. And I can see that the lead group—now just a few of them—are down by the lake at the very end of the course. I know I shouldn't stand to watch, but I can see Krista still in the pack as they hit the sand, and they're only seconds from the finish. I look behind me. There are a few girls who are closing in on me, but I think I can hold them off even if I wait. And I really want to see how it ends.

Suddenly, Krista dives out to the outside of the pack and makes her move and I completely freeze, before embarrassing myself and jumping up and down shrieking, showing that clearly I have energy to spare, even if my legs are exhausted.

She's going to do it, I think. She's going to win the damn thing. And for a few strides, it seems like no one can even respond. She gets a couple of meters ahead, when one of the blond racers, the one in the orange singlet, her hair in pigtail braids (I hated her the minute I saw her) busts out from the front of the group and sprints up to join her.

For a second, when Krista notices that she has another racer next to her, she tries to attack, but with only 100 meters to the finish, the blond counters her easily. They're running side by side, racing to the finish line. The other girls are now meters behind and it's just Krista and the blond.

The seconds stretch into what feels like hours as Krista's arms are pumping wildly and her feet are kicking up a sand cloud behind her. I can sense the other racers closing in on me, but I don't care.

"GO, KRISTA, GOOOOO!" I scream, but I know she can't hear me. They smash into the final meters, almost touching, and I think she has it.

Then, the blonde lunges.

I've never seen anything like it. She must be a beach volleyball player or something in her off season, because her body arcs through the air like she's going in for a digger to hit the ball, but her fingertips just snare the tape a millisecond before Krista breaks through on the other side. I feel like my vision has never been clearer, I can almost feel Krista's disappointment, can feel how she's feeling.

And then, I snap back to the moment, and I can hear the breathing from the girls making their way up the hill. I was only stopped for a few seconds, in reality, but it feels like I've had a break and am about to start a whole new race. And I do—I bolt down the hill, feeling like I'm flying, channeling that finish line energy. I can feel my hair streaming out behind me, I can feel my whole body pounding up and down as I power down the hill and carry the momentum into a right turn onto the flat section that signifies the final kilometer of racing. I've lost the girls behind me, and the girls who I was with before I paused are suddenly in view again, not too far ahead.

I lower my head and charge. In seconds, I'm on their heels, and we burst out into the sand and sunlight, our feet churning up the beach as we move as a single unit. I still feel like I'm flying, still moving on this sudden newfound energy.

I edge around to the side of the group, and realize that I'm more than okay to run around them. I speed up to the front of the herd. I'm in the lead.

We hit the final stretch, just 25 meters to the finish according to the sign.

My breath is coming in short, hard bursts as I pick my feet up as high as I can, pumping my arms furiously.

When I hit the finish line ahead of my group, I feel absolutely elated. No, I didn't win, but I did more than I thought I could. And I don't even have the chance to collapse, because Krista has grabbed me in a huge hug before I have a moment to catch my breath. And that, more than anything else, takes my breath away more than any sprint would.

Are we best friends?

I doubt it. But at the moment, I'm thrilled beyond belief. Miss C and my mom and Krista's mom are elbowing their way through the crowd as well, and we're suddenly all hugging and crying at the same time. More than just a race, it feels like we've put a dramatic finish on a terrible season, ending on a high point.

Sure, I admit, I was secretly hoping to surprise myself and come out in the top ten or something somewhat miraculous, but from the first minute of the race, I realized that wasn't happening. Still, I finished and I wasn't last, I wasn't huffing and puffing (too much) and that feels good.

I put out my hand for a high five and Krista smacks it hard. "Amazing job!" she says, and really means it.

"You too," I say. "You almost had it!"

"Ehh, it was better than I expected," she says, looking a little bummed but not as disappointed as I would have thought she'd be.

"You should both be proud," Miss C says. "For so many reasons."

On the ride home, I'm definitely not expecting Mom to be as happy as she is, but she seems genuinely proud of me. I guess she really is okay with me trying my hardest, even if my hardest isn't nearly as fast as I'm sure she'd prefer. I can tell she's trying to come up with honest compliments without lying about how talented I am at running. I know I'm not, and that's just fine with me. But I am weirdly enjoying it—and I think I'll keep doing it, even if I don't need the extra extracurriculars. And even if it'll annoy Krista. Let's be real, I'm mainly doing it because it'll annoy Krista.

After we've dissected the race as much as any human possibly can—God, Mom should get a job as a sports broadcaster!—she abruptly changes the subject.

"So, we don't talk about your dad very much," she says, and I can tell she's trying to sound casual, but she's clenching the steering wheel a teensy bit too hard. She's clearly nervous, and now, so am I.

"And?" I say, trying to figure out where she's going with this.

"I just wondered if you'd been hearing from him lately," she says. "I know he's gone in and out of touch over the years, and I know that can't be easy for you."

It's the first time in a long time that she's mentioned Dad in a very long time, and I'm completely confused. I don't really hear from him, nor do I care to.

"I haven't talked to him in a while," I say. "Why do you care all of a sudden? You never talk about him."

"Well, you know him not being in touch has nothing to do with you, right?" She asks. "It's just him. And I know I can't be both of your parents, but I hope you'll let me know if you have something you're afraid to talk to me about."

"I know, Mom," I say. "We've been over this so many times. As far as I'm concerned, you're my number one go-to parent."

"You're not still secretly hoping that your dad and I get back together?" she asks, and I'm astonished.

"Absolutely not," I say. "What am I, six years old and still believing in Santa? That would be a total disaster. And besides, I love our life the way it is. No boys allowed, right?"

She laughs, but it's a little shaky. "You have no idea," she says. And then, she turns the radio up, signaling that we're officially done with this awkward mess of a conversation.

But before I can totally let her off the hook, I realize I have the chance to be the mature one here. Clearly, she's asking about Dad for a reason. "Mom, you know I'd be okay if you started dating again, right?" I say, trying my hardest to keep my face on the positive side of neutral.

"Thanks, hon," she says, and she looks a teensy bit shifty, like she's hiding something. But she turns the volume up even louder, and I realize that whatever she has on her mind is definitely not up for discussion yet.

chapter
fifty-two

Krista

BACK IN THE REAL WORLD, life isn't quite as neat and tidy as it was in the race. There aren't clear winners and losers, or a finishing time. It turns out that Jess's lawyer has recommended that he not fight the suspension, which is a good thing, and he's out for the rest of the season from the team. It won't look good on his college applications, Elle's mom tells us, and I admit, I feel a brief pang of guilt over that. There are a lot of good memories with him from when we were kids, and even this year before everything went sideways—but I try to swallow that guilt and remember that it's not my fault at all.

The guidance counselor at school has been replaced by one who actually specializes in dealing with sexual assault and harassment, not just resumes and college applications, and I've been talking to her a fair bit. It helps.

But what helps the most is that cross-country practice is now led by Miss C since Coach 'retired early,' (AKA 'was forced out by the school board') and even though there aren't any more races on the calendar for the season, I'm still there every afternoon, and so is Elle.

The day before he left, Coach came over to us after practice and apologized. It was awkward and gruff and I don't think he meant a word of it, but at least the other kids on the team got to see it happen and I think it made them a little less pissed at us since even Coach admitted to some wrong-doing.

However, Miss C, as it turns out, is a brutal taskmaster. What Coach had in gruffness and a hard-man-style of work ethic is nothing on her matter-of-fact take on sprint intervals, longer post-workout stretch sessions, and shorter, harder hill repeats. Having her take over has probably made the team faster, so it's too bad it didn't happen earlier in the season.

Even as we line up for our warmup strides now, she yells at us to drop and do ten pushups.

"Are knee pushups okay?" Elle asks, dropping down.

"Absolutely not," Miss C says. "Here, come use a bleacher and stand and put your hands on this first step."

"Why can't I do knees?" Elle asks.

"This will teach you to eventually do an actual pushup, knees won't," Miss C promises.

"But I don't want to do an actual pushup," Elle points out.

"Tough," Miss C tells her, and blows the whistle. "One. Two. Three..." she counts off as we dutifully work our way through the pushups. I collapse after five. Turns out all the running in the world has not prepared me for this.

After we're warm (read: sweating like pigs), she sends us out for two mile-long efforts with a five-minute walk break in between.

My first mile feels absolutely terrible. Mile-efforts are the worst kind of painful, since you have to go really, really hard for about six minutes. One minute is easy to push through. Anything after two starts needing pacing, which I admit, I still don't have.

When I double back for my recovery walk, I almost bump into Elle as she closes in on the mile marker on the trail ahead. A few months ago, I would have ignored her, I realize. Now, I grin and cheer her on.

"You've got this!" I yell. "SPRINT!"

She does. It's definitely not the smoothest sprint but she does speed up.

I high five her when she jogs back to me and slows to a walk. "Holy crap," she says. "That was awful."

I nod. "But how good do you feel now?" I ask. Now that my breathing has relaxed, the mile-effort has given me the runner's high boost of endorphins, and I feel like I'm almost floating along on the path as we walk.

"Pretty great," she admits. "It's weird that running can simultaneously suck so much but feel so good at the same time."

"That sums it up," I agree, looking down at my watch. "Now, let's finish this last mile."

She groans but picks up the pace as I accelerate away from her down the path.

When I get back to the school, I collapse dramatically onto the grass, gasping for breath. Of course, Miss C is somehow right there and pulls me back up and orders me to walk a lap of the track to cool down so I avoid tightening up, which just feels cruel.

Once everyone has made it back, Miss C reminds us that there's only one run left this season, and it's our traditional long one—nothing too hard, she promises, just a seven-mile loop of the trails done at an easy pace. After that, we're going to have to train on our own if we want to be ready for next season.

We all moan and protest a little at the length of the run, but I don't really mind. Time spent winding through trees and on the dirt, dodging roots and rocks? Nothing feels better than those moments.

chapter
fifty-three

Elle

AS WE'RE TRIPPING our way back from the last long run of the season, finally having hit the glorious 'time to walk for cool down' phase and collecting our bags from by the fence that leads us back to the school, I notice two familiar people in the distance. It's not quite my worst-case fear being confirmed, but it's definitely in the top-10.

"Umm, Krista?" I say, walking over to where she's crouched down by her stuff.

"Yeah," she says, still looking down and rummaging in her bag for her sunglasses. She pulls them on but still stays down, looking at her phone instead of me. I didn't expect us to be super-tight best friends, but I'm guessing she thinks I'm trying to create some kind of bonding moment and wants to avoid it.

"Krista!" I say, trying to snap her to attention. "Is that your mom?"

"Where?" she says, still not looking up.

"Making out with my mom," I say in a slightly more panicked tone.

Her head pops up and she scowls at me. "No, she isn't."

I point. She looks over and her jaw drops.

"Oh no."

"My sentiments exactly," I say.

"I KNEW this was going to happen," she says, and starts stalking towards them. "I told her not to go there."

Chapter Fifty-Three

"Hey, what about me?" I say, grabbing her arm. "My mom is straight!"

Krista just looks at my pityingly. "Clearly, not entirely the case," she says.

"Well, maybe we should leave them alone," I say, hanging on to her arm as she tugs away.

"Wait, why aren't you more pissed or freaked out?" Krista demands, dragging me along with her towards them. They haven't noticed us yet, and I don't want them to.

I don't know how to explain it. My mind is racing and I want to be pissed, I know I should be shocked, but all I can think about is how happy and chill Mom has seemed lately. If this is why... well, I can't be that upset, honestly. It's definitely weird, but it's not bad.

"I mean, if she's happy, she's happy," I say weakly.

Krista glares. "Great. So what, we're going to be sisters? This is like some twisted Parent Trap kind of situation?"

"God, I hope not," I say. "But let's not be overly dramatic. It's probably not a big deal, and the worst thing we can do is make them start thinking long-term. And if we confront them now, they'll have to start getting all 'what does this mean,' and 'where are we going with this,' and then they'll either break up and my mom will be miserable, or they'll end up deciding that they're madly in love and moving in together and then we're stuck with each other."

She thinks this over for a beat and nods. "You might be right. But if they're still together in a month, we're going to have to do something about this. I don't want to spend senior year sharing a room with you."

I had not really thought about that possibility.

Krista sighs hugely. "They do look happy, don't they?"

They really do — and my mom has spotted us and waved for us to come over. "Truce?" I say, holding out my hand. Krista looks annoyed, but shakes my hand.

"Fine."

We walk over to our moms together, and we're both trying our best to look loving and supportive as they hold hands. "Obviously, we have something to tell you," my mom says as we get closer.

"Oh God, they're getting married," Krista mutters under her breath and I bite back a chuckle/gasp of horror (I'm not sure which way that would have come out).

"We're just dating," Krista's mom says quickly, accurately reading Krista's expression, and we both relax our shoulders in unison. She's grinning, but she looks nervous, like she might be sick, but at the same time, she looks happy. Sort of the way Krista looks before a race start, come to think of it.

"I kind of guessed," I say, looking at my mom, who at least has the good sense to blush about it. "You've been way too happy lately."

She grimaces. "I'm sorry we didn't tell you sooner," she says. "We just wanted to make sure this was a real thing before we told you. It's a pretty big change."

"I'll say," I respond as sarcastically as possible.

"You guys aren't going to, like, move in together or anything crazy, right?" Krista bursts out. Yeesh. Way to be cool about this, Krista.

Her mom laughs. "Not at the moment," she replies, leaving the door open for future drama.

"Thank God for small favors," Krista mutters and I grin at her. I'm not quite ready for Krista to be my sister, but I think we're back to being friends.

chapter
fifty-four

Krista

9 Months Later…

"THIS YEAR'S cross-country team captains will be…" Miss C rolls her eyes at the annoying junior who does a loud drumroll. "Krista and Elle!"

Elle is standing on the other side of the team huddle, sporting dark purple tights and a light gray school t-shirt. Her hair is carefully done up in Game of Thrones-worthy braids that must have taken her hours to do in the morning, and her makeup is flawless. My black leggings have a rip on the knee that's been patched with a piece of fishnet stocking, and my mandatory school t-shirt was sized up and I chopped the arms off, so it bags down the sides to show my long-line black sports bra. My hair has grown out just enough to scrape it back into a proper ponytail, finally, which feels like I've made the official jock transformation.

I haven't, of course. But I think there's a middle ground between angsty emo kid and varsity track runner.

I catch Elle's eye and simultaneously, we both do an exaggerated eye roll. Of course, I'm not an idiot: I know Miss C did this entirely on purpose. It's bad enough that Elle and I are already spending most Friday nights together for 'family dinner' while our moms make googly eyes at each other over my mom's ultra-healthy meals, and that we've ended up at Sunday brunch at least once a month as well.

At least Elle's mom is a really good runner, so we've gotten in a few

238

training sessions together and she's given me a lot of really helpful tips. So, there's that. And I know my mom has been teaching Elle how to cook—her mom might be fast, but she's not so great in the kitchen. I hate to admit it, but our moms seem to be really happy together, and while I wanted to stay mad about it or break them up, it's hard when they both seem so stable and right together.

"Well," Elle says, "Why don't we get right into it? Everyone circle up for warm-ups!"

I guess the bright side of Elle being co-captain is I'll save my vocal cords from needing to yell all the time.

As we get ready to lead the team through warm-up stretches, Miss C comes over to us. "You're going to be okay with this, right?" she asks.

We both grumble our yeses.

"Good," she says. "I didn't do this to torture you... not entirely, anyway. I thought it was time for some female leadership now that I'm head coach, and Elle, you're great with newer runners and Krista, you can hold your own with the fast guys, so I thought it made a lot of sense."

Much as I hate to admit it, she's probably right. I still don't have to like Elle, and she doesn't have to like me. In the last few months, we've bonded over a few things — like the same taste in cheesy TV shows — but fought just as often about everything from what she likes to read to how I do my makeup. We're not going back to our BFF days when we were 12, but it's less because we hate each other and more because we're different people now, and we can't be the same friends we used to be. We might be something better.

"I absolutely, positively still don't like you," I say to her.

"Ditto," she says, and holds out her hand for a fist bump.

"So, you're coming over for dinner tonight?" I ask as we touch knuckles.

"Absolutely," she says. "After I meet up with Jan for coffee. He's going to be so excited about us being co-captains!"

I roll my eyes, but smile. They've been dating for a while now and I've not only had to watch them make googly eyes in the hall at school and before practice, I've also had to sit through dinner with them on a couple of our family nights lately. On the bright side, he never fails to bring me egg rolls, which are normally on Mom's 'unhealthy foods' list. So he's great in my book. And it's nice to see her a bit more chilled out and enjoying her time in high school instead of freaking out about the future.

Me, on the other hand? Boys are definitely not on the radar right now, since I left a lot of stuff until the last minute, whereas Elle probably had her college applications drafted in eighth grade. (Actually, I know for a fact that she did.)

NYU applications are coming up and I'm starting to plan out my essay — I'm not sure exactly what I'm going to say on it, but I have a few ideas. Between what we said in our speech and what I wrote for the paper, we're both getting a lot of attention from actual magazines and newspapers, so I'm pretty sure my application is going to look really strong no matter what I write about. I'm thinking I don't want to just rehash what happened in the last few months, though.

What I might want to write about is the role that female friendships (and a lack thereof) can have on our high school lives. Jane messaged a few days ago and I bounced a few ideas off of her and that's the one she says sounds the most collegiate and the least goofy — and can avoid linking to any clips of me falling on my face or screaming on national television.

The good: Laughing with Elle as our moms hang out in the kitchen and we re-watch our favorite *Buffy* episode on opposite ends of the couch.

The bad: Reliving that *GMA* nightmare in GIF form, thanks to a new crop of memes that comes up nearly monthly.

The ugly: The aftermath of us telling the principal about Jess, the team losing States because we were down a coach and a key runner, and the few girls on the team that still refuse to believe us — or if they do, they're keeping it quiet because they're pissed that we lost States and potentially cost them scholarship funding. Which, I admit, would make me bitter too. But would I do it all again?

Absolutely.

The biggest thing that I've learned this year is that it's easy to let a small argument completely change the course of your life—and that isn't always a bad thing. If Elle and I had just sat down and hashed through our issues after Homecoming four years ago, we might be completely different people. But at the same time, had we stayed friends, maybe we wouldn't have both grown in the ways that we did. Maybe it was okay that we let go of our friendship for a while to let ourselves grow up in different directions. Maybe it's okay to not focus on fostering friendships, and to let things evolve on their own. And maybe if you can both grow on your own, when you do get pushed back together, you'll be better than ever.

And, of course, that a run through the forest won't solve a problem, but it will help you find a solution.

afterword

Writing this book has been more difficult than any of my other books, since it gets a lot more personal and honestly, a little darker than any of my middle grade works. I didn't set out to write it this way, I just wanted to write a fun book about running! But as I thought about stories I hear from young women I chat with regularly, talk honestly with friends about past experiences, and reflect on my own teen years, it was the direction that felt right for this story to go.

I often write about three key themes. Girls in sport is the obvious one, and something I'm passionate about in my real life as well as in my writing. It's why I started my company, Strong Girl Publishing and why I wrote the *Shred Girls* books. And through all of the fiction I write, you may notice that there are two other themes that emerge: there are the concepts of identity and female friendship.

For me, growing up I was a nerd, a punk kid, a bookworm. These identities became more and more solidified over time, and because I was so set in maintaining that 'alternative' identity, I was adamantly against anything athletic that might add the label of 'jock' or 'popular kid,' or even—heaven forbid—'normal.' So, I refused to sign up for cross-country, play volleyball in gym class, or do anything that might be deemed 'sporty.' (Sound a little like Krista? Yep, that was me.)

At the same time, I never quite fit in with the alternative crowd either—I always felt like I was trying too hard. I remember mornings in high school, how the punk kids would all gather in a certain alcove and I would always fumble in my locker until it was too late to walk over to them for fear of not having the right thing to say. That's part of why I wrote Krista the way I did: I think when we look at other people, it seems like they've slotted into a box perfectly. But when you dig deeper, you realize most of us don't really feel like we belong in any one specific niche. We're all faking it.

Twenty years later, I finally understand that we contain multitudes —and that's a good thing. I don't have to give up my punk rock-ness to run a marathon, nor am I any less of a bookworm because I love bikes. I'm still a nerd—I just spend a lot more time outside moving my body than I used to. But I'll still talk about comic books for days.

And finally, this book is about female friendship. It started out as a bit of a cheeky nod to my original best friend, Lindsay. Like Elle and Krista, we were best friends since we could remember. Of course, this book almost instantly veers away from how our actual friendship played out, though we did have the occasional fight over boys. We did host a backyard 'water war.' And we did realize that a guy would never be worth a friendship. But because of that whole 'identity' thing, we unfortunately did drift apart as we got older. We stayed in touch, but not as much as I wish we had.

Lindsay was killed in a car accident almost 15 years ago. Not a day goes by where she doesn't cross my mind once, whether it's a dumb inside joke I'm remembering, an old memory resurfacing, something as small as the way we signed off on letters to each other. I have a strip of photos of us from a photo booth (a real one, back pre-digital camera days!) that sits in my bathroom as a constant reminder of the pure joy of some of those teen year moments together. She's the person who taught me the value of female friendship, and for that, I will be forever grateful.

As I wrote this book, one thread I knew I wanted to bring in was that friendships get rocky—sometimes in incredibly serious ways. But I think that even at their most combative, Elle and Krista deeply cared about each other, even when they wished they didn't. That's how I felt about Lindsay—no matter how far apart we drifted in life, she was a constant I could count on. She was family.

This is a bit of a different afterword, but it's one I've been thinking about writing since the first *Shred Girls* book. So, do me one simple favor, and give your best friend a hug today... even if you two haven't spoken for years.

And Lindsay, wherever you are—you will forever be my best friend.

XO,

Molly

One final note: Everything I wrote about in terms of sexual assault in this book is sadly statistically accurate. Visit RAINN for the statistics about sexual assault in the US and to find resources if you need them: https://www.rainn.org/statistics/children-and-teens

about the author

Molly Hurford is the founder of Strong Girl Publishing and has been called a chronic book writer by her friends. She's a journalist by trade, writing and speaking about all things cycling, running, nutrition and movement-related. When not actually outside, she's probably writing about being outside and healthy habits of athletes and interviewing world-class athletes and scientists for The Consummate Athlete podcast and website.

She runs and rides in Ontario, where she lives with Peter, her husband, and DW, her mini-dachshund, who she definitely used as a character in the Shred Girls series.

She's the author of multiple books including 'Fuel Your Ride' and the Shred Girls series. Molly is a little obsessed with getting people—especially girls—psyched on adventure and being outside. Those passions combined are what prompted her to start Strong Girl Publishing, in order to reach more young girls and help them find and stay in sports and outdoor adventuring.

also by molly hurford

Shred Girls: Lindsay's Joyride

Shred Girls: Ali's Rocky Ride

Shred Girls: Jen's Bumpy Ride

The Strong Girl

You can also find more books written for girls in sport by young women athletes at Strong Girl Publishing. Visit StrongGirlPublishing.com to learn more!